DEVIL RISING

The Heart of a Gunman

R B CONROY

CCB Publishing
British Columbia, Canada

Devil Rising: The Heart of a Gunman

Copyright ©2007 by R B Conroy
ISBN-13   978-0-9784388-8-3
First Edition

Library and Archives Canada Cataloguing in Publication

Conroy, R B, 1944-
Devil Rising: The heart of a gunman / written by R B Conroy.
ISBN 978-0-9784388-8-3
I. Title.
PS3603.O57D49 2007   813'.6   C2007-907152-X

Cover image by Alton Vance: www.NHisLight.com

Publisher: CCB Publishing
British Columbia, Canada
www.ccbpublishing.com

TO MY WIFE CHERYL

Thank you for your total devotion to my work.
In my life, you make all things possible.

and

TO MY EDITOR TRACY JONES

Thank you for making Devil Rising a better book.
Your advice was invaluable.

Prologue

"You damn four-flusher!" The huge, swarthy man was in a rage as he tossed in his hand. The tattered cards landed face up, tobacco juices dribbled down his scraggly beard. His beady eyes cast a jaundiced stare at the startled young buffalo hunter. "You slid that queen off the bottom. I have jacks up, now give me that pot!" His filthy hands reached for the shiny coins.

The young hunter slammed his forearm on the table, blocking the angry wolfer. "You saw my hand mister, queens pat!" He glared at the bigger man. "Pot's mine!" The gathering crowd gasped as the slight young man challenged the menacing giant

Playing stud at a nearby table, Jon Stoudenmire grimaced as he watched the angry brute shout insults at his friend Ed Morgan. Concerned, he quickly folded his hand, gathered his winnings and moved closer.

As Jon approached, the big man was staring daggers at his partner, his face red with anger. "I'm tellin' you for the last time runt, hand it over!"

"Like I told you Mister, pot's mine!" Ed said bravely.

The bravado of the smaller man surprised the angry wolfer. Eyes locked on Ed, he slid his hands slowly off the table. Fragments of food from his dinner dangled from the front of his grimy shirt. He smelled like the rotten buffalo meat he had poisoned earlier in the day. He was smelly, ugly, and mean. Ed stayed calm, carefully stacking his chips.

Suddenly, the onlookers screamed and pressed back as the huge man leaped up, leaned over the table and grabbed the young hunter by the collar. He pulled the startled youngster out of his seat and punched him square in the face. Crack! Ed's nose busted open as he flew back against the side of the tent. Broken glasses, bottles, and coins were flying everywhere as the big man kicked the table aside. Stunned and disoriented, blood spewing from his nose, Ed staggered around helplessly, groping frantically at the tent ropes to keep from falling. The powerful blow had knocked him senseless. Unable to defend himself, he was raw meat for the wicked giant.

Jon became enraged watching the beating. He knew Ed could no longer protect himself from this charging bull. Moving quickly into the fray, Jon planted his legs firmly between his dazed friend and the wolfer. The startled crowd now saw a young man who might be a match for this monster. Jon was thick built and muscular, not nearly as big as the nasty wolfer, but an imposing figure in his own right.

Jon's chest heaved, his anger grew as he spoke to the wolfer, "Listen up mister, if you lay a hand on him, I'll beat you senseless." The crowd groaned, the air was thick with tension.

The wolfer, alarmed by the fury in Jon's eyes, suddenly lunged forward for an attack. Jon quickly jerked to the side letting the big man stumble and almost fall. Arms flapping backwards, the big oaf struggled to right himself.

"Damn you!" the infuriated wolfer shouted as he spun around and once again charged full force at Jon. Jon saw his opening; he ducked left as his right arm flew forward. With one mighty blow, his fist crashed into the ogre's forehead, right between the eyes. A loud "pop" reverberated throughout the saloon. The big man stopped dead in his tracks, he was jumping around, screaming in pain and holding his face.

"I can't see!" he shrieked.

Blood squirted from between the staggering man's dirty fingers; his forehead began to swell around his eyes. But Jon was not finished. He let loose with another mighty blow, his fist buried deep in the big man's stomach.

"Uggh! Oh no!" The wolfer folded over in pain. One hand grabbed his belly; the other squeezed his nose, trying to stop the bleeding.

Whack, whack! Jon gave him two more blows to the back. The giant man grimaced; he was moaning and teetering and ready to fall, but Jon wasn't through with him just yet.

"Ain't so tough now, are you?" Jon taunted the huge bully as he prepared to administer even more punishment. Jon circled his prey, like an animal preparing for the kill. He moved sideways as he stalked the nasty brute. Suddenly his leg flew forward. There was a loud cracking sound as Jon's boot crashed into the wolfer's knee cap, shattering it.

"Gawd!" he screamed as his huge body crashed onto the hard dirt floor of the saloon. His eyes were bulging, just narrow slits now. Blood was gushing from his nose. His knee cap was shattered and his ribs were busted.

But Jon was still not ready to quit; in a state of uncontrollable rage, he wanted more. In a fight with young Jon, there was no quarter asked and no quarter given. He stood over the fallen giant preparing to unleash ever more punishment. Suddenly he was shaken out of his rage by a voice from out of the crowd.

"Stop Jon, you're killing him!" Ed screamed as he ran over to where his good friend was standing.

The sound of Ed's voice was the only thing that could have stopped big Jon. He was straddling the fallen man, holding him up by his collar. Jon looked over at Ed; sweat was dripping from his forehead, his chest heaving as he stood shaking over the massive brute. He was in a fit of rage and waiting to come out of it.

"It's okay Jon, it's okay!" Ed said calmly.

Jon just stood there for a moment with his arm cocked, fist clenched. Ed and the others waited anxiously; Jon slowly let the big man's bloody shirt slide through his fingers. He watched as the huge body fell to the floor with a thud, his arms flopped to the side.

"He's had enough," Jon said quietly.

There was a collective sigh of relief among the patrons in the bar. Jon took a couple of steps backward, bent down and picked up his hat. He looked around the room at the people. With all eyes on him, he felt he had to apologize to the folks.

"Sorry, but this man had a whuppin' coming and I gave it to him." Jon was almost whispering, his breathing labored as he spoke to the shaken bystanders. "Just send me the bill bartender," Jon said as he glanced over at the stunned barkeep. "I'll take care of the damages." Other than some sore knuckles, Jon had nary a scratch on him.

Ed's white silk shirt was stained red with blood, his nostrils stuffed full of cotton as he approached his good friend. "You okay?"

"Yea, I'm a might better off than he is," Jon said quietly as he glanced down at the fallen man.

"How are you doing, Ed?" he asked, anxious to change the subject.

"I'll live my friend. Why don't you and I head on back to camp?"

Jon nodded as the two young buffalo hunters put their arms around each other and slowly walked toward the front of the saloon tent, pride and dignity intact.

"No charge, Jon!" the bartender shouted at the departing warriors. "That damn wolfer has been causin' trouble in here all week. He got what was comin' to him." The other patrons all nodded in agreement as the tough, likeable young hunters walked out of the saloon and back to camp. A couple of bargirls hovered over the battered wolfer, tending to his wounds.

Many times over the years, Jon would think back to that hot summer evening in the buffalo camps in the Red River Valley, Dakota Territory. Each time he was tried and each time he won, he would remember that day, when he came to the defense of his good friend Ed Morgan. It was the first time he had become that angry or violent; it was the first time he had seen the devil that was buried so deep inside of him. That explosive event, coupled with so many others during his adult life, would continue to haunt Jon Stoudenmire as he made his way through the towns and outposts of the early West.

The powerful youngster grew into a tough, seasoned gunman and made quite a name for himself in the rough and rowdy early frontier. After twenty years of hard living and violence, he decided to escape to his vineyard in central California. During his long journey through the hot Sonoran Desert, he stopped at Logan's Crossing, a small mining town to stock up. To his surprise, he met up with his old friend Ed Morgan for the first time since their buffalo hunting days. The bond was still strong between Ed, a popular local miner, and the weathered gunman.

After dinner one evening, Ed made Jon an offer. With the support of the County Commission, he asked Jon to stay on as County Sheriff. The town felt Jon's reputation as a gunman would come in handy when facing down the many unsavory characters in the desert town. Jon, short of ready cash, agreed to take the job on a short term basis. He asked Ed to be his deputy; Ed gladly accepted. Jon's dream of going to his beautiful vineyard nestled in a lush valley near the Sierra Madre Mountains was put on hold.

Chapter 1

The cool winter breeze sent a chill down Pecos Street. Local residents scurried to get inside on this unusually cold day in Logan's Crossing. Quiet conversation and laughter could be heard coming from inside the Barbee Saloon, a safe haven from the unexpectedly cool weather. Inside, Sheriff Jon Stoudenmire and a few of his closest friends enjoyed a game of five card stud.

"Are you going to make a play or just sit there and look at your cards all day?" big Jon needled his good friend, Ed Morgan. The aging gunman, now lawman, was on a roll and didn't like being held up. His eyes squinted through the curling smoke from his Havana.

"Alright, alright, I call," Ed replied. Three shiny silver dollars bounced on the table as the trusted deputy called the bet. "Just consider this another donation to our chief law enforcement officer here in Mesquite County," he said sarcastically.

Jon gulped down a shot of whiskey and slammed the glass on the table. "I can't think of a more worthy cause." He tossed his hand on the table and pushed he cards apart.

"All black, queen high," Jon announced as the spade flush became visible to the other players. They just shook their heads. It looked like another winner for big Jon.

"Well, you better get that fixed," Ed said as he quickly laid down his hand. "Full up, Jacks and threes!" Ed snickered as he leaned forward to rake in the pot.

"There's over two hundred dollars in that pot!" someone shouted.

"Yea, it's a good one alright, but I still ain't well by a long shot," the smiling Ed replied.

"Quit complaining, you no account sidewinder!" Jon barked as he watched his friend drag in the biggest pot of the day. "You're about the luckiest varmint I've ever seen!"

Ed just smiled as he carefully stacked the pot full of silver dollars.

"If I keep winning like this, I'll be able to quit my deputy sheriff's job and become a professional. Don't you think so, Jon?"

"I wouldn't make any rash decisions. I've seen people starving before and it ain't a pretty sight." Jon grinned as he carefully flicked his ashes in the small metal tray.

"Yea, yea, starving my foot," the feisty Ed retorted not wanting Jon to get in the last word.

Just then a soft, gentle voice interrupted the two friendly combatants. Elizabeth Thompson, the beautiful owner of the Barbee, had just returned from a visit to the bank and was approaching the table. Once a renowned actress from New York City, for reasons unknown, she had moved west to open the Barbee a year earlier. When Jon arrived in town, the sparks flew almost immediately between the seductive actress, better known as Libby, and himself. They were soon a couple.

"My oh my, you boys are at it again. If I didn't know better, I would actually think you didn't like each other," Libby said as she walked gracefully over and put her arm around Jon's big muscular shoulders.

"You sure are a sight for sore eyes, Miss Libby," Jon said. Smoke curled up as he punched out his cigar and laid it in the ashtray. He slid his arm around her tiny waist and gently pulled her a little closer. "How's my girl?" Jon checked his hole card with his free hand, still waiting for his up card.

"Just fine, thank you honey."

Libby looked stunning in her full length dark blue gown and white neck scarf. A gold earring dangled from each ear and a delicate gold necklace seemed to draw attention to her bare, well proportioned shoulders. Her long auburn hair was combed upward into a bun, adorned by a blue onyx hair pin. The delicate features of her beautiful face were lit up with a never ending smile. To all these men way out in the Sonoran Desert, she was indeed a sight for sore eyes.

"I'll let you fellows finish your game, I've got plenty to do around here. And don't forget Jon, you promised to take this girl to dinner tonight. So don't lose it all," Libby said flirtatiously.

Jon beamed at his lovely Elizabeth.

"Oh don't worry Libby." Camp Wilson, stable hand and part time deputy, jumped into the conversation. "If Jon goes bust, one of us would be happy to fill in. How about it, boys?" The other men smiled, there heads rapidly nodding in agreement.

"Now just hold on there," Jon exclaimed loudly. "It'll be a cold day in Hades before this lovely lady goes to dinner with one of you claim jumpers."

"Claim jumper, is it? That's it, put 'em up Sheriff." Young Camp jumped up, his fists rotated in front of him, challenging Jon to a mock fight. Everybody at the table joined into a spontaneous round of laughter, as the lawman put his hands up, palms forward in defeat; all the while grinning from ear to ear at his young friend's antics.

The fun didn't last long. Suddenly two shots rang out and screams could be heard coming from the street in front of the Barbee. The shots seemed to be coming from the area around the general store, caddy cornered from the saloon.

Jon jumped up instinctively; gathered his coins, stuffed them in his jeans.

"Excuse me Darlin'." Jon tipped his hat to Miss Libby as he made a hasty exit out the door.

"Please be careful Jon," Libby pleaded, as Jon rushed toward yet another possible shootout. Libby and the others were close behind.

This town sure is changing, Jon thought. The wooden step creaked as he stepped down off the boardwalk. Since the nearby Brockston silver mine busted open, it seemed like every conman, card shark, rustler, rounder, and gunslinger had decided to call Logan's Crossing home. The now famous town had become a magnet for all sorts of bad actors. A new raucous saloon had recently opened down the street.

Jon's heart raced as he charged across the dusty street toward the hardware store. As he got closer, he could see chubby storeowner Bill Webster looking down at the ground. A crowd quickly gathered; their faces told Jon that someone was badly hurt.

Jon's eyes went to the ground; he saw the long slim body of his deputy, Jack Malone, lying on the street. Jon felt like he'd been punched hard in the gut. Jack's white cotton shirt was stained red with blood.

Doc Fletcher arrived and dropped down on both knees next to the wounded deputy. He snapped open his black leather bag and yanked out his stethoscope. He ripped Jack's shirt open and placed the end of the scope on Jack's chest. His fingers pressed around on his ribs and stomach, checking for internal injuries.

"How's he doing Doc?" Big Jon knelt down next to his deputy.

"He's lost a little blood Jon, but I don't think they hit any vital organs. The bullet passed clear through his side; he should be okay." The doc took the stethoscope from around his neck and stuffed it back in the bag.

Jon leaned down and laid his big hand gently on his friend's shoulder. "Doc says you're going to be okay, so hang tough, Partner. I'm going after the sidewinder that shot you directly, so do what the doc tells you, okay?"

Jack nodded, too weak to talk.

Jon stood up and spoke to the store owner, "What happened here Bill?'

"A couple of... a...a bad apples tried to rob the store and then they shot Jack here when he...a... came to help!" The store owner was very upset, still very much shaken by the sight of Deputy Malone taking a bullet to the chest.

"Just calm down a little Bill and give me as many details as you can," Jon said calmly.

"Sorry Jon." Bill took a deep breath went on. "These two culprits have been working a claim on the edge of the canyon for the past several months. Poor old Will Harmon's claim, the one he was working when he was murdered. Everybody told them that the claim was burnt out, but they wouldn't listen. They bought them an outfit and went to work. The vein went bust after awhile. They owed money to a lot of people here in town, including me. I told them they could pay me so much a week, but that didn't work out. So I cut them off the other day and told them not to come back until they paid their bill. When they came in the store today, I refused to sell them anything and they got real mean. One of 'em pulled a Derringer out of his inside vest pocket and put it to my head, while the other one went around the store throwing stuff in a canvas bag." Bill stopped for a minute to collect his thoughts.

"What happened next?" Jon pulled out his Army Colts and spun the cylinders to be sure they were fully loaded.

"I started yelling at the varmint who was stealing all of my stuff. Someone heard the commotion and went and got Deputy Malone. When Jack ran over to see what was going on, the lowlife who was holding the gun to my head let Jack have it point blank. I yelled and he hit me over the head with the butt of his gun. I fell to the floor like a sack of potatoes. I been seeing stars ever since. One of my customers told me they threw all the stuff they took on a pack horse and high tailed it out of town."

"They won't get far," Jon promised.

"I don't know, Jon; the customer told me they took a whole lot of bacon, flour and jerky. I think they're planning on doing some serious travelin'."

"Thanks for the info Bill, are you okay?"

"Yea, I'm going to be fine, got a sore head, that's all," Bill said as he rubbed the back of his bald head.

Jon turned his attention to the crowd of onlookers. "Let's all go home now, folks, Jack's going to be okay. No use hanging around here." People grumbled as the crowd began to slowly break up. Libby came close to Jon and laid her hand on his shoulder. He smiled at her as his eyes squinted into the sun.

"Promise me you won't take any unnecessary chances out there Jon, promise me," Libby exhorted her lover. "You've got more than just yourself to worry about now!"

"Don't you worry your pretty little face Libby, I'm going to be fine," Jon said confidently as he yanked the billet straps tight and loosened the bridle a might on his faithful companion, Babe. "I hate to rush off Darlin', but I've got to catch a couple of varmints who have a pretty good head start on me. I'm going to grab some supplies and go after them right away. I'd like to catch them before dark if I can."

"Godspeed," Libby said quietly, trying to control her emotions. She knew that when the lead started flying, someone could get maimed or killed - even a man like Jon. That's what tormented her.

Jon smiled and winked at her as he hurried up the rickety stairs to the general store. He grabbed several strips of jerky, a few cans of beans, a bag of flour and a few canteens of water off the shelves and arms full, he quickly left the store. Ed had rushed down to the livery stable and was waiting out front with Babe. Jon quickly stuffed the goods in his leather saddle bags and mounted his anxious steed; he stopped for a moment and spoke to Ed.

"Malone's down. Ed, you need to stay here and mind the store. I can take care of these two lowlifes myself."

"If you say so, Boss," Ed said disappointedly. "But be careful. Someone said the older one is Zing Fuller, a gunman from down Pecos way.

"Thanks Ed; I've heard of him," Jon replied as Babe leaped forward to begin his pursuit of the shooters. He glanced down at the fresh tracks heading south from town toward the Gila River. "Let's go girl!" He spurred Babe on, anxious to make up for lost time. He hoped to catch the culprits before dawn, but the winter sun was setting fast in the reddish-gray sky. He had to hurry.

As he rode along, the trail suddenly curved and dropped down a steep bank toward Black Rock Creek, a small tributary that had splintered off of the Gila. Jon moved quickly, but carefully, down the sharp incline. At level ground, Jon spurred the big mare forward toward the creek which was slightly swollen by recent rains. He pulled up suddenly.

"Whoa girl, whoa!" Jon shouted. Babe reared up and pushed backward with her hind legs, her front hoofs knifed into the muddy bank. Hoofs slipping, she climbed up the bank to level ground.

"Okay girl, it's okay," Jon said softly, as Babe pranced nervously. Jon quickly examined the tracks leading to the stream.

"Looks like an old Indian trick to me, girl."

The tracks had taken a sharp turn to the east just before entering the stream. This should indicate that the savvy varmints had gone into the creek and then traveled east, but upon closer examination, Jon eyed a deep hoof print just above the water line on the opposite side of the creek. "That print's pushing west; they turned on us and went west. Let's get after 'em!"

Jon rode rapidly alongside the creek looking desperately for any evidence of the lowlifes that shot his friend, Jack Malone. After a while, the desert ironwoods, creosote bushes, and cat claws were growing thick along the bank of the creek.

"The brush is getting too thick, we're going to have to go in," Jon whispered. Babe whinnied as he prodded her into the stream.

Neigh! Neigh! Babe suddenly reared up, almost throwing Jon off; a spotted Gila monster slithered up the muddy bank. Jon patted Babe's neck and continued on. The creek began to narrow and the bushes got thicker as Jon struggled forward in the icy creek. Soon he was in a darkened, eerie, tunnel-like space. He was surrounded by thick brush on one side and a steep incline of slippery boulders on the other. It seemed like forever until a sliver of light appeared up ahead signaling the end of the shadowy channel. Jon picked the twigs and stickers off his brown felt hat and denim shirt, tossed them aside and continued on.

"Let's find that sunshine," Jon whispered. He rode toward the light and then pulled up. Babe's ears pricked as she pranced in the gurgling stream. She was warning her master. Jon listened closely; he could hear men's voices off in the distance.

"It has to be them girl," Jon muttered. "We haven't passed any abandoned campsites or seen any other hoof prints along the way. Let's go girl."

Jon felt crowded and trapped as he inched forward through the creek. Thick brush and slippery boulders bordered the dark passageway. He looked around for a way out but couldn't find an opening. One thing for sure, there could be no turning back for big Jon. Trapped or not, he was moving on. Those men had to pay for shooting Jack; he would see to that. There would be no quarter asked, no quarter given.

Jon struggled along the stream toward the voices. As he got closer he decided to look for a way out of the creek. He jumped into the rushing water and waved his hand in front of Babe's eyes, signaling her to stand still until she heard his whistle. Jon felt the cool water on his legs as he sloshed through the gently flowing stream. He heard the voices again; they were on both sides of the bank. *An ambush!* he thought. Jon stepped over and moved quietly along the north side of the stream next to the thick brush; he was soon just fifty yards from the culprits. He ducked down in the shadows of the brush and leaned forward. He could see the two men standing on opposite sides of the creek talking to each other. The well dressed older man had to be Zing Fuller, the other man was too young.

"Wonder if that deputy's dead?" the younger man shouted.

"Don't know," came the reply from the other side. Jon watched as the nattily dressed Fuller popped a couple of bullets from his gun belt and slid them carefully into the cylinders of his six gun. Jon knew that Fuller was a dangerous man.

"His eyes were as big as saucers when I let him have it," the young man boasted.

"I reckon so. He thought he was playin' with amateurs," Fuller replied.

This conversation infuriated Jon. He knew what kind of man Jack Malone was and he knew that he wouldn't have shown any fear to these lowlifes. The "eyes as big as saucers" comment was the wrong thing for big Jon to hear. These cowards had shot Jack without warning and they were about to face a deadly shootout with an angry Jon Stoudenmire.

"Better quiet down now," the older man remanded his younger counterpart. "Won't be too long before that sheriff's gunna be here. Somethin' must have spooked his horse a little while ago, I heard a whinny. He should be here anytime."

"Yea, I guess he's a pretty bad hombre." The young man seemed jumpy as he hocked a big one on the ground.

"That's what I hear," Fuller replied. "Now let's both just shut up and hide in these rocks before he gets here."

An angry Jon wanted revenge, but he knew he had to be careful with these two. Fuller sounded like a pretty hard case and was reportedly good with a gun. The younger man sounded nervous and kind of jumpy. He was the one who shot Jack. In a tight spot he would more than likely shoot first and ask questions later. His kind was predictable - trigger happy and very dangerous, but predictable. The older man would be less nervous and more calculating.

The two men had settled in and been quiet for some time when Jon decided to move out from behind the bushes and cross the creek to the other side. Jon had to be careful, both were packing rifles as well as six guns. Jon moved over and looked up at an opening in the brush at the top of the steep incline. He dug around in the bank for a foothold, and found some fairly good size rocks pushing out from the bank about half way up. He placed his boot firmly against the first rock, reached up and grabbed hold of a protruding root. He leaned back and pulled to see if the root would hold his weight. Nothing broke loose so he decided to go for it. He fell back again and pulled hard on the root. With a mighty effort, he yanked himself up to the next rock. Another root became visible on a higher rock. Jon grabbed hold of it and pulled as hard as he could again. His body flew up and out of the dark creek bed. He rolled to a stop on the ground above the creek. He quickly scanned the area to get his bearings. Jon spotted some large rocks approximately forty yards away near the water, close to the area where he had heard the young man's voice. He moved toward them, careful not to alarm the trigger happy youngster. Jon stopped and listened for any sounds. Not hearing any, he moved quickly and quietly over to the base of the rocks. Jon dropped down on one knee and leaned against the large rock. His head jerked back as something flew by his face.

"Phftt." A small cloud of dust plumed up as a brownish fluid hit the ground next to him. The nasty varmint had hocked one over the rock near Jon, exposing his location.

Jon leaned against the stony surface and slid quietly around to the back of the rock. The kid was busy watching the creek, his back to Jon. Jon continued to inch his way around the large rock to a crevice leading up to the top. He pushed his back against one side of the crevice and his feet against the other, and then slowly scooted up the hard surface. When he finally reached the top, he quietly rolled over to a kneeling position and leaned forward far enough to see the young scallywag staring at the stream below, clueless that he was being watched. He reached in his shirt pocket, pulled out the chaw and ripped off a big chunk.

Jon looked down at the varmint for a second and then broke the silence. He spoke very calmly and very quietly, not wanting to alarm him.

"I got a dead bead on you partner, just stay real calm and listen carefully." The young fellow froze. Jon continued, "Pick up that rifle lying in front of you and throw it over that rock on your left side." The nervous youngster did as Jon asked. Jon went on. "Now carefully slide that six gun out of your holster with two fingers and throw it over the same rock." The jittery shootist reached down with two fingers to lift his gun and then it happened. At the last minute, he opened his hand, grabbed the gun and yanked it from the holster. He quickly rolled to the right and moved up to his feet; wide eyed, he lifted his gun for a shot. Before he could right himself, Jon squeezed off two shots. The bullets blasted into the frightened youngster's gut; he reeled backward.

"I'm hit, damn it, I'm hit good!" he screamed. His

body fell with a thud to the ground, jerked a couple of times and fell still.

"That's for shooting Malone," Jon said quietly, his six guns smoking. He jumped down from the large rock and kicked the boy over on his back. The young man's arms flopped to the side, his head fell sideways; blood trickled from his mouth. Jon grimaced; he looked so young up close.

Jon was angry and conflicted as he quickly climbed down from the rock and moved around the formations toward the creek. Always hard on the outside, he bemoaned the killing of the young man. *He was just a youngster, I could have winged him!* a voice screamed inside Jon's head as he hurried down to the creek toward the older man. There were two chest high rocks near the creek; Jon quickly ran and ducked down behind them. His gun was still warm as he popped two fresh bullets into the empty chambers.

Jon, certain that the other man had heard the shots, had to be careful. He figured the cagey gun hand would lay low and wait in ambush. *This one's going to be tougher,* he thought. He felt agitated and at a disadvantage. More than likely, the other varmint had taken a position back in the rocks. If he rushed him, Jon would be an easy mark. He thought about waiting him out. At most he figured the wily poke had a couple of strips of jerky, possibly a small canteen of water. That stuff wouldn't last long. Eventually the nasty bugger would have to try and get to his pack horse. Jon had plenty of supplies and water and could hold out much longer. When the cagey gun came out for food or water, he could let him have it. A good plan, but there was one problem - Jon was very anxious to get back to town and see Miss Libby. The thought of hanging around these rocks for a few days was unacceptable. He had to figure something out.

* * *

Beads of sweat formed on Fuller's forehead as he lay still contemplating his next move. He had heard all about Sheriff Stoudenmire and his legendary anger. He was more than a little concerned about facing big Jon. An experienced gunman, he wasn't as fast as Jon and he knew it. He was startled as a deep voice bellowed into the rocks. "Can you hear me up there, Mister?" Jon hollered.

"Yea, yea, I can hear ya." Fuller tried to sound tough.

"Your partner's not around any more. He's lying up there in the rocks with two bullet holes in his belly," Jon said forcefully. "I'm the law around here. My name's Jon Stoudenmire and you're under arrest. I want you to throw your guns out by the creek and come out with your hands up. One false move and I'll use you for target practice. Do you understand?" Jon said menacingly.

"I hear you Sheriff, but how do I know you won't kill me anyway?" he replied. Fuller felt very isolated in this desolate spot so far from town. Jon could kill him and then tell everyone that it was self defense. He also knew that Malone was a friend of Jon's and that Jon could get furious when you messed with his friends. Fuller was still undecided when Jon shouted back at him.

"You're right Mister; you don't know what I'll do for

sure. Make your call!"

Fuller was starting to worry; he was damned if did and damned if he didn't. He yanked his red plaid handkerchief from around his neck and wiped the sweat from his brow. He tapped the barrel of his Uberti on the palm of his hand. After a few agonizing minutes, he spoke up.

"Okay Sheriff, okay. I'm coming out with my hands up. Don't shoot!" the nervous man pleaded. His rifle and six gun flew out of the rocks and landed on the creek bank where Jon could see them. Fuller stood up and walked slowly out from between the huge rocks, hands in the air. His brow was sweaty; his heart was pounding hard as he came into full view of the big lawman.

"Don't worry; I never kill an unarmed man. Not even a snake like you," Jon said. Both of his pearl handled Colts were drawn and pointed straight ahead as he stepped out and moved up to the edge of the creek.

"Move on down here where I can get a good look at you," Jon ordered.

Fuller walked toward the creek; he stopped at the edge of the water near his discarded six gun.

"Kick that gun in the creek and then come over here."

The water rippled as the shiny six gun slid into the creek. Fuller grimaced as his leg went into the icy water. His red leather boots sank into the mud under the water as he struggled to the other side. He was shivering as he continued to slosh across the narrow brook. Cold and scared, he reached the other side and looked up at the big lawman. Jon's muscular two hundred pounds and six foot plus frame looked huge; his blue eyes looked dark and menacing as he squinted into the slices of sun that filtered through the trees.

"Now you listen to me you ugly snake," Jon said angrily. "You're alive for one reason and one reason only. I heard you and your friend talking and I know you didn't shoot Malone. If I thought you did, you'd be dead already. You understand?" Jon said threateningly as he yanked Zing's hands behind him and cuffed him.

"Yea, I understand," Fuller grumped.

"Now we're going to ride back to town and find you a nice warm cell. And I'm hoping and praying that between here and town, you try something, so I can let you have it," Jon snorted; he seemed disappointed that he hadn't been able to kill the Fuller sooner.

"Don't worry Sheriff, I ain't stupid," Fuller said as his lips turned into a nasty grin.

Jon whistled for Babe. She came lickety-split down the center of the creek. He collected the other horses and helped Fuller mount his steed. He carried the youngster's body over and dropped it on the pack horse, it fell limp, arms dangling to the side. Jon mounted up, looped the pack's leather rein around his saddle horn and headed back to town. There was just enough daylight left to make it back to town before dark.

Chapter 2

Piano music drifted out the window of the Barbee as Jon and Babe rode slowly into town. It was almost dark now. Camp, shoeing a horse by the light of a kerosene lamp, rose up when he saw Jon coming. A dejected Zing Fuller looked over and gave the young stable hand an ugly stare as he rode past on the lead horse. The dead gunman's arms dangled to the side of the following pack.

"You okay?" Camp shouted.

"I'm fine Camp, see you at the Barbee tomorrow at the usual time," Jon shouted.

Camp stuck his black thumb in the air and quickly went back to work. He had a stable full of horses that needed shoeing by morning.

"Sheriff's back, one dead and one alive!" a young boy playing in the street shouted.

A few folks gathered along the side of the road to greet their returning hero. Jon sat tall in the saddle as he tipped his hat to the crowd. He rode slowly toward the jail, keeping a close eye on Fuller.

"Whoa girl!" "Whoa!" Babe's head jerked back as they stopped in front of the jail. Deputy Morgan came running out to meet him.

"Any chance?" Ed asked, shocked by the sight of the young man's body.

"Not a chance," Jon replied. "How's Malone doing?"

"Not so great, but Doc Fletcher seems to think he'll make it okay. Lost a lot of blood, but he's a pretty tough hombre."

"Might have to get someone to fill in for Jack while he's mending," Jon replied.

"Okay Jon, looks like we're gonna need all the help we can get round here."

"Make sure this poor fool gets a proper burial. He's only a kid, it's a shame." Jon sounded distressed as he spoke of his most recent kill.

"Sure thing Boss, you better clean up a little and get down to the Barbee. Libby's been coming down here every twenty minutes to check on you. I'll send one of the boys o'er to the Barbee to tell her you're okay."

"Thanks Ed." Jon smiled at his loyal deputy. He tied Babe to the hitching post and hurried down to the Westwood Hotel to spiff up a little.

The floor boards creaked as Jon walked to his room at the end of the hall on the second floor. He turned the key, and the door fell open. Jon stepped in the room and quickly closed and locked the door behind him. Steam rose from a pan of hot water sitting next to the bed. *They're spoiling me,* he thought, as he tossed his hat on the bed and slid his hands into the water. He splashed his sweaty face, it felt great. He grabbed the cotton towel off the brass bed rail and patted his face dry. His black leather vest and denim shirt came off. He slipped on his white silk shirt and brocade vest, slapped on some cologne and took a quick look in the mirror. "You handsome devil," he mumbled as he grabbed his hat off the bed and hurried down to see his girl.

* * *

Libby's eyes kept glancing at the door as she waited for her big lover. She reached under the bar and pulled up a small bottle of expensive perfume and carefully dabbed it on a few key spots on her neck. She liked being Jon's girl, even with all the uncertainty. *Why do I always fall in love with the wrong men?"* she thought, as she carefully placed the perfume under the bar.

The door opened, Jon walked in slowly and stopped. He looked around the room for Libby. She smiled and waved; his face lit up with a big grin as he straightened his hat and headed for the bar.

"How's the prettiest girl in town?" Jon said as slid up on the bar stool.

"Just fine! And how's our big handsome local Sheriff?" Libby said enthusiastically. She carefully lifted a bottle of Early Times out of the rack, the amber liquor splashed into Jon's glass.

"I'm doing okay," Jon replied.

"Well I guess all my worrying was for nothing." Libby's pulse rate jumped as Jon's big hand slipped around her delicate wrist.

"I'm right sorry 'bout that Darlin'. But I can take care of myself alright; try not to worry too much." Jon smiled and winked at the happy saloon owner. He lifted the shot glass to eye level. "Here's to the loveliest lady this side of the Gila River." He downed the shot of Early Times and smiled at Libby. He paused for a moment as his eyes went to the center of the empty glass as if in deep thought.

"Forgive me for worrying so much!" Libby said, interrupting his thought.

"You're forgiven, Sweetheart," Jon said quickly.

"Dinner?" Libby asked.

"Thought you'd never ask!"

"I had Sam set us up in the back room; it will be quieter there," Libby said, as her face broke into a warm smile.

"Sounds good!"

Libby slid effortlessly around the end of the bar; she grabbed Jon's hand and led him back to the separate room. The candelabra's flames reflected off the shiny silverware as they entered their private retreat. Always the gentleman, Jon slid Libby's chair out and waited for her to be seated. He tossed his brown felt hat on the table and sat down next to her.

Sam arrived with two glasses and a bottle of imported wine; he carefully poured the expensive wine into the delicate glasses.

"Ready to order or do you need some time?" Sam asked.

"Well if Libby doesn't mind, I'm pretty much starvin'," Jon replied.

"That's fine, I'm a little hungry myself," she replied.

Sam reached inside his apron and pulled out the green order pad.

"What'll it be?" he asked.

"Venison parmesan over pasta for me, Sam," Libby said softly.

"How bout a big t-bone steak with fried potatoes," Jon said.

"Scalloped corn's good tonight, Jon, and you need some veggies." Sam grinned as he lectured his good friend.

"Okay Sam." Jon laughed.

Sam hurried off to the kitchen.

Libby lifted the glass up to her lips and took a sip. "Somebody said there was gun play out there today. Is that right, Jon?"

Jon looked down at the table, he seemed distressed. "Yea, the young fella, the one who shot Jack, was kind of trigger happy," Jon said.

"And....." Libby said.

"And...I ah had to kill him." Jon was upset; it was the same old feeling, but now for the first time in his life he wanted to talk about it.

"What is it, Jon? What happened?" Libby said, very concerned.

"I.....uh.....I gave him every chance to back off, but he still went for his gun! I had no choice!" Jon's voice trailed off as he talked of killing the young man.

Libby looked intimately toward the powerful gunman. Her hand gently stroked his thick forearm. "Are you okay?" she asked.

Jon's eyes began to well up, they glistened as he spoke. "Yea, I guess I'm just....." his voice trailed off once again.

"You're just what, Jon?" Libby asked. She had never seen her big, fearless lover so vulnerable before.

Jon looked over at Libby. His face filled with pain. "I'm just tired."

"Tired of what, Jon? What are you talking about?" Libby's eyes darted up and down Jon's face, looking for any sign of the answer. He seemed genuinely upset; it wasn't like him.

"Tired of all the killing, tired of living with this rage inside of me!"

"But Jon, you never killed anybody that didn't deserve it. I don't understand!" Libby sat up, upset and confused by the revelations coming from this tough, decent man.

"Yea, but it's still killing! It gets to you after awhile. That fella today was just a boy, barely eighteen years old Libby! His face keeps running through my mind. His eyes were pleading with me not to shoot, but I blasted 'em anyway. I felt no remorse, only anger and rage at what he had done to Malone. I wanted him dead; all I could think about was killing him. There's something inside of me Libby; it's like there's a devil or something deep down in my heart!" His rugged face was full of remorse.

Libby jumped up and rushed over and laid her soft body against his muscular back, her cheek pushed against his shoulder. Upset herself, she wanted very much to comfort her shaken man.

"I love you Jon, you're a good man!"

Jon, sensing the distress he was causing Libby, stood and put his arm around her waist and pulled her warm body next to his. He held her tightly, gently caressing her.

"I'm sorry I upset you Libby," he said tenderly. He

pulled her closer and tighter. Spurred on by the passion of the moment, they continued to embrace. "I love ya baby, you know that," Jon whispered softly in her ear as he gently stroked her lovely auburn hair.

Libby slowly pulled back and looked up at Jon. She slipped her hands gently around his face; she held him tightly. "Now, you listen to me Jon Stoudenmire! I understand about the killing, it must be an awful feeling to have to kill someone! But you were given this anger for a reason. Your anger has helped so many people in so many ways. I know how upset you can get Jon, I've seen it. But you use your fierceness in the right way - to help others. No decent person need ever fear you."

"Thank you, Libby," Jon said softly. "It's just...."

Libby interrupted, still anxious to sooth his pain. "I'm sorry dear, but you've beat yourself up enough for one evening. Sam just signaled me that dinner is ready. What do you say?"

"Okay baby." Jon yanked the red handkerchief from around his neck and gently dried the tears on Libby's face.

"I love you," Libby said softly.

"I love you too darlin'!"

Chapter 3

"And may the Lord bless his tortured soul. Amen!" A warm breeze blew across the barren hilltop as Jon, Ed, and Pastor Toms performed a brief burial ceremony for the young gun killed by Jon the day before. Ed kneeled down and pounded a cross in the dirt above the grave. The name Dusty Fry was crudely painted on the small wooden edifice.

"Thank you Pastor Toms," Jon said. "I appreciate it."

"You're welcome Jon; it's a shame. Such a young man," the elderly Pastor replied as he shook his head.

"Yea, I wish I could ..."

The Pastor interrupted, "I know you do, Jon. But the boy had no kin and you helped send him off. It was a fine gesture, Sheriff."

Jon nodded. The Pastor climbed in his buggy, the leather cracked, "Gitty up!" he shouted, and the buggy jerked forward toward town.

"I've got to be going Jon, I promised Will Banks I'd help him round up some strays," Ed said as he dropped the hammer in the saddle bag. "You okay?"

"I'll be fine; see you later at the jail." Jon smiled at his old friend. Ed's leg flew up over his Buckskin; he tipped his hat and rode off to the Banks Ranch.

Jon's heart was heavy as he stood and watched his friend ride away. Alone with his thoughts, the memories of past gunfights and the sounds of death flooded through his mind. The screams, the pain, the violence; it was a recurring theme. He yearned for the simpler days, when he was a younger man. His mind wandered back twenty years ago when he and Ed Morgan first met on the plains of North Dakota. He thought of the whys and wherefores of his life, and how life's bumpy road had led him to where he was now. As he mounted Babe for the trip back to town, he thought back to that first day in the buffalo camp.

* * *

The bay's nostrils had flared as she reared up and almost bucked Jon off. "Whoa girl! Whoa!" he tried to calm his frightened steed. The horrible stench of rotting buffalo carcasses piled on the edge of the compound had spooked the jittery horse as they rode into camp. Just twenty-one and fresh from a year long stay in Dodge City, Jon was young and restless and looking for a new adventure. A couple of old timers had told him that buffalo hunting camps in the Red River Valley would be a good bet for a young man like Jon. Fearless and a crack shot, Jon packed up his belongings in Dodge City and headed out to the Dakota Territory, determined to make a go of it as a buffalo hunter.

Jon remembered reining his horse around toward a large tent where several men were standing in line. Others were eagerly exiting the tent and counting their take for the day. Most of them were heading for the saloon tent, some fifty feet away. *It won't be long before those boys will either drink their money away or lose it in a poker game,* Jon thought. *What a shame.* Jon was no fool when it came to money. As he moved into the camp, he saw a group of runners talking loudly and playing poker around a campfire. The old timers in Dodge told Jon to use the name runner, not hunter, while in camp - only green horns used the name hunter. Always proud, Jon didn't want to be branded a green horn, even if he was new to the fine art of buffalo hunting. Suddenly a fight broke out between two of the runners in the card game. Jon stopped for a second to watch as the two ruffians slugged away.

"Don't you ever try that again, you lowlife!" one of the men shouted as he leaped out of his seat and dove toward the other player. Money and poker chips were flying everywhere as the two ruffians rolled around on the ground kicking and punching.

Then suddenly, as quickly as it had started, the fight ended. One of the men jumped up, dusted off his jeans and headed back to the game. The other man shouted something at the retreating pugilist and then followed suit. It was just like nothing had ever happened. Both were laughing and joking as they picked up their chips and got back to poker.

Quite a rambunctious group, Jon had thought, *I should fit right in here.* Jon could down a drink and deal a hand with the best of them, but he always knew where to draw the line. Growing up on a farm in Indiana, his Pa had taught him early on the value of a dollar.

Anxious to get over to the mess tent and get some grub, Jon first had some business to take care of. The old timers in Dodge City had told him the only way to make money in the buffalo camp was to avoid the middle man and get your own outfit. An outfit consisted of two wagons, one large and one small, with metal frame boxes. It took metal frames to withstand the great weight of the buffalo carcasses. The large wagon required twelve mules to haul the dead buffalo back to camp; the smaller wagon required six mules and was used around the camp for lesser loads. A couple of horses, the usual bedrolls, cooking utensils and a tent completed the outfit. A typical setup would cost about two thousand dollars, a lot of money for a man as young as Jon. But Jon was no ordinary young man. Through a combination of hard work and well-honed gambling skills, he had been able to save almost five thousand dollars during his stay in Dodge City - a small fortune.

Jon's horse was prancing nervously. Finally Jon got up the nerve and blurted out at one of the departing hunters, "Pardon me sir, but do you happen to know of anyone who is looking to sell their outfit?" The old runner frowned as he looked up from counting his cash.

"Kind of' young to be lookin' to get your own outfit, ain't ya fella?" the old timer barked, his skin dark and cracked from all those long days in the hot sun.

"Could be, but I really don't think so," Jon shot back.

"I don't either," remarked a young man just leaving the tent. "You look plenty old enough to me."

"Well thank you, and to whom do I owe this pleasure?" Jon immediately liked the friendly young man who had jumped into the conversation and was anxious to learn more about him. Jon smiled and nodded at the old timer, sending him on his way.

"Ed Morgan's the name, just in from Missouri Territory and looking for a partner." The young fella spoke confidently as he approached Jon. "Could that be you?"

"Now hold on there friend. I wasn't really lookin' for a partner," a surprised Jon replied with a nervous chuckle. "I was trying to get my own outfit."

"Well, I understand Mr...?"

"Stoudenmire, Jon Stoudenmire," Jon responded quickly, a little taken back by the aggressiveness of this young hunter.

"You see Jon, you got a big problem. I been checking around for quite awhile and as far as I can tell, there's only one outfit for sale in this camp and it's been promised to me. But I only have half the money it's going to take to buy it, so I need a partner to cover the other half. You look honest enough to me, so are you in or out?" the young runner pushed on, barely giving Jon a chance to think.

Never one to make rash decisions, Jon was really being pushed by this young Missourian. He wanted more time, but he also wanted to get his own outfit real bad. He liked this brash young tenderfoot and decided to trust his instincts and give it a shot, but not before a little more friendly bantering. Years later, Ed would confess that even he was surprised by how forward he was that first day.

"Now just hold on there fella, I don't even know if you can shoot straight or not. I might be tying into somebody that couldn't hit the broad side of a barn from fifty feet. I might end up shooting all the buffs and then you'll want to split the profits." Jon's eyes narrowed as he looked over at the young runner.

Without saying a word, Ed carefully lifted his .50-90 Sharp Carbine up out of its saddle holster and raised it carefully to his left forearm. Jon wondered what the heck he was doing, as he leveled the large rifle for a possible shot. Ed then took direct aim at a big sign hanging some hundred yards away, next to the Wells Fargo Tent. It seemed like an eternity before Ed gently squeezed the trigger on the beautiful rifle.

Boom! came the blast from Ed's .50-90. All eyes turned to look at the distant sign. Splinters flew as the bullet hit the soft pine edifice. It was a long way off, but it appeared to Jon that the "e" in the Wells Fargo sign was pretty much gone.

"You still think I can't hold up my end?" Ed said confidently, the smoke still spewing from his Sharp's barrel.

Jon couldn't believe his eyes. *This kid can really shoot,* he thought. *I'd better just knock him down a notch or two.* Jon, without saying a word, slid his .50-70 Carbine out of its saddle holster; lifted it up to shooting position and took careful aim at the same distant sign. A crowd had started to gather after Ed's shot; some of the men in the camp had picked up on what was going on. They had quit doing whatever they were doing and started moving closer to where the two young men were squaring off.

Suddenly there were two loud blasts from Jon's Carbine. Hs head jerked back, his horse reared up as the percussion from the shots reverberated throughout the camp.

The growing audience hastily turned to look at the distant sign to see how the youngster had done. No splinters flew this time; it appeared as though Jon had missed the sign completely.

"Looks like you were off a little my friend!" Ed shouted. "Let's go check it out!"

Ed leaped abroad his mount as he and Jon raced toward the sign. Their horses jumped to a stop right in front of the sign. Both men craned their necks to try and see the result of their handy work. Sure enough, the "e" had a great big hole in it. Just as Jon had thought, Ed had made a perfect shot. The pressure was on Jon now as the two young men scanned the rest of the sign. There were oohs and ahs from the arriving crowd as they began to see the results of Jon's marksmanship. Upon closer examination, two precision like holes could be found in the middle of the "a" and the "o" of Wells Fargo.

"Lordy be, did you see that?" one of the old runners exclaimed loudly. "Them young fellers sure can shoot!"

Both men began laughing hysterically as they reached out to shake hands and cement their new partnership. The crowd that had gathered began to applaud the young sharpshooters as they dismounted and went inside the tent to pay the frightened owner for the damage to his sign. Soon the two young men emerged from the tent, smiling from ear to ear.

"What you say we get that outfit we were talking about a few minutes ago?" Jon said with a smile.

"Sure 'nuff, Partner. Sounds like a great idea! I'll meet ya here in the morning."

Jon nodded and headed for the mess tent.

The next day the two young men met and purchased their new outfit. After a few small repairs to a back wheel on the large wagon, they were ready to start shooting some buffs and making some money. But as Jon thought back, he remembered that it wasn't quite as easy as they reckoned it would be. These cocky young hunters had a few lessons to learn along the way.

He remembered the first day of the hunt. He and Ed had located a herd of buffalo only a few hours from the camp, just up from the Red River northeast of camp about five miles.

"Hold on there, Jon," Ed ordered as they approached the buffs.

Both of the young runners reined their horses to a stop. Jon looked puzzled as he glanced over at Ed.

"What's the matter; did you wet yourself or something?" Jon kidded his new partner.

"No, smart aleck! I just want to know how we're going to shoot these buffs?

"With our guns," Jon laughed. "How else?"

"You really are a green horn," Ed replied. "I sure hope nobody heard you say that or they'll never call us runners again, even if we are crack shots."

"Okay, okay. Go ahead!"

"There's two ways of shooting, Jon. The stationery method, where we lay down behind our horses and shoot the buff as the run by; or there's the running method where we ride into the herd on horseback and shoot them that way. I could do it either way, what do you think partner? "

"Oh, the running method for sure," Jon replied, cheeks still a little pink with embarrassment.

"Okay big Jon, running it is. Let's get at it. We're not doing any good standing around talking about it."

As they approached the herd of about three hundred buffalo, the huge animals became nervous and began to move away from the two youngsters. Jon signaled to Ed that he would ride in first. By now the frightened buff were almost at full gallop. Jon was more scared than the buffalo as he rode into the middle of the herd - a little too far in, he would think later. There were buffalo all around him and they kept bumping into his horse and knocking him sideways, all the while they were picking up speed. Jon had basically seen only pictures of buffalo and was amazed at how big they were as he raced among the giant behemoths. He was holding on for dear life and trying to get his rifle out.

It was at this point that Jon learned the first important lesson about buffalo hunting - beware of prairie dog holes! Now just a few hundred yards into the hunt, Jon was being knocked silly in the middle of the rampaging herd. Suddenly, he felt his horse go out from under him.

"Oh my God, oh my God!" Jon screamed as his poor horse stepped into a prairie dog hole at full gallop. The horse went down and Jon went soaring through the air, right into the middle of a bunch of stampeding buffalos. It was at this point that Jon's instinct to survive, that would serve him so well throughout his life, kicked in. The chances of making it out of a fall like this alive were slim to none, especially for a beginner. But somehow Jon was able to grab hold of the mane of a large bull buff as he flew over the frightened animal. With a mighty effort, he yanked himself down on top of the two thousand pound beast. With Jon holding on for dear life, the frightened buffalo went kicking and snorting down the trail. After several minutes, the huge animal grew tired and ran off to the side of the pack. This momentary detour allowed Jon time to jump to the ground, safely out of the way of the other rampaging buffalo.

Ed arrived on the scene shortly after Jon got off the buff.

"You alright?" Ed shouted nervously.

"Yea, I think so," Jon said quietly, skin pale and eyes wide.

He laid motionless for several minutes, staring at the sky.

A little concerned, Ed yelled at his new friend, "Try moving your arms Jon."

"Okay!" Jon lifted his arms up and down.

"Your arms are okay," Ed barked. "Now move your head from side to side and back and forth."

Jon's head rocked back and forth.

"Head seems okay," Ed said. "Well, your arms are okay and you didn't break your fool neck. Now try to get up on your legs," Ed ordered, looking nervously at his pal.

Jon's big hand went up to Ed, beckoning for his assistance. Ed leaned down and grabbed hold; his horse pushed backwards as he pulled the muscular young man to his feet. Jon walked around gingerly, testing his legs. He was limping a little, but otherwise everything seemed okay.

Ed shook his head. "I swear, there aren't too many people who could come out of that alive. What the heck happened out there?

"I was riding along in the middle of all of them buff, when all of a sudden my horse went out from under me and I went flying. Next thing I knew, I was on the back of a big bull holding on for dear life," Jon explained, as he limped around holding his leg. Except for some soreness in his right leg, Jon appeared to be in pretty darn good shape.

"Why'd your horse fall?"

"I don't know for sure, but I think she may have stepped in a prairie dog hole. By the way, how's my horse doing? Is she alright?" Jon queried Ed as he dusted himself off.

"Well I'll be, you just about got killed and you're worried about your darn horse," Ed chuckled.

"You're darn tootin', she's a good one. Don't want to see her get hurt."

"I checked her out on the way over here; she looked fine to me. A little scared, but fine," Ed replied, reassuring his friend.

"Good, glad to hear that." Jon sounded relieved. "I guess we both learned a lesson today, Ed. Watch out for prairie dog holes!"

"Guess so, Jon, but I learned another lesson."

"What's that?"

"Always let your partner go first."

Both men joined in a lively laugh on that one, but Ed could not help but be impressed with the toughness and resourcefulness of his good friend. *This is one tough hombre*, he thought. *What he just did was amazing.*

Lesson one was in the bag now but there were more lessons to come. Jon thought back to another lesson the two young runners had to learn, and it was all about ammunition. Not the kind of ammo they were using but how much. He remembered a talk he had with Ed after their first day out hunting.

Ed had just got back from the skinner and fur company, and Jon had a few questions about their first harvest.

"Well, how'd we do Ed? Can I buy that ranch in Colorado now?" he joked as he looked at his partner's long face.

"Hardly. We got six hundred for the skins and our ammo cost seven hundred," Ed said dejectedly.

"What the heck's going on?" Jon asked, a little shaken by the news. He and Ed had just been thinking about how many buffs they had to get to have the kind of payday they wanted; they never even thought about the cost of the ammo.

"I talked to some of the other runners in camp and they said that our kill rate should be about four buffalo for every five shots."

"Hmmm.....what's our rate Ed?"

"It took us three hundred shells to kill two hundred buffalo; we got a long way to go, big partner."

"I guess so. You got any suggestions?" Jon was open to about anything at this point.

"Yea, I think we should get ourselves a couple of .40-45 Remingtons. They're more accurate, especially at over a hundred yards. And most of our shots are about two hundred or better. Also, we need to switch to English Powder; it's cleaner and creates more energy."

"Let's get at it, Ed. I didn't come clear out here to lose money. Let's get those guns and powder and see how we do partner." Jon patted his good friend on the back. "We're the best shots in camp. If we can't do it, nobody can."

The next time out, the boys got a hundred buffalo with a hundred and fifteen shots. And it only got better from there. It wasn't long before they had days where they only had two or three misses. They loved their new Remingtons and the English powder was giving them greater velocity and a clearer look at the buffs. The money started rolling in.

Now that lesson number two was in the bag, Jon thought back to the third and final lesson the boys had to learn. And it was about something totally unexpected; something called a poison vial. One day Ed had taken their harvest over to the skinner in their large wagon. To his surprise, the skinner had offered him some unsolicited advice.

"You boys got your poison vials yet? You're gonna need 'em," the skinner shouted to Ed.

"Poison vials, what the heck are you talking about?" Ed was a little confused by what the scruffy old skinner was saying.

"You heard me right, I said poison vials. All you runners are having to go farther and farther from camp to find good herds. And there's Injuns out there that would just love to do you in. And if they do, they're going scalp ya, and cut your privates out, and generally chop your body all up. They believe that if they cut you up bad enough, you won't go to the happy huntin' grounds. And believe me, Youngin', those Injuns don't want no buffalo hunters goin' to their happy huntin' grounds. So you better take a vial of poison with you next time out. And if you happen to run into some Injuns and if they're about to let you have it, just you take out your poison vial and drink it. The Injuns won't scalp you or cut your privates out if you're already dead." The old skinner was kind of grinning as he looked up at the startled young runner.

"Well, that's good to know I guess," Ed retorted, kind of shaken by the revelations from the skinner. "I guess I just don't like hearing things like that."

"Nobody does, but that's the way it is out here. This ain't no Sunday picnic 'round here, Young Feller," the old skinner said emphatically.

"I'll talk it over with my partner," Ed said quietly, still trying to comprehend everything the old man had just told him.

That evening while he and Jon were sitting around the campfire, Ed decided that it would be a good time to bring up the ugly news he had received earlier in the day. Jon remembered the concerned look on Ed's face as he explained to him in some detail the awful necessity of carrying a poison vial in case they were attacked by Indians.

"Sounds like something we ought to do, don't you agree, Jon?"

"I reckon I do; there's just one problem."

"What's that?"

"You better hustle around a get yourself one, 'cause I already got mine. I like my privates the way they are, so I went and got me one the other day. I guess I plum forgot to tell ya." Jon laughed as he raised his hands playfully to protect himself from what he knew would be the coming assault from his surprised companion.

"You went and did what? You snake!" Ed shouted as he jumped over the campfire and dove on top of his big friend, the two youngsters rolled around on the ground kicking and fighting.

"Why didn't you tell me, you gizzard lovin saddle bum?" Ed screamed.

"I would of, but I didn't get one either. I'm just kidding. I was just spoofin' you," Jon shouted as his buddy kept on with the punishment. "I don't have one! I really don't!" Jon yelled as he tried desperately to rip loose from the wiry Ed.

The two friendly combatants were laughing hard as they finally began to tire of their frivolity. They looked around for their bedrolls and the chance to get a good night's sleep. Their chests were heaving as they chuckled and mumbled insults at each other as they crawled under their wool blankets. They were soon fast asleep on the cold, hard ground of the dark solemn prairie. Jon heard the screech of a distant hoot owl as he drifted off to sleep.

Jon smiled to himself as he thought back to that day and the mock fight over a poison vial. It reaffirmed to him what great friends he and Ed had become during those early days on the plains. It was a friendship that was sorely tested one evening when both of them decided to go to the saloon for a night of fun and gambling.

Even as a young man in the camps, Jon spent a fair amount of time at the saloon playing poker. He had become a pretty accomplished gambler during his tenure in Dodge City. Most of the fellows he played against in Dodge City were very good players, many of them professionals. Jon found the pickings pretty good in the camp, playing against a bunch of amateurs. Many of them had walked right off the plow to the camps and had little if any experience with the fine art of five card stud. Jon had been making almost as much playing poker as he was hunting buffalo. Ed did some gambling also, but only occasionally. One evening Jon preformed the usual ritual, politely asked his partner to go with him to the saloon.

"I swear Partner, you're going to read your life away! Why don't you put that book away and have some fun for a change?" Jon said as he straightened his brown felt hat and prepared to leave.

"Well, you know what Jon, I might just do that tonight. I haven't played poker for awhile. I'm getting a little rusty. A night of five card stud and black jack might do me some good," Ed answered as he closed his book.

"Hey, that's great. We'll have a good time. You need to enjoy some of that money you been making anyway," Jon said as the two young men left their camp and headed for the card game.

The saloon tent was the largest in the camp and was right in the middle of all the chaos. It was a favorite hangout for the runners after a long day of hunting or working around their campsites. It was a makeshift setup with several poker tables, three faro tables, and a roulette wheel. The largest edifice in the tent was a long, old oak bar that was a castoff from the Oriental Saloon in Dodge, a little beat up, but it looked fine. The men were just glad to have a place to drink and play cards, and maybe get lucky with one of the girls brought in from Dodge. The owners found out early on that a few whores in the bar could really improve business.

The patrons sounded particularly boisterous on this sultry July evening. *Maybe it's the heat*, Jon thought as the two young runners entered the tent. He greeted several of the regulars lined up at the bar. They were a motley crew, all dressed up and looking for a good time.

"How you fellas doin tonight?"

"Pretty darn good Jon. I suppose you're here to take our money again?"one of the boys shouted from the end of the bar.

"I sure hope so." Jon laughed.

"Who's that handsome fella with you?" one of the hookers asked as she smiled at Ed.

"Oh that's my partner, Ed," Jon replied as he introduced Ed to the hooker and several of the boys at the bar. Ed seemed embarrassed by it all and looked for a table to start playing some poker. Jon spotted an open chair at his regular table and sat down for an evening of beer and poker. Ed found a game at a nearby table. As Ed pulled his chair out to sit down, he looked over and nodded at Jon. He looked nervous and a little unsure of himself.

The cards weren't going Jon's way. It seemed like every time he had a shot at a big pot, he would take a bad hit and go bust. He was still way ahead for the season, so a bad night now and then was no big deal. On the other hand, every time he looked over at Ed, he appeared to be raking in another big one. He had eight or ten good size stacks of chips sitting in front of him. *More power to him*, Jon thought. If he was getting shut out, there was nobody he would rather see doing well than his friend Ed.

Jon had noticed a rather large, bearded man at the bar when he and Ed first came in. He knew most of the guys who frequented the saloon, but he didn't know this fella. He was being very loud and obnoxious and seemed to want to be the center of attention. *Probably a wolfer*, Jon thought at the time. Wolfers were the scum of the earth and Jon had little use for them. They were the men who came in after a kill and poisoned the buffalo meat left behind by the runners. When the wolves and coyotes would come in for dinner, they were greeted by a big pile of meat full of strychnine. After they had their dinner, they rolled around on the ground for a few hours and died a horrible death. The wolfers would then move in and start skinning them right where they fell. Then they would then leave the poisoned carcasses of the wolves and coyotes behind for the other smaller animals and birds to eat and also die a slow, painful death. They would later sell the skins and move on to the next harvest area and create the same ugly scenario all over again. This line of work attracted the very worst the West had to offer; it took a real bad person to want to become a wolfer. The wolfers usually stayed away from the runners, skinners, and other men in the camp. While the others tolerated the lowly scallywags, they didn't want to associate with them. It was an unwritten rule that the wolfers were not welcome in camp, except during the day to pick up some supplies. Occasionally, a bold or stupid one would venture into camp after dark to spend some time in the saloon. The large man at the bar looked big enough to hunt bears with a stick. If he was a wolfer, he probably wasn't too worried about what the runners thought about him being in the camp after dark.

It wasn't long before the big man had joined Ed's game. This was not a good sign; Jon didn't like it. Ed, on the other hand, didn't think a thing about the big man joining in. He always thought the best of everyone and had a difficult time separating a good man from a bad man. Jon could see trouble coming from a mile away and this guy spelled trouble.

"Is that big loud fella over there at the next table a wolfer?" Jon inquired of one of his playing partners, attempting to verify his intuition about the big lout.

"Sure enough is," was the answer. "He's from the Black Hills area over 'round Deadwood. I hear he's one mean varmint. Someone said he beat a man to death in Deadwood with his bare hands over a two dollar bet."

"You don't say," Jon replied. "Sounds like a real fine fella."

"Yea, he's a bad one. He shouldn't be in here anyway, being a wolfer and everything. I guess he's so big he doesn't give a damn," the other man said quietly, not wanting the big man to hear him.

"I guess not," Jon said as he threw his hand in. "I fold."

Worried about Ed and what was going on at his table, Jon was not able to concentrate on his cards any longer. It didn't take too long before his concerns about Ed were proven right; things were starting to get ugly over at Ed's game. The conversation between the players had become very animated. The big bearded man was arguing with Ed about a pot Ed had just won. Jon listened as he accused Ed of cheating. Jon knew better than that; Ed Morgan was as honest as the day is long. Jon excused himself, gathered up his chips and quickly moved over to the end of the bar, right next to Ed's table for a better vantage point.

Suddenly, without warning, the big wolfer suckered punched Ed. Overcome with rage, Jon interceded and violently beat the huge man senseless. The savageness of the beating was unnerving to the patrons in the saloon. Even in the rough and tumble buffalo camps, a beating of this brutality was rarely seen. At the sound of Ed's voice, Jon backed off and let the battered man fall to the ground. There was a sigh of relief throughout the saloon. Jon apologized to the stunned crowd as the two tough young runners headed back to their camp, pride intact.

Soon the trouble in the saloon was a distant memory as the two boys continued to do well with their hunting. But even though things were going well, Jon was starting to get a little bored with the routine and was finding it more and more difficult to get up for the hunt.

Ed could have kept at it a little longer but he also was growing tired of the long days on the range and the dirt and dust also. So they both agreed that enough was enough and decided to sell their outfit and move on down the road. Only trouble was, it would be two separate roads.

Ed was looking to find a wife, buy a nice piece of land somewhere, settle down and raise a family. Jon was looking to see a little more of the world. He wanted more adventure and excitement and a chance to use his poker playing skills in a few more of the many frontier towns that dotted the western landscape. Settling down was not in the cards right now for Jon.

He thought back to that day when he and Ed sold their outfit for a good profit to a couple of young runners in the camp. They reminded Jon very much of he and Ed when they first came to the camp two years earlier. Excited and filled with anticipation, Jon hoped the newcomers would do well. Later that evening, they gathered up some wood and built their last fire. It was a windy, cold evening on the Dakota prairie as they sat by the campfire for the last time.

"You got any kin up Ellsworth way?" Jon leaned close to the fire and rubbed his hands together as a cool northern breeze sent a chill up his spine. Ed had said earlier that he wanted to head up Ellsworth way and Jon was wondering if there was a family connection in the Kansas town.

"Couple of cousins and an uncle, that's about it," Ed replied as he threw a couple of logs on the fire. "We lived there for awhile when I was just a boy. I always liked the area, folks are nice there. Ever since then, I've thought that it would be a good place to settle down. How about you Jon, where's your kin folk?"

They had been so busy trying to make a go of it in the camp that they never got around to talking about their families. Now that they were parting, it seemed to be something they wanted to know.

"I got a little sis out in Denver. Last time I heard she was working in a laundry. She's the only kin I got left, except for a couple of cousins; both of my parents have passed away. Daddy died in a farm accident shortly before I left Indiana. He was up in the hayloft pitching hay in a wagon and lost his balance and fell. His head hit the hitch on the wagon and it killed him.

"I was always in awe of my father; I couldn't believe how quickly he died after the fall. Just a matter of a few minutes, his head swelled up and his eyes almost popped out of his face. He looked frightful," Jon said matter-of-factly.

"My mama died from pneumonia when I was just sixteen. She got real sick that winter with the flu and then she caught pneumonia and died. She was a fine woman, I really miss her."

"What kind of man was your father Jon?"

"Hmmm...well, he wasn't a very happy man that's for sure. I got a good beating about every day. He said the beatings would make me tough, but I hated it and I hated him." Jon's voice trailed off. "How about your folks Ed?" he asked, anxious to change the subject.

"They're fine. Both of them are still farming back in Missouri. I plan to visit them for awhile after I leave here." Ed seemed surprised by what he saw next when he looked over at his friend.

Jon's big calloused hand was trembling; his trigger finger wiped a tear away from his eye. "I'm going to miss you buddy, I want you to know that! I'm really going to miss you!" Jon's big heart was breaking as he opened up to his departing friend. "You've been like a brother to me Ed, I'll never forget ya." Jon's voice was shaking; he was almost whispering now.

"Now don't go getting sentimental on me Jon or we'll both end up bawling like babies," Ed replied as he started to tear up. "I wish we could go on forever friend, but things change. And I guess we just have to go our own way now."

"I guess we do," Jon said quietly as he scribbled on the ground with a stick, not wanting the pain of looking his departing friend in the eye. "I guess we just have to go our own way," Jon murmured as he laid back, pulled his hat down over his eyes and prepared to go to sleep for the last time on the cold Dakota prairie.

Ed sat for some time and looked at the flickering flames as they danced nervously in the dimming campfire. Then he too lay down on the cold, hard ground for his last night's sleep in the buffalo camps.

Jon remembered how somber and melancholy the two young hunters had been that final evening as they sat by the campfire and reflected quietly over their two years together. All of the trials, tribulations and challenges that they had faced together in the camp had indeed made them very close. They had taken on a very difficult situation and had overcome enormous odds to make a go of it. All the struggles and shared experiences helped form the character of both men as they made their way through life. The lessons learned and experiences shared would never be forgotten.

Jon and Ed were pretty subdued the next morning as they loaded up their pack horses and prepared to leave. They were still trying to absorb the totality of the situation. Neither one knew what to say. Finally Jon broke the ice. "You better name one of them little ones after me, you hear me!"

"I promise I will, Partner, I promise! Jon Jr., no doubt about it," Ed said enthusiastically. "And may your hole card always be an ace, my friend!" Ed said as he walked quickly over to bid his friend farewell.

"Thank you, Partner!" Jon said sincerely as he approached his friend with his hand outstretched. The two shook firmly, quickly embraced, mounted up and rode away in opposite directions. Both were nursing a very heavy heart as they turned without cue a few hundred yards down the trail and tipped their hats in a final farewell. Jon rode on toward Cheyenne and the gambling haunts in that railroad town while Ed headed back toward Missouri for that visit with his folks. A powerful and defining period in these two young men's life had just come to an end. Little did they know on that cool September day in the Dakota Territory that they would meet again many years later in a little mining town far out in the Sonoran Desert.

Chapter 4

The dust flew as Jon playfully kicked an empty tin can under the wooden walkway. He glanced at the "Military Discount" sign that hung next to the red, white, and blue barber's pole as he hurried up the stairs. It was time for Jon's bi-weekly haircut and some friendly jawin' with his good friend Tom Baldwin, popular barber and President of the County Commission.

Busy sweeping the floor, Tom didn't notice Jon come in.

Jon looked around, admiring the little shop. Several colognes, scissors, combs, shaving mugs, and the ever present straight razors were lined up on the shelf just behind the chair. A beautiful oval mirror with beveled glass hung above the shelf. Jon glanced toward the back, looking for Tom's brown and white Bassett hound. He smiled as he spotted the docile hound lying motionless by the back door. The only sign of life from the chubby beast was an occasional swat of the tail.

"Well hello Jon, how the heck are you?" Tom grinned as he caught a glimpse of the big lawman.

Commissioner Baldwin looked distinguished in his red plaid vest, white cotton shirt, and black shoe string tie. A pair of small, round lenses hung precariously on the end of his rather long nose.

"I'm just fine, Tom, good to see you again," Jon replied.

"Sit down Jon, please." The natty barber pointed to the chair.

Jon's big body fell into the leather chair; his head nestled into the soft head rest. The breeze from the large black cloth felt good as it flew over Jon's head.

"You know Jon, I always kind of hate to cut your hair."

"Oh yea Tom? Why would that be?"

"I don't like messin' with perfection!" the friendly barber quipped.

"Ha, ha, ha!" Jon shouted. "That's a good one!" His big hand slammed down on the leather arm. "Wait till I tell the boys about this one."

"Gotcha that time Sheriff," Tom said with a grin. "The usual?"

"Yea, just don't trim too much off around my ears, I don't want them to stick out," Jon said, still chuckling.

"Okay, okay lover boy, don't worry!"

Tom got more serious as he picked up the scissors. "I'm glad you came in today, I been meaning to talk to you."

"Oh yea, what about?" Jon asked.

"Did you know our British friends Alex Faraday and Clive Cook have both thrown their names in the hat for County Commissioner?"

"No I didn't, but they seem like nice enough

hombres. They bought that big mansion out by the mines, didn't they?" Jon asked.

"Yea, they seem to have plenty of money and they're very popular around here. They could win, you know."

"Are you worried about that Tom?" Jon asked.

"Well, I'm not sure. I was talking to an old friend of mine who just came here from up Kansas way. He stopped in for a haircut the other day. He was a bartender in Ellsworth before coming' out here. He's a talker, seems like he always knows what's going' on."

"What'd he have to say?"

"Rumor was in Ellsworth that Alex hired Butch Canady, a nasty gunhand, and he'll be arriving here in a day or two. I guess the question is, why would he need to hire a gunman? He doesn't seem to have any enemies that I know of." Tom seemed genuinely puzzled.

"Alex has been doing pretty well down at his saloon, maybe he feels he's making so much money he needs protection."

Tom's foot tapped the foot lock, the chair spun to the right. "Maybe so, but something doesn't feel right about this Jon. Maybe you ought to look into it."

"Okay, Mr. Commissioner." Jon grinned. "I'll kind of check things out a little. Faraday and Cook came here from Denver. I'll send a wire to my sheriff friend up that away and see what I can find out. One thing for sure, that Canady is one mean bugger. I spent some time with him in Dodge City years ago and he's pure evil."

"We need to stay on top of this," Tom said warily.

Jon grimaced. "Sure do."

"Well that's enough of this kind of talk Sheriff. How

bout a shave?"

"Sounds good, partner!"

Tom hit the release button on the cast iron chair; Jon went perpendicular.

"Hold on there!" Jon shouted, feet in the air, laughing like a fool.

Chapter 5

Steam rose as the hot black liquid splashed into the metal cup. "Thank you Ed," Jon said. The pot banged as Ed strolled over and dropped it on the cast iron burner. Jon was nestled in the corner of the office behind his large oak desk. He took a sip of coffee and sat back to admire the new jail the town had built him. From this vantage point, Jon could see everyone coming and going from the jail. He also had a good view of all but one of the cells. That cell sat around the corner and was used to house harmless drunks, vagrants etc. The deputy's desk was smaller and just to the right of the front door. A local seamstress had made some appropriately masculine brown curtains to adorn the windows at either side of the door. The four small cells featured steel plate ceilings lined with railroad ties, thirty-two inch stucco walls, and two hundred pound, riveted steel doors. Jon was particularly proud of several pictures of local dignitaries that hung in various places around the room. One was of himself.

Deputy Ed Morgan was at his desk doing some

paper work when he noticed Jon admiring the room. "Nice office, ain't it, Jon?"

"Yea, yea, it's pretty darn nice alright."

"You know, the other day I found some pocket mice back there in the supply room. They were trying to get in our bags of coffee and sugar," Ed said as he looked over at Jon.

Jon was genuinely annoyed at being brought out of his delightful trance by his good friend. "Oh, oh well, is that so? Ah, what the heck did you do about it, Ed?"

"Well I uh, took the picture of that big ugly sheriff off the wall and sat it back there in the supply room for a couple of days. And you know what?"

"What?"

"I ain't seen a mouse since," Ed said, with a grin.

"Why you no account claim jumper!" Jon shouted. "You know I hate that picture, Libby makes me keep it up there because she painted it!" Jon grabbed a book off his desk and started to throw it at Ed. Ed was heading for cover under his desk. Suddenly, the front door swung open; Fred from the telegraph office rushed into the room.

"Sorry to interrupt," the prim and proper Fred announced, obviously taken aback by the silly behavior of the two law enforcement officials. "But your message from Sheriff Taggart in Denver just arrived and you told me to bring it right down."

"Yea, I certainly did Fred. And thank you for bringing it down so quickly." Big Jon said nervously. He could feel his face turning red as he set the book on his desk. Ed was smiling from ear to ear, obviously delighted at the predicament his good friend had gotten himself into.

"That'll be two dollars Sheriff."

Jon's hand slipped into his front jeans pocket and pulled out two silver dollars. "Thank you Fred," Jon said. The wire slid across Jon's desk. Fred left the jail, nose in the air.

Jon sat back and began reading the lengthy telegram from Sheriff Taggart. Several minutes later he looked up and made eye contact with Deputy Ed.

"Well, what is it? Let's have it." Ed was anxious to learn more about the two popular Brits who had opened the Faraday Saloon six months prior.

"It seems like I should have checked on these boys a little sooner!" Jon scowled.

"It's that bad huh?" the deputy replied.

"Pretty bad. It seems our friends from Britain were quite the movers and shakers in Denver."

"Oh yea? What'd Sheriff Taggart have to say?"

"Taggart says they came to Denver about three years ago from Boston area. They both got their citizenship while they lived in Boston. As soon as they got to town; Faraday, the one with the money, bought a saloon in downtown Denver. He claims his ancestry goes back to some low level British royalty. Taggart says they were both very popular when they first arrived in Denver. It wasn't long before Clive Cook was getting politically involved. He ran for sheriff and was narrowly beaten in a runoff with a local man. The new sheriff liked Cook and appointed him to be one of his deputies shortly after taking office. When the sheriff was mysteriously killed, the town asked Clive to take the job. That's when the trouble started." Jon paused and took a hard drag off of his Havana; the smoke drifted to the ceiling.

"So now Faraday owns a saloon and has local law enforcement in his back pocket," the savvy deputy surmised.

"Exactly Ed. Cook started going around fining the other tavern owners for housing prostitutes and permitting gambling, while turning a blind eye to his friend Faraday's operation. Faraday was doing the same thing, but not being fined for it. Nobody noticed at first. There were ordinances against gambling and prostitution in Denver but nobody abided by them; an occasional fine was levied, which served as a form of excise tax. The town used the money to fund worthwhile projects. But when the other owners found out they were the only ones being targeted, the crap hit the fan. They were angry, afraid the two curly wolves would run them out of business."

"So what happened next?" Ed asked.

"The City Council stepped in and fired Cook for influence pedaling. They closed Faraday down by using that same ordinance against gambling and prostitution. Faraday tried to fight it for awhile, but after several threats were made against his life, he and Cook finally decided that it would be in their best interest to leave Denver."

"So they picked our little boom town out here in the desert as their next project," Ed said disgustedly.

"Sure looks that way. And if they win two seats on the County Commission, they'll almost have control of the whole county. They'll need one more vote, so they'll try and buy off one of the other commissioners. If he refuses, they'll use Canady to threaten him or his family.

One way or another they'll get their damn vote. Then they'll fire me and hire a new sheriff of their choosing, probably Cook or Web Norton. And before you know it, they'll control everything round here. And then they'll be trying to force Libby out of business so they can take over all the gambling and prostitution. Then they'll move on to the next town and do the same thing. Soon they will control all the gaming in the entire area." Jon frowned, shaking his head.

"How do we stop them, Jon?" Ed asked.

"Well, the election's almost over. Faraday and Cook will probably be our two new county commissioners. And to tell you the truth, I'm not entirely sure what to do about it right this minute. But one thing's for sure, Ed!"

"What's that Boss?"

"It's going take more than those two snakes to take this town over!" Smoke rose as Jon angrily snuffed his cigar out it the small metal ashtray.

Ed just shook his head in disgust.

"Watch the prisoner Ed, I'm going down and talk to Camp Wilson about filling in for Jack for awhile. With all that's coming down around here, we're going to need another gun. Camp's helped me out a few times before. He's good with a gun and a tough little hombre. I think he'll jump at the chance."

Jon quickly cleared his desk, took his gun belt off the peg, pulled the belt tight, and tied down. "I'm going to stop at the school first and check on the election. See you in a few," Jon said as he headed out the door.

Babe was prancing nervously in front of the jail as Jon approached. He quickly untied, mounted up and headed for the little one room school on the edge of town. The big lawman reined to a stop in front of the makeshift polling place. His fast approach startled some of the voters.

"Sorry folks, didn't mean to startle you," Jon said with a smile.

"No problem Sheriff," an older man replied. "What can we do for you, Jon?"

"Oh I was just kind of curious about how the vote was coming along. You got any feel for it, Jeb?"

The old man looked up at Jon. "Most of the folks I've talked to are voting for those British fellas; they're right popular around here you know. I'd say they're the ones to beat."

"Yea, I'll bet they are, thanks for the info," Jon replied. He tipped his hat to the folks and rode to the stables to talk with Camp. He was out front talking to a customer as Jon approached. He looked lean and muscular in his blue denim shirt, jeans and buck-stitched chaps. The youngster shook hands with the departing customer and turned to greet big Jon.

Camp smiled at his friend. "Howdy Jon! What brings you down to this end of town? You droppin' Babe off?"

"No Camp, we got us more serious problems right now," Jon replied.

Camp's eyes narrowed as he looked over at Jon. "Oh yea, what's up?"

"It looks like our friends from Great Britain, Mr. Faraday and Mr. Cook, are turning out to be a couple a bad actors. Seems they got a habit of trying to take over all the gambling and prostitution in whatever town they ride into. They did their darndest to take over everything in Denver, but the locals got wind of it and ran them out of town. They're trying to get elected to the County Commission here so they can throw me out of office and put their own man in. Doesn't look good Partner."

"Hmmm! That's kind of surprising. I don't know em, but everybody says they're right decent fellas," Camp replied.

"Yea, those two are smoother than silk. I kind of like them myself."

Camp nodded as he replied. "Sorry Jon, but I'm kind of running behind; what can I do for you?"

"Okay, I'll get to the point. Malone's down and we're kind of short handed right now. I need a good deputy real bad." Jon looked with anticipation at his young friend.

"Hmmm...a deputy, huh?" Camp's hand rubbed the stubble on his chin. "We're kind of busy right now, but I'm sure the owner, Pat, could fill in if necessary."

"Is that a yes? I haven't got all night."

"I know, I know! Pat's out at the McLennan ranch shoein' some horses. I'll talk to him soon as he gets back. If it's okay with him, I'll finish things up here and be down."

"Sounds good, Camp! I want to pay Faraday a visit this evening and I'd like for you to go with me."

"Okay, Sheriff." Camp nodded and smiled as he hurried back to the stables.

Jon rode back toward town. Almost at full gallop, he came to a sudden stop in front of the Barbee; dismounted and walked hurriedly into the saloon.

"Give me a shot of Early Times Sam," Jon ordered.

"Comin' up, Jon," Sam replied. "You're kind of in a hurry big guy, something comin' down?"

"Yea there is, Sam, I'll tell you about it later," Jon said hastily. "Is Libby around?"

"Who wants to know?" Libby's mouth curled into a smile as she shouted across the room at her big lover. "What's up?"

Jon downed his shot, slid a silver dollar across the bar to Sam. He walked over to where Libby was standing near the faro tables. Taking her gently by the wrist, he led her over to a table around the corner from the door. They both sat down.

"Tom Baldwin asked me to look into Alex Faraday's past a little bit; so I wired my sheriff friend in Denver. Looks like he and Cook had concocted a scheme to take over all the saloons in Denver, but before they could do their dirty deed, they got thrown out of town. So they packed up and headed our way. I think they want to do the same thing here," Jon said.

"Hmm, doesn't really surprise me; something just didn't feel right about those two," Libby replied.

"I'm going to deputize Camp and then we're going to ride out to Faraday's tonight and have a heart to heart talk."

"Please be careful Jon, these men could be dangerous," Libby said softly as she placed her hand tenderly on Jon's forearm.

"At this point, I got no quarrel with Faraday and Cook. We just need to come to a little understanding before this thing gets out of hand." Jon smiled warmly.

"I understand, but just be careful anyway, alright?"

"Alright pretty lady. I got to be going," Jon stepped behind Libby's chair. She pulled her beautiful red cotton gown up slightly and stood up, as Jon carefully slid the chair out of the way.

"I'll stop by later and fill you in," Jon said.

"See you then, handsome." Libby winked at the embarrassed lawman as she turned to greet some miners.

"By handsome!" "See ya cutie," some of the patrons shouted at the red faced Jon as he hurried out of the saloon.

"I sure wish she wouldn't do that," Jon whispered to Babe as he hopped aboard and hurried down Pecos Street to the jail.

Chapter 6

Jon set the steaming plate of sausage and beans on the small wooden shelf next to Zing Fuller's bunk. Fuller lay still on his bed until Jon left and pulled the heavy riveted steel door shut and turned the key. Zing took the hot plate of food off the shelf and sat it on his lap. "Bout time!" he mumbled.

"What did you say?" Jon shot back.

"Uh, I said thanks." Fuller's thin lips cracked into a smart grin.

"Don't thank me, Fuller, thank the cook at the Barbee. He's the one does all the cooking."

Suddenly the front door swung open.

"Still need that deputy?" Camp Wilson said as he hurried in the room.

"Sure do, Camp," Jon replied, smiling at his young friend. "I thought you might show up, Pat owes me a favor or two."

"He told me to take all the time I needed, so let's get at it," the anxious recruit replied.

"Okay Camp, I need to swear you in."

Camp walked over to Jon's desk and put his right hand on black leather Bible Jon kept on the corner of his desk for such occasions.

"Just follow after me."

"Okay."

"Do you Camp Wilson swear to uphold the laws of Mesquite County to the best of your abilities?"

"I do."

"And do you Camp Wilson swear to stay sober and not use foul or profane language when acting as a deputy of said county?"

"I do," Camp replied as Jon pinned the metal badge on the pocket of his blue denim shirt.

"Heck, if he can do all that, he oughta be sheriff," Deputy Ed Morgan chimed in as he walked out of the supply room.

"Now there you go again!" Jon laughed. "Just pipe down Ed and look after the jail while Camp and I pay Faraday a visit."

"Will do Sheriff," Ed said as he winked at Camp.

Jon and Camp hurried outside, mounted up, and headed west out of town toward the Faraday mansion, an hour's ride away.

The desert landscape was showing its stuff as the two riders galloped down the winding trail. The globe mallow, desert lilies, mariposa, and the awesome saguaro cactus were in full bloom on this cool winter day. The delicate beauty of this desert scene was in sharp contrast to the violence that would soon befall this isolated mining town.

Suddenly, a solitary rider flew past. Jon reined to a stop. Babe reared up a little as the rider charged on, head down and chaps flapping in the wind.

"What's that all about, Jon?" Camp shouted as he pulled up next to Jon.

"Looks like Web Norton, one of Faraday's boys. He's probably going into town to meet the stage and check on election results. Might be Butch Canady's greeting party."

"I've heard Canady is one nasty varmint," Camp replied.

"Yea he is, we don't need people like him around here." Jon's eyes narrowed as he spoke of the nasty gunman. He could feel the darkness growing inside of him.

"I've never met these hombres, what can you tell me about em Jon?" Camp asked as they rode on toward the ranch.

"Well, Alex Faraday is an educated and cultured man. He's kinda tall and lean and he has a thin face and a small wisp of a mustache. He's got black shiny hair and it's always combed and parted on the left. He looks rich and always dresses to the nines. He likes silk shirts and fancy vests.

"How about Cook?"

"Cook's his right hand man. He was a bare knuckles boxer back in England and held the light heavy weight championship of Great Britain for awhile. He's a big guy and looks like he weighs two hundred plus. These two are like fire and ice, but they make a nice team. Faraday's smart and comes up with their crooked schemes. Cook's pretty handy with a gun and makes a great enforcer for Faraday."

"You think they'll be out here?"

I hope so. My guess is they're holed up at Faraday's enclave waiting for the results of the election. Local custom discourages candidates from being in town during the vote, except when casting their own ballot. They voted in the morning and then rode back out here. They'll be surprised to see us, I guarantee you that."

"Is that the mansion up ahead there?" Camp asked.

"Sure enough is."

"Quite a place."

The two lawmen rode slowly toward the front of Faraday's sprawling estate.

"I just saw somebody looking out one of the back windows, they probably know we're here," Jon surmised as he dismounted and tied down. Jon walked up to the double oak door on the front of the mansion and slammed the gold knocker a couple of times. He could hear someone hurrying toward the door. Suddenly, the door swung open as Clive Cook stepped out.

"Sheriff Stoudenmire, what a nice surprise! And you also, Mr. ....? "

"Camp Wilson," he replied.

The big Brit nodded at Camp. "Welcome Mr. Wilson, I take it you gentlemen are here to see Alex?"

"If you don't mind, Clive," Jon replied.

"Well certainly. Mr. Faraday is in his study. Come right in." Cook stepped back and waved his arm toward the study at the end of the long entryway.

"Thank you kindly," Jon replied as he and Camp walked toward the study.

They looked around at the plush leather chairs and large oil paintings of kings and queens that decorated the beautiful oak hallway. Jon pointed up at a huge antler chandelier hanging from the vaulted ceiling; he smiled as Camp craned to see the large edifice.

The three men reached the end of the hallway; Jon stepped aside as Cook moved forward and grabbed the large knocker on the den door. He pounded it several times, announcing their arrival. The door swung open almost immediately.

"Why hello, Sheriff, what a surprise! Please come in," the ever-gracious Faraday exclaimed, motioning with his thin hand for the men to enter.

"Sit down, gentlemen, please sit down," he said politely as they approached his desk.

"Thank you Alex," Jon replied as he and Camp sat down in front of Faraday's large cherry wood desk.

"And to what do I owe this pleasure?" Faraday asked as he eased into his leather chair.

"Oh we were just out riding and thought we'd stop in and say hello," Jon replied. He glanced over at Camp who was trying mightily to keep from laughing.

"Well I know better than that Mr. Stoudenmire, and I'm a very busy man, so..."

Jon interrupted the uppity Brit. "You're right Alex, you are a busy man. With the election about over and a guest coming and all, I'm sure you have plenty to do," Jon said as he looked directly at Faraday.

"Guest? I don't know what you mean Sheriff."

"Let's not play games here Alex. The sheriff in Tombstone wired me just today and told me that Butch Canady had spent the night there and was on his way to Logan's Crossing to work for an old friend. That friend is you Alex and it concerns me very much. Butch Canady only knows how to do one thing and that's kill people. I'm just wonderin' why you hired a man like that to come here to Logan's Crossing."

The muscular Cook, standing to the right of Jon, moved closer as Faraday spoke up.

Faraday's eyes narrowed. "That's none of your affair, Sir. So I would suggest that you mind your own business." Alex appeared confident with his enforcer, Cook, nearby to protect him.

"Now you listen to me, Faraday. When somebody brings a hired gun into Mesquite County, that's definitely my business."

Cook moved even closer to Jon; he was now standing just a foot away. The tension in the room was thick as Camp sat up in his chair, hand on his peacemaker.

"Tell Cook to back off, Alex," Jon said calmly.

"I don't believe that would be proper, Sir. I think the proper thing would be for you and your young friend to leave immediately." The stuffy Brit thought nobody could match his powerful friend.

"Tell him to back off Mr. Faraday, the sheriff is starting to get mad and you don't want to see that!" Camp warned.

"Oh my, I'm sure that Clive is just shaking in his boots, young fellow. The man's a famous prizefighter for God's sake. Now if you boys would..."

"Let's go!" Clive Cook shouted as he slapped his large hand on Jon's shoulder signaling him to get up and get out.

"Take your hand off me!" Jon said as he started to slowly get up from his chair.

"I'm not playing around with you Stoudenmire!"

Cook's right hand went toward his six gun.

Jon's hand folded into a fist. He quickly turned and blasted the big Brit with a mighty blow to the gut.

"Ughhh!" The big man's eyes almost popped out of his head from the force of Jon's powerful punch. Jon had Cook back on his heels, writhing in pain and gasping for breath. He quickly raised his right arm high above his head and with a violent downward motion he slammed his right elbow into the huge man's rib cage.

"Ahggg!" Cook shouted as he fell hard to the floor holding his side and his stomach. Jon looked hard at a shocked Faraday; his eyes were wide as he watched his huge enforcer roll around in pain on his expensive rug.

Jon shouted at him. "I know what you're up to around here Faraday. Let this be a warning to you and your hired guns. If you try to move in on this town, you're gonna have to go through me!" Jon exclaimed. Faraday was speechless.

"Don't forget what I told you!" Jon said sternly as he and Camp backed out of the den and into the hall.

The Brit nodded nervously as he continued to look down at the battered Cook.

The two lawmen turned and walked through the beautiful hallway, spurs jingling, and out the front door. They yanked the leather straps loose, mounted up, and rode rapidly toward town. As they rode along the dusty trail, Jon felt himself becoming very angry at the developing showdown. The arrogance of the wealthy Brit in the face of the law infuriated Jon. His anger was rising; the darkness was starting to come, darkness that would be the precursor to another orgy of violence. Violence propelled from the very soul of this tormented lawman. The beating of Clive Cook just whetted his appetite; there was a devil rising up once again in Jon, out in the dirt and heat of the desert.

Chapter 7

The polls had just closed as Jon and Camp came thundering into town. They reached the front of the jail and dismounted. They hurried up the wooden steps and went inside.

"Any news Ed?" Jon asked his trusted deputy.

"Nope, it's a little early. The polls just closed. It will be a little while before the ballots are all counted. How'd it go out at Faraday's?" Ed asked.

"Not too well, Ed," Jon replied. "Faraday didn't want to talk about Canady. When I brought him up, he tried to throw us out."

"Oh boy! I'll bet that didn't go over too well," Ed's eyes were wide with anticipation.

"Sure didn't. Cook grabbed my shoulder and I let him have it a couple of times."

"A couple of times? Oh my! Is he dead?" Ed exclaimed.

"Not quite." Camp joined the conversation. "But when we left he didn't look too good."

"I heard he's a boxing champ or something," Ed

said, always amazed at the great punching power of big Jon. "A couple of times. Wow! He'll be laid up for awhile!"

"I had to teach him a lesson. Least now they know I mean business," Jon said quietly, a little embarrassed by all the talk.

"Better watch your back side partner, a man like Clive Cook has a lot of pride and you humiliated him in front of his boss. I got a feelin' you'll see him again," Ed said, eye brows raised toward his boss.

"Thanks for the warning, Ed. We're going down to the Barbee and grab some dinner. I'll have Sam send you down a plate." Jon and Camp turned to leave.

"You're all heart!" Ed bellowed.

As they walked down to the Barbee, Jon thought about his visit to Faraday's enclave. *Faraday's a proud man, he won't give up easy. This will be a tough fight.*

Camp interrupted Jon's thoughts, "Hey Jon, is that Canady over there talkin' to Web Norton?" he asked. Two men were standing in the street near the one room school. Norton was an average sized man; the other man was small and thin.

"Yea, that's him," Jon said as he and Camp came to a stop on the wooden walkway. Jon leaned against a support post and looked across the dusty street at the two men.

"He's doesn't look that mean to me," Camp quipped.

"Don't let his size fool you Camp. He's mighty quick on the draw and he ain't afraid of nothin'. He'd kill his own mother if the price was right. Butch Canady is one bad man."

Jon told Camp about his time with Canady in the

Kansas Territory. "I spent a couple of years in Dodge City after leaving the family farm in Indiana. Still wet behind the ears, I heard a lot about a local gunman named Butch Canady. And what I heard wasn't good. He was a gun for hire. Several enemies of the sheriff in Dodge came up missing. Everyone knew who did it, but of course nothing was ever done about it. I saw him shoot a dog dead on the streets of Dodge just for barking too loud. Canady has a big empty hole inside of him and the only way to fill it is to hurt someone or something else. He is a very bad man.

"What do you want to do for now, Jon?" Camp asked.

"I've had enough fun for one day, Camp. We've got plenty of time to deal with Butch Canady. Let's go have some dinner."

"Yea, he'd probably say somethin' wrong and you'd let him have it and I'd have to take him to the Doc!"

Jon lifted up Camp's Sonoma straw hat and ruffled the young deputy's hair as both men had a good laugh.

Their fun was short lived as shots rang out from over by the little school house. People were screaming and running to get out of the way.

"Looks like Canady's making his presence known already," Jon said as he jumped down from the walkway and ran like a shot toward the trouble. Camp was close behind.

As Jon got closer he could see Canady standing over a young man waving his smoking six guns in his face and threatening him. At one point he kicked the fallen man in the groin. Jon drew his six guns as he got closer. He pointed them directly at Butch Canady's back when he reached the scene.

"Sheriff Stoudenmire here Butch, don't make any sudden moves or you're a dead man," Jon said calmly.

"My oh my, Jon Stoudenmire. Haven't heard that name for a coon's age, how are you, Jon?" Canady asked. He stood very still, not wanting to alarm the sheriff.

"Listen real close Butch. I want you to slowly slide those six guns back in your holsters. If those guns go any way but straight down I'll blow your damn fool head off." Jon sounded tough and commanding.

"No problem Jon, I ain't lookin' for no trouble," the nasty gunman said as the white handled Cimarrons slid slowly out of his thin fingers and into the awaiting holsters.

"Now, put your hands up and turn around slowly."

Butch felt the metal barrel of Jon's six gun poke into his rib cage.

"Okay Jon, stay calm. I don't want no trouble with you," Canady replied as he slowly turned around.

As he turned, Jon had forgotten how strong he looked face on. Although a small man, he looked muscular and wiry. He had a square face, dark from the sun, with thin lips and a flat nose. His eyebrows were thick and bushy; his eyes looked black and empty. His face was accentuated by a thin black handle bar mustache. He was a tough looking hombre.

"What seems to be the problem here, Butch?"

"Seems like this fella over here says I killed his brother a while back in the Nebraska Territory. I said he was a liar and he drew on me. I shot him in the arm Sheriff, it was self defense. Web here will testify to that fact, right Web."

"Yea, it was self defense alright," Web replied nervously.

"Is that true, young fella?"

"Yea, I drew on em alright. He shot my brother in cold blood and he's gonna pay for it," the young man shouted.

"Are you just passin' through?" Jon asked the youngster.

"Yea, I'm on my way to Tombstone to visit family."

"I want you out of town by midnight tonight or I'll throw you in jail for attempted murder. It's for your own good. So get your supplies and get on out of town," Jon said as Camp threw the young man his hat.

"There'll be another time, Mr. Canady," the youngster shouted as he brushed his jeans and hurried off.

"Well thank you Sheriff, you kept me from havin' to kill that young fella," Canady smirked; a brown stain popped in the dust as Butch spit on the street.

"Listen to me, Canady. I know why you're in town and I know what you're up to. You would have killed that boy in a minute, but you got a job to do and you haven't been paid yet." Jon detested men like Canady. He wanted to put a bullet in his belly in the worst way.

"You win this time Sheriff, but I'm gonna be around for awhile. So I'm sure we'll meet again," Canady said coldly.

"I sure hope so, Butch! I'd like nothin' better than for you and I to go one on one."

Canady's mouth curled up in a wicked smile as he mounted his horse and rode toward Faraday's saloon with Web Norton close behind.

"Sure seems like a nasty critter," Camp said.

"One of the worst. Gotta keep a close eye on him," Jon replied as he slid his two Army Colts back in their holsters.

"Let's get some grub!"

The man with the striped hat pounded the Honky-Tonk piano. Turkey in the Straw resounded throughout the saloon. The gambling hall was buzzing with activity; laughter filled the air as Jon and Camp entered the Barbee to get little grub and wait for the election results.

"Howdy boys," Sam the bartender slid a couple of shots of Early Times in front of the two lawmen.

"Howdy Sam." Jon walked over and took his usual spot at the end of the bar. He could see the room better from there. Just in case some unhappy relative of one of the men he'd killed happen to show up and try to get even.

"What was the gunplay all about?"

"Alex Faraday's hired gun winged a guy out there," Camp replied.

"What's the guy's name?' Sam asked.

"Butch Canady and he's a bad one," Camp replied.

Suddenly two shots rang out by the front door.

"Listen up everybody!" the smallish election official shouted, six gun still smoking. "The results are in!" The official's small hand slipped inside into his vest pocket; a crinkled up piece of paper appeared. "For County Commissioner the results are! Alex Faraday 474. Clive Cook 387, Paul Nettles 212, Dave Carson 123, and Jeb Harter 82. Our two newly elected Commissioners are Alex Faraday and Clive Cook. Since the positions are vacant due to a death and sudden retirement, their terms will start immediately, thank you!" There was nice applause and several 'here, heres," as the official hurried out the door.

"That doesn't surprise me," Jon said disgustedly. "They just got what they wanted."

"Yea, they're going to try and take over now and the town doesn't even know it, it ain't right!" Camp complained.

Jon looked warily through the swinging doors at the scene outside. Norton and Canady rode by at full gallop, anxious to get the news of the election to Alex Faraday. The billowing dust from their horses' pounding hoofs darkened the street. As the dust cleared, Jon could see the sun setting under the surrounding hills. It was a calm and beautiful scene. *Those men must be stopped!* Jon thought as he looked out at the quiet street.

Chapter 8

Alex Faraday paced as he awaited the results of the election. Even though he and Cook were the favorites, he was nervous about the pending results. A few minutes later, he heard riders approaching.

"Clive, somebody's here!" Alex shouted as he leaned out of a large side window.

Alex saw Cook rush from the stables, holding his sore stomach.

An anxious Alex was already coming out the front door. He looked intently at Web. "Well, for God's sake man, say something!"

"It was a sweep Alex, you both won!" Web Norton replied.

Butch Canady dismounted and tied down; he appeared disinterested.

"I dare say that's the best news I've heard in some time," Alex replied. "And I'm sorry, is this gentleman Mr. Canady?"

"Oh yes, sorry Alex, in all the excitement I forgot to introduce you," Web replied.

"It's certainly a pleasure to meet you, Mr. Canady. Welcome to the ranch," Alex said graciously, extending his right hand to the gunman.

"Good to meet you Alex," Canady said quietly, he gripped Faraday's outstretched hand for a quick shake. "Hope I can help out around here."

"Well I'm sure you can, Mr. Canady. We have a lot of things to get done and your services will be a big part of that." Alex grinned at the notorious gunman. "Now, will you all join me in my study for a touch of brandy?" The Englishman gestured toward the study.

Nervous conversation filled the room, as Clive clumsily poured each man a snifter. Alex leaned back and stuffed some Scottish Blend tobacco into his Aldo Velani pipe. He turned slightly to his left and struck a match on the stone fireplace just behind his chair. He lit up and began to explain his plan to take over the gambling and prostitution in Logan's Crossing. "Gentlemen, we have a wonderful opportunity here to all become very wealthy men. We now have two of the five County Commissioner positions. And since the Commission rules by majority vote, all we have to do is convince one of the other Commissioners to see things our way and we'll have this town in the palm of our hand." He smiled smugly, proud of how he had duped the local people into voting for he and Cook.

"How do the other Commissioners feel about things?" Norton asked.

"Well, Tom Baldwin is the current President of the Commission and he's a pretty straight arrow, I don't see much hope with him. Of the other two Commissioners, Jed Orton and Bill Hancock, I believe Orton is our best bet. His mine burned out a couple of years ago. He tried a couple of other veins, but they didn't produce much. I'm sure he's very short of cash. I think with the right proposal, Jed would be happy to side with us. Bill Hancock is pretty well off; he would be difficult to buy."

"Sounds like a cozy little plan Faraday, but what if Orton can't be bought?" Butch Canady asked. His dark eyes narrowed as he sipped the brandy.

"Well Mr. Canady, that's where you come in. Your job will be to convince Jed to see it our way."

"And what if he still doesn't want to cooperate, what then?" Canady pushed on.

"Well then, I guess we'll just have to eliminate him," Alex said coldly. "Then there will be a special election and we'll run Web here to fill his spot. Web's lived around here all of his life, he would win easily."

A hush came over the room. The men looked intently at their boss.

"No problem Alex, but the sheriff isn't going to take Jed's death sittin down. And he's got a horse in this race, Web tells me the pretty owner of the Barbee's his lady friend."

"You are correct, Mr. Canady. Sheriff Stoudenmire is a very substantial adversary indeed. He knocked Clive senseless the other day with just two punches."

Clive's large face and bald head turned bright red.

"And yes, there is a strong bond between he and Miss Thompson," Alex continued. "That's all the more reason I hired you Butch. And just so there is no misunderstanding, Mr. Stoudenmire is part of your responsibility. I'm sure Clive wouldn't mind giving you a hand if the circumstances called for it," Faraday said.

Clive nodded in the affirmative.

Canady frowned a little as he replied, "You should of told me Stoudenmire was the sheriff before I came here. He's one bad hombre, most people that mess with him end up dead." Canady fidgeted with the diamond cluster ring on his left hand.

"I hired you to do a job Mr. Canady and I'm paying you very well. Whether you like it or not, Sheriff Stoudenmire is part of your job. Can you handle this or not?" Faraday was looking carefully at the gunman.

Canady paused for a moment and then spoke up. "I'm in alright Faraday, but my price just went up to a hundred a week plus expenses."

"What?" Faraday exclaimed.

"You heard me Faraday, take it or leave it."

"Alright, alright, we've got a deal," Faraday said reluctantly. "It's too damn late to find anyone else, but you'd better get the job done."

Suddenly, Web Norton jumped in the conversation, "I'm gettin' kind of worried Boss."

"Worried, Web? About what?"

"Camp Wilson's been hangin' round with Stoudenmire a lot lately. He's been deputized once or twice. He's young and fearless and good with a gun."

"Okay Web, so what?"

"Well.... I'll tell you what! Stoudenmire's also got Morgan and Malone when he gets better. Those are four darn tough men. Clive and Web are plenty good enough, but I think we're gonna need another gun," Web said somberly.

"Ummm...I see what you mean my friend. It's a point well taken. The only problem is, this is all getting just a might expensive," Alex replied.

"I understand Boss. But I think I might be able to get us a gun pretty cheap. Maybe for a few hundred dollars of bail money," Norton had a sly look on his face.

"Well that sounds promising, go on."

The brandy snifter plopped on the end table; Web smacked his lips and continued. "Stoudenmire just arrested Zing Fuller today for the shooting of Deputy Malone. The sheriff shot and killed the other fella in a showdown near the river. He's the one who shot Deputy Malone. They ain't got much on Fuller; bail should be low. We could offer to pay Fuller's bail if he joins up with us. Then we'd just offer board and room and a chance for his freedom when his hearing rolls around. He's got nowhere to go, he'd probably take it."

"An interesting idea Norton, do you think Stoudenmire would go along with it?"

"The sheriff's department is broke after building that new jail. They could probably use the cash. Besides, if we get the judge to set a low bail, Stoudenmire doesn't have any choice in the matter."

"That is interesting. What's the story on Fuller?" Faraday asked as he downed the last sip of brandy and poured himself another.

"I know a little about him," Canady chimed in as he lifted a crinkled cigarette out of his shirt pocket, lit up and waved the smoke away from his eyes. "Luke Short hired him as an enforcer at his saloon in Dodge. He's tough and good with a gun. Not one to trifle with. I'd try and get 'em if I were you."

"Alright, let's give it a shot," Faraday said. "Clive,

why don't you, Web and Butch ride into town tomorrow and find out what the situation is with Fuller. If he's in, you can go up to three hundred on bail. Any more than that, and we will do with what we got."

"Okay Boss," Web replied.

"Well, that's enough conversation for one evening. Gentlemen, why don't we all retire?" The handsome Brit led the group toward the lavish dining room.

* * *

Back in town, Jon and Camp were finishing dinner at the Barbee as darkness settled in over the desert town.

The cool beer flowed into Jon's dry mouth. He gently sat the empty mug on the table and sat back. He reached inside his leather vest and pulled out a fresh cigar. He struck a match on his belt buckle and took a long, hard drag off the yellow-blue flame. He squinted a little through the smoke and spoke to Camp. "Things are heating up around here Camp. Faraday's going to move fast now that he and Cook have been elected. We've got to stop 'em dead in their tracks."

Camp chewed his last bite and pushed his plate forward. "Good grub tonight," he said as he nervously played with the gold ring on his shooting hand. "I agree Jon, things seem to be movin' awful fast around here. What do you think they're gonna do?"

"I think they're going after Jed Orton first, and sooner rather than later. He's had some tough times lately. His mine went bust last year. He tried a couple of smaller veins on the short side of the mountain and they dried up pretty quick. They'll play on Jed's troubles and try to bribe him. Jed's had a checkered past, a little gambling here and there. He got involved in some rustling down El Paso way a few years ago. He's been trying to go straight ever since he came to town, but it's been a struggle for him. I'm afraid he's an easy target. Back when things were going good at the mine, he bought a little chicken farm just outside of town. It's not much, but it keeps him going."

"What about Tom Baldwin and Bill Hancock?" Camp asked.

"Baldwin's a dead end for them, he's too honest. Hancock's got plenty of cash, otherwise I don't know much about him. He's new to town." Jon's eyes squinted, the smoke curled around his fingers as he punched out the cigar in the metal ash tray. "We've got a little time before sundown. Orton's place is just outside of town a couple of miles. Let's ride out and have a heart to heart before Canady gets to him."

"Sounds good, Boss." Camp gulped down his beer and banged the glass mug on the hard oak table top.

Jon grabbed his hat and stood up. He weaved his way between the tables and out the front door. Camp was close behind him..

He and Camp mounted up and rode toward the edge of town. Jon heard a shout. He glanced over and saw Camp pull up suddenly and stop at the livery stable. He pulled up and watched as Camp ran over to the stable door, reached inside and yanked his six guns off a peg. He strapped on, tied down, and jumped back on his mount.

Jon shouted at Camp, "Good idea, Camp! You never know what we're going to run into out there. One thing's for sure, Faraday and Canady aren't going to let some little chicken farmer stand in their way. They'd kill him in a minute. Let's ride; the sun's running out on us!"

Babe leaped forward, the race was on to Jed Orton's. The two lawmen charged out of town toward the setting sun. A few miles down the road, Jon suddenly pulled up.

"Whoa! Whoa!" Jon had reached a fork in the road. Camp pulled up next to him.

"What's up Jon, did you forget how to get there?" Camp joked.

"Take a look at this, smart aleck," Jon said. Camp quickly dismounted and walked over to where Jon was standing. "We've got some fresh tracks coming from Jed's place. Looks like somebody may have beaten us to the punch. The tracks take the west fork toward Faraday's compound. That snake Canady may have already visited Jed."

"Nothing we can do about it now, Jon," Camp retorted.

"Yea, let's ride on in. It's startin' to get dark already." The two riders once again hurried on toward the commissioner's farm.

White feathers flew in the air as startled chickens scurried to move away from the fast approaching riders. They could see Jed throwing scratch on the ground in the bantam chicken yard as the chicks raced to get into the coop, safely away from the thundering hoofs. Jed, a large heavyset man with a red pock-marked face and furrowed brow, dropped the metal feed bucket over a fence post and walked over to greet Jon and Camp.

"Welcome, Gents," Jed said as Jon and Camp found

a couple of empty posts and tied up. They walked over and shook hands.

"Howdy Jed, good to see you again," Jon said warmly.

"Jed." Camp nodded and tipped his hat to the chicken farmer.

"You boys are just in time. I was just gonna clean out the laying hens' coop. I could use some help." Jed kind of smiled at the two visitors.

"Oh, well ah, no thanks Jed," Jon said, surprised by the levity from the big man. "We'd love to, but it's starting to get dark and we need to be heading back to town shortly."

"Okay Sheriff, I'll let you off the hook this time." Jed's belly jiggled as he laughed.

Jon went on. "The sun is setting fast Jed, so I won't beat around the bush. I'm sure you know that Alex Faraday and Clive Cook have been elected as the new members of the County Commission." Jon waited for his reaction.

Jed looked stoic as he calmly replied. "Yes, I know, they're very popular around here, but I really don't know much about them. One of their hired hands stopped by to see me just a little while ago. Said his name was Butch. He said Faraday was counting on my vote and then he rode off." The whole fence shook as Jed slammed the small gate shut and hooked the latch.

"I'd say hired gun's a better description," Jon said evenly. "He's a real bad actor from the Kansas Territory named Butch Canady. Some say he's killed as many as fifteen men."

"Seemed friendly enough, but I guess you never

know. Oh and, you don't mind if I keep on feeding, do you? I got some hungry layin' hens," Jed said. The hens raced over as he dumped the scratch into the metal feeding trays.

"No, go right ahead Jed. I'm going to want my eggs and bacon at Auggie's in the morning." Jon laughed as he explained about Faraday and Cook. "Up Denver way, the two scoundrels tried to take over all the gambling houses by getting Cook elected Sheriff. Once Cook got elected, they went around shutting down all of the saloons, except for Faraday's. The saloon owners screamed bloody murder and the town council fired Cook and sent him packing. They landed here. Looks like they might be wantin' to do the same thing here they tried to do in Denver."

"And they need my vote, right?"

"Right!"

"They think I'm desperate. They think they can bribe me, right?" The chickens scurried about as the remaining scratch sprayed into the pen from Jed's bucket.

"Right. I'm afraid you're right Jed," Jon replied.

Jed got real quiet for a minute as if deep in thought and then he spoke. "Jon, it's no secret that I've had some tough times lately. My vein went bust last year and I lost it all, the whole kit and caboodle. It really set me back on my heels. I've been stayin' afloat by providing eggs for Auggie's and broilers for the Barbee. The money ain't very good, but it keeps me goin' until I find a good vein. And I know, I've had my share of troubles along the way. But you listen close Jon!" Jed's eyes were welling up a little. "I ain't no cheat and I ain't no crook," he said passionately. The bucket rattled as he hooked it on the side of the feed barrel and popped on the round wooden lid. "Those boys are barkin' up the wrong tree with me."

"I know, Jed. You're an honest man." Jon jumped down off of Babe and walked over and put his arm on the large man's shoulder. "This isn't going to be easy, partner; these men can play rough. But we're here for you, any time."

"Thank you Sheriff. I know what men like that can do if you cross them. And it ain't pretty."

"You let me worry about Canady, okay?" Jon said firmly. "And if he comes back to see you, just play along with him, don't take any chances, alright?"

"Alright, Sheriff, but I'll be okay," Jed replied confidently.

"I know you will, just be careful. And if he threatens you, let me know right away. Okay?"

"Okay."

Jed nodded at the sheriff as Jon mounted up. Darkness was gathering as he and Camp began their ride back to town. The moon was already rising in the eastern sky, making the path bright ahead.

"What do you think?" Jon hollered as he rode along beside Camp.

"There could be trouble with Jed!" Camp shouted, "Let's talk about it at the Barbee."

Jon nodded in the affirmative and let Camp pull ahead as the two raced toward town. Jon was worried about Jed Orton. He was afraid that he didn't fully understand the danger he was in. He would have to keep a close eye on Commissioner Orton.

The bright winter moon shone brightly in the night sky as the two riders arrived in town. Laughing and voices could be heard inside the Barbee. The piano was playing and the kerosene lanterns shined brightly as big Jon pushed through the swinging doors of the popular saloon. Camp was close behind.

"Howdy Sheriff!"

"How you doin' Jon?"

"Good to see you!"

Several patrons greeted Jon as he and Camp moved toward the end of the bar.

"Usual?" Sam asked.

"Sounds good," Jon replied as he lifted up his hat and ran his fingers through his hair. Sam grabbed a bottle from under the bar and poured the two men a couple of shots of Early Times. The two men downed their shots and slammed the small glasses on the dark oak bar.

Sam slid a couple of draft beers down the bar in front of them. Jon pulled out a cigar, bit off the end and lit up. The smoke drifted upward as Jon made another failed attempt at smoke rings.

"Riding kind of late aren't you boys?" the curious Sam asked.

"Yea, we've been out to Jed Orton's place."

"How's Jed?" Sam asked

"He's fine for now," Jon replied. "Canady paid him a visit today."

"Is that right?"

"Yea, they need his vote to run the county. Where's Libby?"

"Her friend Sarah McLennan invited her out to their

ranch for dinner. She said to tell you she'd see you tomorrow. She set the table in the corner of the room for you and Camp. She's stayin' at the McLennan's tonight and coming back in the morning. And by the way, dinner's on her tonight."

"Well you can't beat that! Camp, shall we retire to our favorite table?"

"Sounds good, Boss."

Chairs scooted aside as the two lawmen made their way across the crowded saloon. There were several handshakes and greetings along the way. Jon moved around the back side and slid the oak chair out from under the table. He sat down with his back against the wall as usual. Sam was close behind.

"What are you havin' fellas?" the friendly barkeep asked. "I got some real juicy pork chops and the grits are great tonight."

"Sounds good to me Sam. How about you Camp?"

"You got any stewed tomatoes back there?'

"Sure do! Chops, grits, and stewed tomatoes comin' up. I'll bring ya a couple more beers." Sam hurried off.

Camp picked a pre-rolled cigarette out of the front pocket on his white bib shirt, lit up and took a drag. His light blue eyes squinted as he looked through the smoke at Jon.

"Got a question for you Sheriff."

"Fire away Partner."

"Ed tells me that when he first met you in the buffalo camps, you weren't packin' heat. Is that right?"

"Sure is."

"Why'd you start packin?"

"He didn't tell you, huh?"

"Nope, when I asked him, he said it was a long story."

"Well it sure enough is. You sure you want to hear it?" Jon said as he took a swig of beer.

"This is all I got planned tonight, so I'm game for anything," Camp joked. Beer trickled down his chin as he set the empty mug on the oak table top. He swiped it away with his shirtsleeve. Sam arrived with two more beers.

"Well, here we go!" Jon said good-naturedly. He leaned back, took a long, hard drag off his Havana, smoke drifted to the ceiling as he began to tell his story. "It's been a lot of years ago my young friend, but I remember it like it was yesterday."

Chapter 9

"After Ed and I parted ways in the buffalo camps, I headed on down the trail to Cheyenne. I wanted to test my gambling skills at some of the famous haunts in that old railroad town. I liked Cheyenne and stayed on there for several years.

One day I was playing black jack in the McDaniel Saloon on Fifteenth Street and I noticed a couple of scruffy looking hombres standing at the end of the bar. When I first looked at them, a chill shot up and down my spine--something wasn't right with these boys. I smelled trouble coming. It was kind of dark in the corner where they were standing so I couldn't get a good look at them. Before long, one of them called me out - he was a mite upset about something. 'Hey Stoudenmire, you remember me?' He sounded real mean; the saloon got kind of quiet all of a sudden.

"'Can't say as I do!' I said, kind of egging him on a little. 'If you quit hiding in that corner, I could see you better,' I said, trying to make him mad.

"'I ain't hidin' from nobody Stoudenmire,' he

shouted. He sounded real mad, like I insulted him or something. Then the two of them came out from the bar and walked toward my table. They looked dirty, smelly, and mean.

"The first man had an eerie look to him - long scraggily hair and a thin, evil face. He looked kind of familiar, but I still wasn't sure who he was. The other one was a step behind; I never got a look at him. As the smelly critters got closer, the other players in my game started backing away. They didn't want any part of these two.

"I stood up slowly so they could see that I wasn't carrying. 'Sorry to disappoint you boys, but I ain't packin',' I told them, but it didn't do any good.

"They just kept coming right at me; my heart was pounding pretty good by now. The ugly one came to a stop a few feet in front of me and spoke up.

"Name's Will Sledge, I was there the night you beat my big brother to a pulp in that saloon tent in the Dakota Territory, Stoudenmire. You damned near killed him, he ain't been the same since. He just sits in his cabin and looks out at the sky all day. His leg's all busted up, he can't see right. He's not half the man he used to be. You didn't have to beat him like you did. You coulda let up, but you didn't. It was an awful thing to watch. I was just a boy then, now I'm all grown up now and you're gonna pay!"

"While he was talking, I kind of recognized him. I had seen him there a time or two. Just a kid at the time, he looked quite a bit like his brother, but not nearly as big. Now that he had grown up, he had a real nasty look about him. His mouth kind of curled up in a cruel smile when he talked. I tried to explain why I beat up on his brother.

"'The truth is, Mr. Sledge, your brother was whipping up on a much smaller man. If I hadn't stepped in, he would've killed him. You're brother had a beating coming to him, so I gave it to him.

"'Shut your damned mouth!' Sledge screamed as he kicked a chair aside and moved closer, not wanting to hear the truth about his brother.

"Just then his partner slid a six gun across the floor in front of me. 'Hell's waitin' for you, Stoudenmire, pick it up now!' the ugly man shouted. I wasn't about to try for that six gun, that would have been suicide and I kind of wanted to live a few more years. I just stood real still right beside my table. I wasn't moving a muscle. It would have been cold blooded murder if he shot me in front of all of those people. I gambled that he wouldn't. I've got to admit it was pretty damn tense in there for awhile.

"Suddenly, the swinging doors flew open and the local sheriff came busting in the room. Someone had slipped out of the saloon and ran and told the sheriff about my predicament.

"One of the cowpokes at the bar spoke up. These two hombres are tryin' to bait this man into a fight and he ain't armed.' Will Sledge looked over at the frightened man. He grabbed his hat and hurried out the door.

"'Is that right, fellas?" the sheriff asked.

"The wolfers got as quiet as church mice. They just looked at the sheriff. Surprised by his visit, they weren't sure what to say.

"'I asked you fellas a question and I expect an answer,' the sheriff yelled, starting to get upset. The wolfers still didn't answer. Then as quick as a flash, his two Navy Colts flew out of their holsters. They were pointing directly at the two troublemakers.

"I've got to admit Sledge kind of surprised me with his answer. He may not have been as dumb as he looked. Without missing a beat he shouted, 'I'm just sayin' hi to an old friend, no need for everyone to get so all fire upset.' He looked over at me and smiled. Man oh man what an ugly smile that man had.

"The sheriff asked me if they were really friends of mine. 'Hell no!' I said. 'I don't make friends with snakes.' I looked over and winked at Sledge."

"You did?" Camp had a good laugh on that one.

"Sure enough did Partner," Jon replied.

"Next, the Sheriff told them to unbuckle their gun belts and drop them slowly to the floor. Any false moves and he'd let them have it. The two unbuckled their belts and dropped them. The sheriff told his deputy to go over and pick them up.

"Then the sheriff told them he was booking them for disturbing the peace. I told the sheriff that wouldn't be necessary. I had a better idea.

"'Well let's hear it,' he said.

"I told them I'd fight them both, right then and there, out in the street!

"'Both of them?' the sheriff asked. And I said, 'Yea, both of them.'

I didn't think either one of them would fight me alone after what I did to the nasty one's brother. So I offered to take them both on. I wanted to try and knock some sense into them. With the crowd egging them on, the two agreed to fight me, two against one."

"You're one mean hombre, Boss!" Camp said. "What happened next?'

"A lot of people got excited and ran out to spread the word about the fight. By the time the three of us walked out, a big crowd had gathered. I guess they wanted to see some blood; my blood!" Jon laughed. "I started to wonder what I had gotten myself into.

"When we got to the street, the ugly one, Will Sledge, started yelling at me and waving his fist," Jon recalled. "He was one ornery cuss.

"'No mercy, Stoudenmire, you rotten bastard, you're getting no mercy. Just like you gave my brother.' That's what he said to me. Then he ripped off his leather vest and chaps and threw them on the ground and started moving around with his fist doubled up."

"What'd you say to them, Jon?" Camp asked. Smoke plumed around Camp's face as he lit another cigarette.

"Nothing, I just took off my vest and began rolling my shirt sleeves up."

"So they could see your muscles, right Jon?" Camp teased his big boss.

"Come on Camp, cut that out!" Jon replied, slightly embarrassed.

"Sorry, Boss. Go ahead."

"I really wasn't all that sure I could whip them both at once, but I wanted to try. I figured I'd have to deal with these boys, particularly Sledge, sooner or later. I hoped this fight would get it out of their system. So I wouldn't have to be looking over my shoulder the rest of my life.

"I really never got a look at Sledge's friend while they were in the saloon," Jon said. "He was always kind of behind Sledge."

"And...." Camp said.

"Well, when I looked at him out on the street, all I saw was broad shoulders and a bunch of muscles. My oh my, I thought, I've really done it this time. He was one big man and he was just dying to knock my block off. I was hoping an earthquake or something would come along and get me out of this. Then the sheriff spoke up.

"'Listen up boys! There will be no hitting or kicking in the privates,' the sheriff shouted as he drug all three of us toward the center of the street.

"Is that the only rule? I thought to myself, I'm gonna get killed by these guys.

"The horse and buggy traffic, which was always busy at this time of day, came to a complete stop. Life was a little slow around Cheyenne back in those days. Except for an occasional train coming through, nothing much happened. Watching someone like me get killed, could really break up a day. The sheriff went on, 'You'll fight until one side gives up or until I tell you to quit. And if you don't quit when I tell you, I'm going to throw your butt in jail. Do you all understand?' The sheriff shouted so all could hear.

"We all nodded yes. Then he motioned for us all to come forward to the center of the street. He had us touch knuckles, he stepped out of the way and the fight was on. I can remember it like it was yesterday. Sledge kept saying 'you rotten bastard' under his breath. Those guys wanted to kill me and I knew it. One wrong move and I was dead."

"You must have been sweating bullets!" Camp laughed.

"Yeah I was. Now will you quit interrupting me so I can finish my story?" Jon squinted through the smoke.

"Okay, okay, tell me about the big fight."

"Well those two buggers started circling around, trying to confuse me. I ducked and weaved, moved left and right, trying to keep track of both of them. Finally, Will Sledge jumped in front of me and threw a big ol' roundhouse punch. I fooled him and ducked to the right. At the same time I let fly with two hard jabs right to his hairy old jaw. Those two were a couple a good ones, he was yelping in pain. He started making all sorts of funny faces. All of a sudden something spit out of his mouth. A bloody tooth landed on the ground right in front of me. Blood was trickling down the side of his mouth and everything. Gawd, he was an awful sight. Meanwhile, the other son a gun was moving around behind me, looking for his chance to knock my block off. I think he thought the sight of that tooth falling out and everything might throw me off. But knocking that wolfer's tooth out didn't bother me anymore than if I'd bitten the head off a rattler or something. It's either him or me and I'd rather it be him than me.

"At last, the big lug saw his chance to come at me from the back. He shouted 'Stoudenmire you big pile of buffalo shit, you're going to get it now!' Only problem was, I saw him coming out of the corner of my eye. So at the last minute, I bobbed to the left. He threw a huge punch and missed me about a foot. Boy that made him mad; he called me a damned coward. Well that didn't set

too well with me. I swung around like a house afire and
buried my fist deep in his gut. The ugly oaf folded over
in pain. Then I smacked him with the palms of my
hands on both sides of his head. Just like this!" Jon's
cigar slid into his mouth, his arms moved up, his hands
smacked together to show Camp how he hit the big
wolfer.

"I'll bet that smarted," Camp said. "You probably
popped his ear drums."

"Not sure bout that, but he did start kind of
wandering around in circles holding his head and
screaming. He was stumbling around; I think he lost his
equilibrium. It looked a little comical. If he wasn't trying
to kill me, I probably would have laughed.

"They were getting a little frustrated at this point.
Then, they leaned down and put their heads together
like they were planning something. I told them it wasn't
polite to whisper in front of other people. That really
got their backs up. All of a sudden they both came
charging right at me; screaming, snorting, grunting, and
spitting. They both jumped on top of me, kicking,
scratching, and clawing. Trying like hell to get me on the
ground, so they could finish me off. Sledge was hanging
on my back, grunting and making all kind of noises. His
hand went over the top of my head, he stuck his fingers
in my nose and eyes and yanked backwards as hard as
he could. I think he was trying to rip my pretty nose off.
Blood started squirting from both my nostrils. I reached
back and grabbed hold of the back of his shirt collar. I
pulled him forward as hard as I could and slammed him
on the ground. He was struggling to his feet, when I
gave him two nasty blows to the kidneys. I was younger

then, but I could almost punch as hard as I do now. Those blows to his kidneys were horrible, he fell to the ground and started rolling around, howling in pain.

"Now the big one saw his chance. He let loose of my waist, stepped back and threw a punch right at the side of my head. I ducked down, his big fist bounced off my shoulder. He was madder'n a hornet now. He lifted up his big, stocky leg and kicked me as hard as he could right in the shin. That sent me a hopping, holding my shin and howling in pain. Then the big nasty mudsill tried to kick me again, I let loose of my shin and moved quickly to the left. His foot went flying past me, so I gave him two God awful punches to his rib cage. I think I hurt him real bad with those two, he was all doubled up and wandering around in the street. I clenched my fist and moved over to finish him off. Just as I was going to let him have it, he put his hands up and begged me not to stop hitting him. I pulled back; I showed mercy.

"Boy, he was a sorry sight," Jon said, as his big body slumped down in the chair, elbows resting on the arms of the chair, his hat tipped back a little. His mouth curled up in a little smile as he continued.

"Then the skunk's knees started wobbling, he looked kind of bow legged as he staggered around on the street. He was holding his side and making funny noises. I think I got him with those two."

"No kidding!" Camp joked as his smiling blue eyes looked over at big Jon. "What about Sledge?"

"He was starting to kind of come to. He rolled up on all fours, crawled over to where I was standing, lunged forward and grabbed me with everything he was worth around my leg. He started biting me on the back of my knee--the most tender spot on the leg. Man did that hurt! I yelped in pain and he bit me again. This time he really dug in, he was holding on for bloody murder.

"'Damn you Sledge!' I shouted. Then I grabbed a big wad of his scraggly hair and tried to yank him loose. He wasn't budging. He knew if he let go, I was gonna beat him to a pulp. Pretty soon his jaw muscles begin to tire. I could feel his grip on my leg start to loosen. All of a sudden his muscles let loose and he plopped on the ground. Blood was dripping down the side of his mouth, he was tired and beaten.

"I told him to get up and fight like a man, but he was too weak. I reached down and grabbed him by the shirt collar and yanked him up to where I could see his ugly face. I knew at this point it wouldn't be a fair fight. As mad as I was at the smelly varmint, I didn't want to hit him again.

"'Had enough Sledge?' I asked as I pulled him up to eye level. He stared at me for a minute and then you know what he did?"

"What?" Camp replied.

"The nasty bugger spit right in my face. I ripped my handkerchief from around my neck and wiped off the vile, stinky, slime. For the first time all day, I was truly mad at this man. His eyes got big as saucers, as he waited for me to finish him off. I doubled up my right fist and buried it right in the center of his gut. I'll never forget the look on his face." Jon laughed. "I thought his eyes were gonna pop right out of his ugly head.

"'You devil, look what you've done to me!' he screamed and then he fell down on the street, holding his gut and moaning in pain. I thought about rearranging his face, but I decided to just hit him in the gut."

"How thoughtful," Camp said sarcastically.

"The sheriff came running over yelling at the wolfers. They were rolling around on the street and holding their guts. 'Soon as you boys get to feeling better, I want you to saddle up and ride on out of here lock, stock, and barrel. If I ever see either one of you in this town again, I'll throw your butts in jail.'

"I was kind of smiling as the boys got their lecture. All of a sudden the sheriff turned and gave me a stare that would kill a horse.

"'Wipe that smile off your face, Stoudenmire!' he barked.'Maybe this wasn't your doin', but you're part of it too, and I don't like brawls in the middle of Fifteenth Street. Next time you cause any trouble 'round here, your butt's goin' to jail!'

"I told him that I was sorry and it wouldn't happen again if I could help it. He gave me this real mean stare for a minute and the walked back to the jail.

"Several folks in the crowd came up and patted me on the back and told me it was the best fight they had seen in a long time. One of them said I reminded him of my friend Wild Bill Hickock. That was a real compliment.

"I dusted myself off real good and picked up my hat. The two wolfers were still lying in the street and kind of rolling around. To tell you the truth, I kind of felt sorry for them, so I walked over to lend them a hand. I reached down and grabbed Sledge's arm to help him up. But he was having no part of it.

"'Get your stinking hands off me, Stoudenmire, I don't need your damn help. And if I was you, I'd watch your backside. Next time it ain't going to be no fistfight!' His face looked like pure evil. I knew he meant it. I guess my plan to knock some sense into him didn't work. I had to respect the guts of that nasty bugger. He was one wicked hombre. I also knew that his threat was not an idle one. I was sure this would not be the last time I tangled with Will Sledge and the next time it would be with guns.

"I thought about Will's threats all night long as I laid in that boarding house in Cheyenne. I thought about a couple of close calls I'd had in the local saloons. Next morning I made a decision that would change my life forever. I decided to start packing. It was a tough decision; I had vowed that I would never carry a gun. But out in the real world, things start looking different. Leading the kind of life I was, always running into someone with a gun in his hand. For my own protection, I needed to start carrying.

"I walked over to the M & M gun shop in Cheyenne that morning and bought two pearl handled Army Colt 45 revolvers - same ones I got today. My days in the buffalo camp in Dakota Territory made a man out of me. My days in Cheyenne made a gunman out of me."

Beer splashed on the table as two mugs slid across the oak table top. "Dinners will be up in five! Sorry for the hold up, it's been a little hectic around here." Sam had just arrived with a couple of refills. The empties clanged together as Sam hurried away.

"No problem Sam," Jon shouted at the departing tender.

"What's it like, Jon, being a gunman and all?"

"It ain't easy, Camp. That's why I've got my back against the wall now. I never know when the son, brother, or father of one of the men I've killed is going to show up and put a bullet in my head. Just like Jack McCall did to my good friend Wild Bill in Saloon #10 in Deadwood. I've got to be on my toes all the time." Jon looked down as the foamy beer swirled slowly around in the thick glass mug.

"Every time I walk by an alley, I'm kind of leery. I don't know if someone's waiting there to shoot me. That's why I walk down the middle of the street sometimes, so they can't take me out from the alley. I'm always on guard; and I'm always on the move, trying to keep one step ahead of some swine's bullet. I can never call anyplace home. Most respectable women don't cotton to me much. I can't blame them. What kind of husband and father would I be? Always on the run, always inches from death."

"Libby's respectable," Camp said nervously.

"You bet your bottom dollar she is. But she's different. She's a strong woman, and she knows all the risks of being with someone like me. She's willing to take them, but it's real hard on her. I worry about that a lot."

"You don't paint a very pretty picture, Boss." Camp flipped his shoestring tie nervously, surprised by the revelations from his hero.

"Yea I know, but it could be worse."

"Worse?"

"I could be dead,"

"Ah, nobody could kill you Jon, you're too good."

"Nobody's that good!" Jon's eyes darted to the left as the swinging doors banged open. Two wranglers rushed in. "Just like that Camp, I have to watch everybody that comes in this place. I'm just never sure who's out there or what will happen. It ain't good."

"You ever think of givin' it up?"

"Yea, I was heading to my vineyard in California when I stopped in this God forsaken town." Jon's head tipped back as he took a swig of beer.

"Will you be safe there?"

"Pretty safe. Most people on the shoot, don't like to cross the mountains. I should be alright there. I can quit carrying and start a new life."

"I'll be sorry to see you leave," Camp said quietly, the thought of Jon's moving on saddened the young stable hand.

"Thank you Camp, I appreciate that. And don't worry, I'm not leaving for awhile. We still got that Faraday mess to clean up. And by the way young fella, I been meaning to tell you something."

"What's that?"

"You remind me of somebody," Jon said directly. He leaned forward, folded hands and arms on the table pointing toward Camp.

"Oh yea, who's that?" Camp squirmed in his seat a little, surprised by the direct attention.

"Me!" Jon replied, his eyes never left Camp.

"Well, uh, thank you Jon." His face turned red with embarrassment.

"No, don't thank me my friend, it's a curse. I hear you shooting down at the stable every day. I see how quick you've become with a gun. It's no good son. If you keep it up you'll be a lonely frightened man. Always on the run. Never trusting anyone."

"Don't worry Jon. That's not what I'm after. I..."

"I know, that's what they all say, but I could talk my fool head off and it wouldn't do any good. The day you decided to strap those six guns on, it was already too late. No one can tell you now, not even me. I just hope you have as few scrapes as possible along the way. And promise me you'll stay on the side of the law."

"Did you, Jon? Did you always stay on the side of the law?"

"Not always, son, not always. But I want better for you!"

Two plates of food hit the table as Sam arrived with dinner. Steam rose up from the juicy pork chops, grits and stewed tomatoes. The silverware rattled as Sam put the knives and forks next to their plates. Sam sat two cups of hot coffee on the oak table top. "Dinner's served."

"Thank you Sam. I could eat a horse." Jon's fingers slid through the handle on the coffee cup. He raised it up and pointed it toward Camp. "To you, my brave young friend. All the best to you!"

"Thank you Jon."

He and Camp broke bread together in the far off desert saloon. Through the window, Jon could see the evening sun disappear behind the dark, foreboding landscape. The lantern flickered above their table in the darkening room. The talented piano player's fingers danced over the ivory keys, accompanied by voices singing along with the popular melody, *Timber Trail*. Laughter, loud voices, occasional shouts of joy and dismay could be heard coming from the gambling tables. The large wood frame building literally vibrated with the sounds of life - a stark contrast to the shadow of death that lingered so close to this carefree scene.

Chapter 10

"Okay Jake, up and at 'em!" The sheriff frowned as he leaned on the heavy door waiting for the scruffy drunk to leave the cell.

"Alright Sheriff, I'm comin'." The old drunk rubbed the stubble on his chin as he pulled his thin body up from the bunk. "The grub was good, thanks Sheriff."

"You look a little dragged out Jake. Try not to get too roostered up today, okay?" The bars shook as Jon slammed the door shut and locked it. The door to the supply room swung open; Jon walked in to get fresh coffee.

"I'll try Sheriff, I'll sure try." The small wooden gate next to Jon's desk creaked open as Jake left the cell area.

"See you, Jake." Ed looked up from his desk as Jake neared the front door. Jake staggered backward as the door swung open. Web Norton, Clive Cook, and Butch Canady came hurriedly in the jail. Jake was wobbling; Web grabbed him by the arm to keep him from falling.

"Sorry old timer, we didn't see you there."

"No problem Web, those things happen." Jake

righted himself and hurried out, the door slammed behind him.

"Can I help you with something, Web?" Ed asked.

Web smiled nervously, surprised by Ed's close proximity. "Uh, oh hello Ed, didn't see you over there."

Canady's eyes scanned the room, like someone planning for a breakout on down the road.

"I know." Ed looked impatient. "What can I do for you boys?"

"We're here to see Zing."

"I didn't know you and Zing were friends, Web." Ed's eyes narrowed a little.

"That's really none of your affair, Deputy." Web fiddled nervously with his gold watch chain.

Canady frowned.

"Everything that happens in this jail is our affair Norton!" Jon said, joining the conversation. His leg bumped the wooden gate open. He walked over to the stove, yanked the top off the coffee pot and dumped in the fresh coffee.

"Ain't no law against visiting a prisoner, Sheriff." Canady looked dark and menacing as he spoke to the sheriff. "Besides, Zing and I go way back."

"Make it quick, Canady. You got five minutes."

"Five minutes? Hell you can't do anything in five minutes!" Canady replied angrily.

"The judge got in late last night. We got a bail hearing in fifteen minutes. It takes ten minutes to walk down to the court house. So you've got five minutes. Take it or leave it." There was a loud slam as Jon sat the pot back on the stove. He pushed the black iron door shut with his knee.

"Oh, the bail hearing's in fifteen minutes huh..." Web interrupted. "I thought it was yesterday."

"Supposed to be, but the stage broke down, a wheel busted out at Comanche Pass. Judge Oliver didn't get in till last night. So the hearing's at ten o'clock this morning, fifteen minutes from now, like I said."

"Enough of this chit-chat, we're ready to see Fuller!" Canady demanded, as his left arm leaned on Jon's desk.

Jon stared at Canady as he walked toward the nasty gunman. Butch's arm rose off Jon's desk, he moved out of the way.

"Pardon me Sheriff," he said sarcastically. His thin, muscular frame moved sideways as Jon passed.

Jon stared hard at Canady as he sat down in his swivel chair. "Let them in, Ed!"

Ed walked over and held the gate open. "This way, fellas."

Jon fell back in his chair, his arms folded on his chest. "Leave your gun belts on my desk, fellas."

Canady sneered, as the varmints begrudgingly unbuckled their gun belts and tossed them on Jon's big desk.

The door clicked open as Ed turned the key. "You got company, Zing."

Fuller's narrow, pocked face cracked with a smile. "Howdy Butch, ain't seen you in a coon's age."

Canady's hand reached forward, the two gunmen shook. "Good to see you, Zing."

"This here's Clive Cook," Canady said.

"Howdy Clive, I've heard about you!"

The big door banged shut, the lock clicked. Ed went back to the office area; he picked two cups off the pegs behind the stove and poured him and Jon a fresh cup.

Jon reached in his jean pocket and lifted out his pocket knife. The large blade swung open, Jon snatched a hunk of a wood out of his left desk drawer and began to carve. Ed slid a fresh cup of coffee in front of him.

"What's this all about?" Ed asked.

Jon looked pensive. "Well...I think they're needing another gun."

"So they think if they bail Fuller out, he'll join up with them."

"Yea, you hit the nail on the head, Partner." The knife blade disappeared into the white pearl handle. He frowned as his huge hands engulfed the steaming cup of coffee. "These boys are starting to make me real mad, Ed."

Ed's eyes opened wide. "You don't say!" He knew what that meant.

"Yea, I--"

"We're ready," a loud voice from the back interrupted the tough sheriff.

"Go let them out Ed, before I lose my temper," Jon snarled.

Ed grabbed the keys from the peg, pushed through the gate and unlocked the cell.

There were smiles and handshakes all around as the three men departed the cell. An ugly grin broke out on Canady's square dark face as he brushed by Ed.

Ed quickly locked the cell door and hurried to get their gun belts. Jon's legs dropped off the desk; he pushed his chair backward and stood up.

"Just keep one thing in mind, fellas." Jon spoke calmly, eyes locked on Canady as the men strapped up.

"What's that, Sheriff?" Norton asked.

Canady stared back hard at Jon.

"You may think you got a pretty cute plan here, but you'll never have enough men, I promise you that."

"Just visitin' an old friend, Sheriff, that's all." Canady smirked, hands held high, as he stepped backwards, never taking his eyes off Jon. Canady kept Norton and Cook behind him as they backed out the door.

Ed pulled the curtain back on the front door, and watched as the three varmints mounted up and rode away.

Ed looked over at Jon. "Can they bail him out, Jon?"

Jon's chair banged into his desk; he walked over by Ed and looked out the window as dust from the departing riders drifted by the pane glass window. "Fraid so. Judge Oliver ain't got much to go on. Jack's on the mend, Doc says he'll be up and around in a few days. Besides, Fuller wasn't the trigger man anyway; he just stole some supplies. Bail will be pretty low and Faraday's got the booty. Fuller will be out a here by sundown," Jon predicted, certain that Faraday's camp was arming up, and a showdown was imminent.

* * *

"Watch out, Isaiah!" a little boy screamed. The youngster's little friend dove to the side of the dusty road just in time. The thundering hooves of Canady's big horse pounded the ground next to the little boy as he and the others charged out of town.

"How far to Jed's place?" Web shouted. The bill on Web's hat blew flat as the three men raced forward.

"It's just down the road a ways!" Canady replied. The whip cracked on his horse's hindquarters, Canady pushed him hard.

"Buk, buk, baaack!" "Buk, buk, baaack!" Wings flapped and feathers flew as the chickens scurried to get out of the way of the approaching riders. The two horses came to a stop in front of Orton's small log cabin. Web jumped down, wrapped the leather straps on the peg, walked over and knocked on the rickety door. "Anybody home?" he shouted.

"Who's callin'?" a voice shouted from the back of the house.

"Web Norton!"

Jed rubbed his soiled hands against his cloth apron as he approached the three men. He extended his hand to shake.

"Of course, good to see you Web."

"Hello, Jed," Web replied as the two men shook hands.

"Nice to see you again, Mr. Canady," Jed said.

Butch nodded at the chunky farmer.

"Mornin' Clive."

"Good Morning Jed," Cook said politely.

"How are you today, Jed?" Web asked.

"Not too bad, I guess."

"How's business?" Web asked.

"Well, I'm makin' enough with my chickens to get by, nothing more, thank you. And to what do I owe the pleasure of your visit, gentlemen?" Jed's eyebrows raised a little as he awaited the answer.

Web's freckled face broke into a smile as he replied. "We were just in the area and thought we'd stop in and say hello."

"Well then, how 'bout some coffee? Just made a pot a few minutes ago."

Web's eyes went in the direction of Clive and Butch; they nodded in the affirmative. "Sounds good Jed."

"Come on in." The old door creaked as Jed popped the latch, pushed it open, and motioned for the men to come in.

"Thank you Jed," Web and Cook replied. Canady stayed quiet.

Jed grabbed a couple of metal cups off the wood shelf next to the stove. "Black?" Steam rose as the hot black coffee flowed into the cups.

"Ain't no other way, is there?" Web joked. Canady and Cook nodded.

Jed set the coffee in front of his guests. "Sit down, please."

The wooden stool slid between his legs as Web pulled it backward and sat down. Canady just stood twirling his mustache, staring at Jed. Clive Cook pulled a stool back and sat down.

"Sure nice to have some company, gets awful lonely out here." The large man smiled. "How are you and Alex doing' since you won the election, Clive?"

"Fine, Jed. We're looking forward to working with you on the County Commission." The steam disappeared as Clive blew on the hot coffee, he took a sip.

"So am I," Jed said. "You can tell Alex that, so am I."

"He'll be glad to hear that. We want to see this county move forward, and we're going to need your help to do that. We can see some room for improvement here in Mesquite County."

"Oh, is that right? What kind of improvement you talking about?"

"We think some changes are needed in this county," Clive said nervously.

"Changes? What changes?"

Cook hesitated and then replied. "We're thinking that Stoudenmire fellow is getting a little too big for his britches. Drinking on the job, and shooting anybody that crosses him. We think we need a more measured man as sheriff of this county." The stocky Brit's eyes peered upward, waiting for Jed's response.

"Well, I know the sheriff might take a drink now and then. But I swear, I ain't never seen the man drunk on the job. And he never shoots nobody, that don't need shootin'. I'm afraid I kind of disagree with that one. I think we need the sheriff right where he's at."

Canady grimaced.

"Uh, Jed, you know it's going to take three votes to get anything done around here. And Mr. Faraday and I are really counting on your vote," Cook said.

"There's a lot a things I just might agree on, but getting' rid of our fine sheriff isn't one of 'em." Jed seemed agitated; he yanked the handkerchief from around his neck and wiped the sweat from his forehead.

"Umm, I was hoping you'd look at it a little--"

"Now you listen to me, fat boy," Canady interrupted Cook. "We're asking nice now, but if you keep bucking us, it could get rough around here!" Butch's dark eyes peered at Jed from under his black silk hat. His right hand had a firm grip on his shiny Cimarron.

"No! You listen to me!" Jed snapped back at the gnarly gunman. "You're threatening' me, because you think I'm poor and desperate, you think you can push me around. You're afraid of Baldwin and Hancock; they got money and influence. So you're coming' after me. Well, you're barking' up the wrong tree Mister, cause I ain't no crook." Sweat from Jed's brow dripped down on his canvas apron as he rebuffed the gnarly gunman.

"You better think twice about what you're saying Jed, we mean--"

Before Cook could finish Butch Canady jumped out his chair. He yanked the gun out of its holster and spun it on his finger. Then he grabbed it by the barrel; his leather vest flew open as he raised his arm. The butt of the gun smashed into Jed's skull.

"Hey, what the--!" Jed screamed as his large body flew sideways out of the chair. His head crashed against the iron leg of the black pot belly stove. His hands covered his face, blood started to trickle from between his fingers, he was moaning in pain.

Canady leaned toward the fallen man and raised the gun again.

"Stop! That's enough Butch! We don't want to kill him!" Web shouted.

The gun fell slowly to Butch's side; he looked down at the fallen man. "Let this be a lesson, you best be with us, and not agin us. Next time I ain't going to stop!" He kicked Jed's fallen coffee cup, and the tin mug bounced off Orton's covered face.

"Let's get out of here!" Web said as he pushed away form the oak table.

Canady slowly backed away, eyes locked on his fallen

prey. "Damn chicken farmer anyway!" He dropped his six gun in his holster as he turned and hurried out. The door banged shut.

Inside, still stunned by the clubbing, a defiant Jed Orton whispered, "You go to hell Canady!"

Outside, the three curly wolves mounted up. "Let's head back to town. That bail hearing should be over by now," Web shouted. The leather strap snapped hard against the hindquarters of Web's gray stallion; the horse leapt forward. Canady and Cook were close behind. The broilers squawked and scurried out of the way. The men rode hard toward town, anxious to add another gun to their potent arsenal.

* * *

The swinging door banged against the wall of the Barbee. Jon was in a dark mood as he moved toward the bar for his daily lunch. "Usual, Sam," he barked.

Sam smiled, looking dapper in his red leather vest, white cotton shirt, and bow tie. A bottle appeared from under the bar. Sam poured Jon a shot. The glass slid in front of big Jon.

"What's up, Jon? You look a might boiled today!"

"I don't like the way things are shaping up around here, Sam. Faraday's moving faster than I thought he would. Looks like Zing Fuller might be joining their camp." Jon grimaced, his big hand ducked under his black vest as he snatched a Havana out of his shirt pocket.

"Zing Fuller? Hell, I thought he was in jail for the Malone shooting!" Sam exclaimed.

"He was! The Judge went lenient on him because he didn't shoot Malone. The bail's only two hundred dollars. Clive Cook and the boys were at the jail this morning to see Fuller. They were talking real low, something's up." Jon's head fell backwards as he downed the shot. The thick glass slammed on the bar.

"That's not good!" Sam replied. The Early Times splashed into Jon's glass again. He usually only had one but Sam apparently thought he needed another. "Canady's as mean as they come, Fuller's a nasty gun for hire, Cook is fast and deadly with a six gun, and he's bearing a grudge for that whippin' you gave him. And Web can hold his own with anybody. And guess what?"

"What?" Jon seemed annoyed. His blue denim shirtsleeve slid across his mouth. The empty shot glass hit the bar.

"Even Alex Faraday is good with a gun! He won the rifle shooting contest at the fair last fall. They say he wears sometimes and he always carries a Derringer up his sleeve. I guess he was quite the marksman over there in merry ole' England. Looks like you got your hands full, big guy," Sam exclaimed.

Jon's face pruned as the whiskey went down. "You're just full a good news, ain't you, Sam!"

"All you got is yourself, Ed Morgan, Camp, if you deputize him, and Jack Malone, who's still on the mend. Don't sound good to me, Jon." Sam's eyebrows rose as he awaited Jon's answer.

"What's the old Bible saying Sam? Oh ye...?"

Sam answered, "Men of little faith."

"Yea, yea, that's it. Ye men of little faith." Jon smiled and looked over at Sam. "I can take care of myself,

Sam. Don't you ever worry 'bout that." Suddenly, Jon's blue eyes darted to the left, out at the street. The dust flew as two horses came thundering past. Jon recognized Canady's clay.

"Gotta go, looks like the boys are heading down to the jail with their damn bail papers! Hold that lunch, Sam!" Jon reached in his front pocket; a silver dollar clanked on the bar. "See you later." The front of Jon's brown felt hat was tipped down; he turned and hurried out of the Barbee to the jail.

Cook and the boys tied up out front and hurried in.

Jon approached the jail and stood for a moment by the slightly open door, looking in on the crafty varmints.

"We're here to pick up Zing!" Cook demanded as he tossed the bail agreement on Ed's desk. A startled Ed looked up at the anxious pokes. Without saying a word, he slid his left hand under the inked document and pulled it up where he could read it. He put on his reading glasses and tapped them down his nose with his index finger. His head leaned back as he read it carefully.

"Looks okay Gentlemen. There's only one problem," Ed said, as he peered over his glasses at them.

"What's that?" Cook said impatiently.

"The sheriff isn't here to sign the release."

Just then the front door swung open. The three surprised hombres jumped backward out of the way as the big sheriff hurried in. Butch Canady's thin right hand went instinctively onto the handle of his six gun. Seeing no threat from the sheriff, it fell to his side.

"I guess we just solved that problem Deputy," Canady said. His thin lips were curved in an ugly smile.

Jon gave the varmints a hard look. His leaned over

and grabbed the document off Ed's desk and quickly read it. Ed slid his desk drawer open, pulled out a pen and handed it to Jon. Jon reluctantly took the pen from Ed, poked in the black ink bottle on Ed's desk and signed the crinkled release.

Jon looked hard again at Cook and Canady as he turned and walked over to the cell area. He unlocked Fuller's cell and opened the door. "Get your stuff together Fuller. You're out of here. Your court date for stealing those supplies is a month from this Thursday. Your horse is down at Camp's. You owe him two bucks."

"We took care of that, Zing." Web smiled at their new compadre.

"Thank you, Web," a surprised Zing replied as he gathered up his belongings and hurried out of the cell.

Ed unlocked his lower desk drawer. He leaned down and pulled out Fuller's Uberti and holster. He dropped them on his desk. "Your gun is over here, Zing."

Zing hurried over to Ed's desk. The nasty gunman quickly strapped on his six gun and tied down. Then he turned the door handle and hurried out; Cook, Norton and Canady were close behind. Canady gave big Jon a nasty grin as he walked past.

* * *

Jed Orton's arm slipped off the table top, his body fell hard to the ground as he struggled to get to his feet. His large torso rolled gently from side to side. His swollen right eye was crimson and black, an ugly sight. Suddenly, he rolled hard to the left and came up on one knee. His right arm moved up and thumped on the oak table top. Bracing himself with his right hand, he leaned forward and pushed himself up to a standing position. Woozy, he steadied himself, untied the red checkered handkerchief from around his neck and wrapped it around the deep bloody gash on his forehead. Legs wobbling, he staggered out the door, hopped on his donkey Charlie and headed for town.

"Aw-EE!" "Aw-EE!" the large gray-dun Jack brayed loudly, his short legs moved stiffly and quickly, just short of a gallop as they headed through the barnyard toward town.

"Get me to the sheriff, Charlie, please get me to the sheriff," Jed whispered to his old friend. Charlie's eyes widened, he looked up at Jed as if to say *I'll try*.

* * *

Nearby, Little Bear, a Pawnee Indian, the only survivor of a brutal war with the Cherokees some years earlier, was gathering sticks for a fire. His small wood hut was some hundred yards from the road, just a short distance from Jed's chicken farm and well hidden among the desert ironwood and velvet mesquite. Still leery of retribution from the Cherokee, he lived quietly in the woods, Jed was one of the few people who knew where he lived. Well liked, Little Bear got by doing odd jobs for people in town. Hungry, he was gathering twigs to build a fire and cook the jackrabbit he had killed earlier in the day.

The twigs snapped underfoot as Little Bear slowly prodded through the thick woods. He stopped suddenly, his ears picked up the sounds of Charlie's brays. *Those brays sound different, Jed's in trouble*, Little Bear thought. He slid the stone tomahawk out of the sash around his waist as he hurried through the heavy brush toward the road. Now within fifty yards of the trail, he could see Jed wobbling atop the fast walking donkey.

"Mr. Jed! Mr. Jed!" Little Bear shouted. He frowned as Jed continued on. The leaves flew and the twigs cracked as the strong legs of the aging warrior pushed through the brush. Little Bear's moccasins touched the dusty road outside as he finally cleared the wooded area. His brown eyes scanned the road ahead for signs of Jed; he could see clouds of dust blowing around the bend. He quickly ducked back into the woods, fearing the arrival of more riders. He sat motionless in a thicket of bushes, senses on high alert. He could hear the sound of men's voices at the bend in the road. Jed had run into some riders on the way to town. Charlie was braying very loudly; this alarmed Little Bear. Protective by nature, the donkey's brays meant that his master was in danger. Little Bear's moccasins once again touched the edge of the road; he began to move quickly along side the road toward the voices. The voices were becoming louder and more animated. Charlie's brays sounded like a horrible scream for help. Little Bear's heart was pounding out of his chest, a bolt of fear shot up his spine as the aging warrior neared the bend in the road.

Chapter 11

"Your coffee pot busted or what, Auggie?" Jon shouted as he dropped down in the corner seat and plopped his leg on the nearby window sill. Camp tossed his straw hat on the table and sat down. "There's other restaurants in town, you know!" Camp chimed in.

"Okay! Okay! Try and keep your pants on fellas!" The steam rose from the snout of the black metal pot as the owner hurried over. He sat two cups on the table; Auggie filled the cups and Camp pushed one over in front of Jon. The men raised the cups in a ritualistic salute as they took their first sip.

"Ahhhh! Nothing like that first cup of coffee in the morning!" Jon said. He smacked his lips, his handsome face broke into a smile.

"How you doing today, fellas?" Auggie asked, order pad in hand.

"Okay Auggie, how 'bout yourself?" Camp smiled at the friendly Irishman.

"Just fine, thank you!" Auggie replied.

"How's that pretty wife of yours doing today?" Jon's

lips curled into a mischievous smile as he kidded his good friend.

"Just let me worry--" Auggie was suddenly interrupted by a woman's voice coming from the kitchen area.

"Just fine thank you Jon, and how's our handsome sheriff doing today?" Auggie's wife, Lucy, stuck her chubby face out of the kitchen door and smiled at Jon.

"Wonderful Lucy, good to see you back there! The food always tastes better when I know you're doing the cooking."

"Thank you kindly, Jon. That's the nicest thing anybody's said to me in a long, long time." Lucy's rosy cheeks turned bright red, her eye lashes fluttered as she spoke.

"Don't mention it, darlin'," Jon said as the cherub cook reluctantly ducked back into the kitchen.

Thud! Jon's boot hit the ground as Auggie pushed his big leg off the window sill. "Sit up and behave yourself, flannel mouth," Auggie bellowed.

"Thanks Auggie, I needed that!" Jon laughed. Auggie's thin face slowly broke into a grin, followed by a raucous round of laughter by both men. The laughter increased as Camp joined in. It finally subsided. Pencil in hand, Auggie asked for their orders.

"Okay boys, what'll it be?" Auggie continued to chuckle as he scribbled the men's orders.

"Biscuits n' gravy for me, Auggie," Camp said.

"Got you Camp, how about you, Sheriff?"

"Eggs over, bacon, n' toast for me, Aug."

"Sorry Sheriff, no eggs today."

"No eggs? What are you talking about?"

Jed hasn't been in for a couple of days. I'm fresh out of eggs." Auggie frowned a little.

"What wrong with Jed?" Jon asked, somewhat alarmed.

"Don't know, he just hasn't been in. Sometimes his laying hens don't cooperate, but he usually comes in anyway and tells me about it. Not this time, I haven't seen him."

"Hmmn! You don't say." Jon grimaced. "Give me the biscuits and gravy too, Auggie."

"Nother thing Sheriff," Auggie said.

"What's that?"

"Little Bear always does my cleanin' up 'round here. He hasn't been in for a couple of days either."

"Hmmm! Is that so?" Jon scowled. "Let's eat up and get on out to Jed's place, Deputy."

"Sounds good, Sheriff; things are a little slow at the stable right now," Camp replied. Auggie hurried to put their order in.

The fork clanged on the plate, Jon's big hands rubbed up and down on his belly. "Grub was great Auggie, give Lucy a hug for me." Jon picked up his brown felt hat and pushed away from the table.

"Will do, Jon." Auggie smiled at his good friend.

"Ready to go Camp?"

"Sure am Boss, lead the way," Camp said. He grabbed his straw hat and stood up.

The two men walked to the cash register, paid the friendly Irishman and hurried out.

The leather strap slipped off the peg as Camp mounted up. The strap cracked against the hind leg of his powerful steed. Camp charged down the muddy street toward Jed Orton's place; Jon was close behind.

"Buk, buk, baack!" Feathers flew; the loose broilers squawked and scurried out of the way as the horses galloped past. Jon pulled back on the reins, the mud flew as they came to a quick stop. Jon's eyes scanned the barnyard looking for any sign of Jed. He jumped down and went over to look in the metal feed trays.

"They're all empty, Camp," Jon shouted.

Camp nudged his horse forward as he looked down in the tray. The broilers ran towards them, the laying hens squawked.

"These chickens are plenty hungry, they ain't been fed for awhile," Jon deduced.

"Look over there, Jon!" Camp said excitedly. "It's Charlie, over by Jed's hut!"

Jon jumped on Babe, the two rode quickly over to the hut. He bumped Charlie as he slid off Babe.

"Eee..aw!" Charlie brayed weakly, the flies temporarily scattered off the piles of dung lying beneath her tail.

"Charlie's been standing here without food or water for a couple a days. Somebody tied her down real good so she wouldn't wander into town." Jon frowned. "Something don't smell right round here and it isn't the donkey dung," Jon said solemnly.

"Take Charlie over to the barn and get her some feed and water Camp," Jon ordered. "I'm going to look around a little."

"It's going be tough finding anything Boss." Camp's eyebrows raised, his light blue eyes looked hard at Jon. "That heavy rain yesterday washed all the tracks away." He slid off his horse, untied the donkey's leather straps and walked him over to the barn.

"Yea I know," Jon scowled.   "They might have got lucky."

Chapter 12

Bam! Bam! Alex Faraday glanced up from his desk as the knocker slammed against the huge oak door that led to his study.

"Come in!" "Please come in!" he shouted.

Clive pushed the door open; his barrel chest bumped the door as he hurried into the study. The door clicked shut behind him.

Faraday stuck his pipe between his teeth, he bit down gently; his long narrow fingers pushed the Scottish Blend tightly into the bowl. He struck a match on the bottom of his riding boot and lit up. His cheeks pruned as he took several drags, the curling smoke floated to the ceiling. He looked up at Cook as he approached his desk.

"Good morning, Alex."

"Top of the morning to you, Clive. Please, please be seated." Alex gestured toward one of the two chairs that sat in front of his large desk. "We need to talk.

"Web just got back from town. I guess our friend, Mr. Stoudenmire, and his young cohort from the livery stable just rode out to Jed Orton's place. I'm sure they're doing a lot of snooping around. I need your opinion about this, Clive, it makes me nervous." Puffs of smoke drifted to the ceiling from Alex's pipe.

"I assure you they won't find anything, Sir," Clive said nervously. "We left Jed's body in woods near Little Bear's cabin. The bloody tomahawk Canady used to beat him to death is broken and lying next to his body. We hightailed it over to Jed's chicken farm, picked up some Bantam chickens, ran over to Little Bear's hut and stuck them in his pen. It looks like Little Bear was stealing broilers from Jed. They had a big argument, a horrible fight ensued, and Little Bear beat him to death with his tomahawk and then dropped the busted tomahawk next to the body."

"Hmmm, okay, okay. What about the Indian, uh...."

"Little Bear?" Clive replied.

"Yes, yes, where is he now?"

"Well uh, he knew too much! Zing shot him in the back of the head. We took the body and threw it into Dead Man's Canyon."

"He's dead too?" Faraday seemed surprised.

"I guess so." Cook chuckled. "But don't worry. Web tells me that nobody has ever been to the bottom of that canyon, the walls are too steep." Clive sat still in his chair as he talked of the two murders.

"Hmmm! Well that's good, that's good. Everybody will think Little Bear killed him and then ran off," Alex mumbled.. He stood up and began pacing the room. He knew there had been killings, but hearing the details was another thing.

"What about the hoof prints, my dear man? There

must be hoof prints all over the place." Alex was unnerved, alarmed by his own revelation. He continued to pace.

"No problem Boss! We swept all the tracks away with a couple a big tree limbs. If there was a chance we missed any, the big rain yesterday took care of that!" Clive grinned smugly.

"Yes, yes, the rain! I guess we got lucky there," Alex replied.

"Guess so."

Alex walked back to his desk and dropped into the leather chair. He leaned forward, plucked the ink pen from its holder and punched it in the ink bottle. He scribbled some notes on a piece of paper and handed it to Clive.

"Get Zing and ride into town. Pick up those supplies." Alex pointed at the note. "While you're there, stay awhile and have a drink, nose around a little. See what you can find out. Hopefully the sheriff will be back from Jed's place. Find out what he knows." Alex's thin lips turned up into an evil smile. "We have our chance now to take this town over." He gestured toward the large oak doors sending Cook on his way.

* * *

Babe's ears perked up. The beautiful Palomino came to a sudden stop on the edge of Jed Orton's farm. Big Jon sat up in the saddle, "What is it, girl?" Jon gently rubbed her neck. Babe whinnied, her head jerked backwards. Downwind, the crafty horse had picked up a scent.

Jon spurred her hindquarter. "Take me there girl," Jon whispered, as she galloped forward. Just a few hundred yards down the rode, she came to an abrupt stop. The whites of her eyes were huge as the frightened horse stared into the woods next to the road.

Jon grabbed the saddle horn and jumped down; his feet hit the ground running. He charged into the woods, pushing low lying limbs out of his way. Leaves and twigs from the desert ironwoods crunched under his feet as he stormed ahead. Suddenly he stopped; he saw something up ahead. It was a body. The stench was awful; his stomach started to turn as he moved ahead. He reached the large, swollen body and looked down. He saw the terribly battered remains of Jed Orton. A bloody, broken tomahawk lay nearby.

Jon slid his gun out of its holster and pointed it toward the sky, his thick index finger squeezed the trigger. The loud noise—a signal for Camp to come over--reverberated through the dense woods. Soon Jon could hear hoof beats as Camp rushed toward the gunshot.

He jumped off his charging steed; stumbled for a second then righted himself. Gun in hand he charged into the thick woods.

"Over here!" Jon shouted.

Camp's eyes moved toward the sound of Jon's voice. He struggled to see through the thick brush. A beam of sunlight broke through the trees, the bright sun reflected off Jon's gun barrel. Camp saw the light and raised his hand over his eyes as he rushed toward Jon.

"Oh my--"

"Yea, it's pretty ugly," Jon interrupted. "Somebody

beat the poor bastard to a pulp and left him here to die. It isn't right," Jon whispered. His anger was palpable as he looked down at the mutilated face of the friendly commissioner. Jon's mood was beginning to darken.

"Some Injun must of got him," Camp said as he stepped over and picked up the bloody tomahawk.

Jon frowned.

"What's that over there in that clearing, Jon? Looks like a little house or something."

"Let's check it out," Jon ordered. The two men pushed through the thick brush toward the clearing.

Jon stopped at the edge of the clearing, his eyes examined the area. The only sounds were a few "buk, buk, baacks!" coming from a small pen next to the hut.

Jon stepped into the clearing; he walked over to the hut, gun in hand. Camp was close behind. The barrel of Jon's Colt 45 pushed up on the metal latch, the rickety wooden door fell open. Jon peered into the empty cabin; there was no sign of life. Jon's head dipped down and leaned through the opening, he stepped into the small room. Camp was right behind.

"Well, I'll be damned!" Jon exclaimed. "This is Little Bear's cabin!" His fingers slid through the handle on the old metal coffee pot setting on the stove. "This old coffee pot's the one I gave him for cleaning the cells awhile back." He lifted it toward Camp.

"Yea," Camp replied. "Over there's the hammer I gave him for helping me out at the stables."

"Hmmm!" Jon said softly. He turned and stepped out of the hut. He laid his hand on the metal fence post next to the hut.

Camp stepped out of the hut and looked over at the

bantam chickens in the fenced area. "Looks like Little Bear's been stealin' chickens from Jed."

"Sure looks that way," Jon replied.

Camp continued. "Maybe Jed got suspicious and came over to check things out. He and Little Bear got in an argument. Little Bear whacked him a few times with the tomahawk and then flew the coop."

"Maybe so, but something just doesn't smell right." Jon grimaced. "Get a pack horse out here and pick up the body. I'm going to look around a little bit."

"Okay, Boss."

Chapter 13

The silver dollar rattled as it slid to a stop on the bar top. "'Nother round, Sam!" Zing Fuller ordered, speech slurred.

Sam pulled the whiskey bottle out of the rack and filled the glasses. He frowned as he slid the bottle back into the rack. "That's it," he said. "You boys have had enough."

Zing's thin lips turned down. "Did I hear you right bartender? You tellin' me no more drinks?"

"'Fraid so, Zing. You're both packin' and you're pretty darn roostered up. So I'm cuttin' you off. Maybe they'll serve you down at Faraday's," Sam said, as his hand moved nervously over the shiny bar top. Libby glanced over at the men from a nearby table where she was entertaining some friends.

Fuller's head fell backwards as he quickly downed the last drink and slammed the small glass on the bar. "Now damn it, give me another drink!" The nattily dressed gunman's face was contorted, red with anger. He grabbed the black handle on his six gun and took it out of its holster. The cold metal barrel crammed into Sam's neck. Fuller leaned forward pushing the gun barrel harder against Sam's neck.

"Now bartender, now!"

Sam looked over and saw Jon and Camp, just back from Jed Orton's place, enter the Barbee. Jon raised his hand, Camp stopped. The two men stood quietly listening just inside the batwing doors.

Libby's chair slid out, she rose up quickly. Attempting to calm the situation, she spoke to the wily gunman, "Mr. Fuller, surely--!" Before the lovely saloon owner could finish she was rudely interrupted by Clive Cook.

"I beg your pardon Madame, but we certainly don't need a common bar girl dressing us down, now do we?" The pompous Brit's face broke into a cruel grin.

The angry Fuller's eyes were locked on Sam; he didn't notice big Jon as he came in the room. Clive Cook glanced to the right and saw the angry Sheriff. He reached over and squeezed Fuller's shoulder from the back. Trying to warn the surly gunman, the petulant Fuller pulled away, still focused on Sam.

"I'm tellin' you for the--!" the angry Zing shouted.

Before he could finish, Jon spoke up. "Draw down, Zing!" Fuller's eyes shot right at the sound of Jon's voice. Jon kicked a chair off to the side, as he spread his legs apart. Facing Fuller directly, Jon looked huge and menacing in his dark leather vest and brim-down hat. Camp was slightly behind, out of the line of fire. Jon's head tipped to the side, signaling Camp to get out of the way. Camp reluctantly moved over to the end of the bar.

"No problem Sheriff, we're just having a drink," Clive Cook said sardonically, still smarting from the beating Jon had given at the mansion some days earlier.

Jon was still, his eyes narrow and angry. His arms hung at his side, ready to draw at a second's notice. "Butt out, Cook!" Jon ordered. "I'll deal with you later." His attention went back to Zing Fuller. "I said draw down!"

The vicious Fuller eased the barrel away from Sam's neck; he slid it carefully back into his holster.

"What's the problem here, Sam?" Jon asked.

"I shut 'em off a little while ago and Zing here took exception," Sam replied as he rubbed his neck.

"My friend here shuts you off and you cram iron in his neck? Is that what I'm hearing?"

"You guessed right, Sheriff," the smart aleck Fuller replied, emboldened by the whiskey and Cook's presence.

"First Malone and now Sam. You're always trying to hurt my friends, Fuller!"

Beads of sweat were forming on Fuller's forehead as he turned away from the bar and faced the famed gunman. "I asked this man for a drink and he refused. I ain't leavin' till he gives it to me," Fuller said, as an evil smile broke out his face.

Jon could see Cook out of the corner of his eye. "What about you Cook, you want another drink?" Jon's eyes looked hard at the Englishman.

"No need for gun play here Sheriff," Cook replied, he turned away from the bar toward Jon. His shooting hand hung loose at his side. Nearby patrons began to mumble and move away.

"You snakes listen close. You aren't ever going to take over this town. This town belongs to the people and I'm the law around here!" Jon was very angry, his mood darkened as he spoke. "Worse yet, you've insulted the woman I love!"

Cook's eyes were as big as saucers, unaware that Jon had heard his comment to Libby. Perspiring heavily, he pushed his back against the bar and slowly slid sideways away from Fuller. The frightened Brit carefully folded his arms on his chest. Fuller couldn't see Cook.

Sam threw his towel in the sink and moved down to the end of the bar. Libby and her friends moved quickly to the back of the saloon, isolating the three men.

Fuller stepped away from the bar; the evil gunman spit on the floor as he spoke, "That whore girl worth dyin' for, Sheriff?"

Jon's eyes went black at the drunken man's comment. "You're dead meat, Fuller, the talking's over!"

Fuller's eyes narrowed, his legs spread apart. "Consider this payback for Black Rock Creek," the horrid man threatened. Soaked with whiskey, he showed no fear.

Jon stared right through the nasty gunman.

Fuller stared back; his thin face was full of hate. Suddenly his bony hand reached for his gun. He drew.

Jon's hands went to his Colts like lightning; the guns flew out of their holsters. He pulled both triggers, the bullets blasted into Fuller's gut. The crowd screamed in shock at the gory sight.

"Ugggh! Gawd, I'm hit!" Fuller shrieked. His body slammed against the bar. Blood squirted from the holes in his gut and splashed on his shiny boots. His face was white, eyes full of terror. "Damn you!" he yelled. "Damn you!" He staggered around and fell head first on the floor. His head cracked as it hit hardwood. His six gun blasted harmlessly into the air. His body jerked violently a couple times and fell still, smoke spewed from the ugly belly holes.

Jon hurried over, his foot pushed against the dead man's body. Fuller rolled over on his back; his lanky arms fell limp to the side. The crowd gasped.

Jon turned left toward Cook, he rushed toward the snobby Englishman. Cook's hands raised in submission as Jon approached.

"Common bargirl, huh?" His gun's warm barrel, still smoking, pressed against Cook's neck. Jon wanted to rip this man apart, but he held back. His fingers wrapped around Clive's shoestring tie. He yanked Cook away from the bar and pushed him toward the swinging doors.

"How 'bout some fresh air, Clive?" Jon said as he put his six gun away. Cook stumbled and fought to stay on his feet as Jon pushed him backward. Full of rage, Jon slammed the big man through the swinging door. Cook's big body stumbled down the rickety steps and crashed onto the dirt road. Jon reached down and yanked the man to his feet again. Cook's feet pushed against the dirt street as he struggled to get up. With a Herculean effort, Jon lifted the large man up, carried him over and threw him into a nearby water trough. Water splashed over the sides, as he pushed the nasty Brit under the water. Jon pulled him up, Clive's head popped out of the water. He was gasping for breath; the devil was driving Jon now. He saw injustice with these men; the darkness was coming. He screamed at Clive Cook, "You in the habit of insulting ladies, Cook?" Beads of sweat were dripping from Jon's forehead. "Answer me Cook! NOW!"

Drops of water fell off of the beaten man's oval face. Eyes wide, he whispered almost inaudibly. "No?"

"SAY YOU'RE SORRY!" Jon screamed, his big arms pulling violently on the shoe string tie. Cook's veins were bulging on his neck; his eyes were popping out of his head as he tried to speak. "I'm S...s...sorry." He barely choked it out.

Jon leaned hard backward, his boots pushed against the bottom of the trough. With a powerful effort he yanked the big Brit out of the water. Jon pushed the big man, he stumbled toward his horse. "Get the hell outa here Cook, before I kill you!"

The beaten man staggered over to his waiting mount and struggled into the saddle. He hung to the side of the horse's neck as he rode slowly out of town.

Jon's arm hung at his side as he stepped back from the trough in a trance. Libby rushed onto the street and over to her man, her small delicate fingers squeezed his bicep.

"It's okay Jon," Libby said tenderly as her lithe body moved up against him. He could feel her warm heart beating rapidly against his chest; his arms moved around her tiny waist, as the two lovers embraced. Only Libby knew the pain Jon was feeling; she squeezed him tightly.

"Thank you, darlin'," Jon said softly. "I needed that!"

"Bravo Sheriff, you really let that Fuller have it," a voice from the gathering crowd shouted. Several people pushed around the couple, as they patted Jon on the back. He grabbed Libby's shoulders and gently pushed her back. "I better greet the folks," he said.

Libby smiled. "I guess so," she replied as she slipped away through the pressing crowd. Jon turned to face the crowd.

"'Preciate it, folks," Jon said humbly. "This man was a menace and I did what I had to do. But now it's over, so let's all go on home."

Camp pushed through to the opening in front of Jon. "You okay Boss?'

"Guess so Camp," Jon replied as picked up his gun and dropped it in the holster. "Go tell the coroner to pick up the body. I'll meet you at the jail." Jon frowned. "I think we're going to have some visitors shortly."

Camp nodded.

Another killing; when will it all stop? Jon thought. The agony on the dying man's face kept running through Jon's mind as he walked toward the jail.

Chapter 14

Jon grabbed a couple of cartridges out of his desk drawer and dropped them in the empty chambers on his six gun. He spun the cylinder and snapped it into place; he eased the ivory handled gun back into its holster.

The front door to the jail creaked open. "Howdy Sheriff, needin' any help round here?" said the friendly voice.

"Well, Jack, how in the heck are ya? Good to see you again! Come over here and sit down," Jon said, as his hand motioned toward the chair. The two shook hands as Jack plopped down in a chair.

"How are you feeling?"

"Pretty darn good, thank you." Jack smiled. "The Doc gave me a clean bill a health. If you've got work, I'm ready."

Jon's hand reached in the open drawer. "Here you go, Deputy, been holding it for you 'til you got back." The metal badge rattled as Jon tossed it on the desk in front of Jack.

Jack snatched it up and quickly pinned it on his

calico shirt.

Suddenly the door flew open again and Ed Morgan rushed in.

"Alex Faraday and his boys just came bustin' into town. They look real mad and they're all packin'. Faraday told me he wants to see the sheriff right away," Ed said anxiously.

"Where's he at?" Jon asked.

"Down at his saloon."

Jon pushed up on the arms of his swivel chair; he jumped up and hurried over to the gun cabinet. He reached in and grabbed a .50-.70 Remington and tossed it over to Jack.

"Let's go," Jon ordered.

The three lawmen hurried out the door and headed for Faraday's. Jon's hand went up, they stopped in the street.

"Spread out," he ordered.

Ed and Jack moved to each side of Jon, several feet away. Four horses were strapped to the hitching post out front.

Jon turned to Ed. "Looks like he brought the whole gang to the party."

Ed smiled.

Jon yanked his gun out of its holster, pointed the barrel to the sky and squeezed the trigger. There were two loud blasts as smoke filled the air. The horses whinnied and pranced nervously. Muffled screams could be heard inside the saloon as the music stopped. It got dead quiet.

Jon's eyes searched the front of the building for any sign of activity. Jack held tightly to his rifle. Ed, always cool under pressure, stood still in the street.

After several minutes, four thin fingers appeared on the outside of the swinging door. The door pushed open; Alex Faraday walked out onto the wooden walkway. Dressed to kill, he fidgeted nervously with the ring on his right hand as he spoke. "So good to see you gentlemen and just what are we celebrating with all the gunfire?" the pompous Brit asked sarcastically.

"Ed here tells me you want to see me, Alex," Jon said coolly.

"That's what I like about you Sheriff, you get right to the point," he replied.

"I got things to do Faraday, spit it out!" Jon barked.

"Why yes, of course." Faraday went on, "I understand that one of my ranch hands was killed in cold blood today at the Barbee."

"Ranch hand my foot, Zing was a killer and you know it. He drew first; it was self defense," Jon said angrily.

"Is that so? Well my witness saw something completely different," the uppity Brit replied, nose in the air.

"I really don't give a damn what your witness saw, Alex," Jon shouted.

Faraday tipped his head. Cook, Canady and Norton spread out behind Faraday on the walkway.

Malone cocked his rifle.

Jon eyes narrowed as he walked over and stuck his nose in Clive's face. "Maybe your witness would like to say that in front of me," Jon said menacingly, glaring at Cook. Clive looked away from Jon; he said nothing.

Jon backed down to the street still glaring at the

humiliated Cook. "You've got no witness, there's nothing to investigate, Alex. Zing went first; the whole town saw it."

Faraday looked disgustedly at Cook; he turned back to the sheriff. "How about trying to drown my courageous friend here?" he said sarcastically.

"Clive insulted Miss Thompson. I'm sure that even you wouldn't approve of that Alex," Jon said.

"Well, I guess I have never been one for insulting the ladies," Faraday reluctantly replied.

"We've got a bigger problem here," Jon said, quickly changing the subject. "Jed Orton was murdered today."

"Yes, yes, I heard about that. Have you found that thieving Indian yet?"

"No, seems he disappeared," Jon replied.

"Hmmm, that's interesting. He must have run off. Well, regardless, the other commissioners and I met briefly today; we are planning a special election two weeks from today to replace Orton. I suggest you get the announcement out as soon as possible."

"Your announcement will be out plenty fast enough Faraday!" Jon barked at the haughty Englishman. "And I'm still investigating Jed's death, and right now, nobody's off the table. I want you and your boys to stay in county 'til I'm done. If you try to leave, I'll have you arrested!"

"Why that's ridiculous, you can't do that my fine man. We've done nothing to deserve such restrictions. It's obvious to everyone that Little Bear killed Orton, you have no right--"

"You heard me Alex," Jon interrupted the haughty Brit.

Indignant, Faraday's face turned red with anger as his fingers continued to fidget with his gold ring. He glared at Jon. "Election is in two weeks, no later! Let's go boys!" The four men hurried toward their horses.

Jon stepped forward; he grabbed Butch Canady firmly by the arm. Startled, Canady's square evil face turned and looked hard at Jon. "You're not messing with greenhorns this time, Butch." The corners of Jon's mouth broke into a smile as he spoke to the heartless killer.

Canady yanked his arm free. The four men quickly mounted up and rode out of town.

"Follow them as far as Jed's place, Jack," Jon ordered. "See what you can find out. I think they're knee deep in Jed's murder."

"Will do, Boss." Jack smiled, happy to be working. He mounted up and quickly rode out of town.

Jon looked over at Ed. "Been a long one, partner, how 'bout some grub?"

"Thought you'd never ask," Ed replied.

The two lawmen pushed the door open as they headed for the bar. Jon looked up and saw Libby step out of her room. She hurried down the spiral oak staircase to greet him.

Jon stepped on the rail and leaned on the bar; Ed moved in next to him.

"Evening Sam," Jon announced.

Surprised by the sound of Jon's voice, Sam turned quickly around. "Well hello Jon! Sorry I didn't see you come in." Sam set two shot glasses on the bar and quickly poured the two men a drink.

Jon and Ed downed their shots. Libby arrived and

put her arm in Jon's. "Good evening," she said softly.

A big smile broke out on Jon's face, "Evenin', Darlin'," Jon replied, eyes twinkling.

"Got a minute?" she asked.

"Always my dear," Jon said with a smile. Her hand slid down his arm and grasped his hand. Her slim figure effortlessly negotiated the tables and chairs as she led him to their corner table.

Jon grabbed the back of the oak chair, Libby sat down. Jon sat across from her, back to the wall.

"What's up?" he asked.

Libby leaned forward talking quietly. "One of my regular customers was over at Faraday's Saloon today when Alex and his gang rode in. He was sitting at the end of the bar. The gang sat pretty close to him and didn't pay him much heed. After a couple of drinks they started jabbering quite a bit. Canady said he was itching to take you out. He heard Faraday say that something has to be done about that sheriff."

"Hmmm, doesn't surprise me." Jon grimaced.

"I think Zing Fuller's death kind of frightened them," Libby replied. "They're scared and they think you're a problem; they want you out of the way."

"Sounds like they're getting desperate," Jon replied.

"I'm worried Jon, they're dangerous men. I have awful thoughts all the time!" she said.

"Don't you worry your pretty little face, Libby. I've faced tougher hombres than these before." Jon smiled, put his hand on the side of her face and gently stroked her cheek. "I'll be fine."

"Do you think Little Bear killed Jed Orton?" Libby asked, wanting to change the subject.

"Not sure. I found pieces of black cotton on some of the velvet mesquites by his cabin."

"Canady?" Libby said quickly. "He always wears black."

"Yes I know, but I can't prove it yet. I got Jack trailing him right now."

"I hope you find something out. How about some dinner? I've got lamb chops and dressing tonight."

"It smells great!" Jon said.

"I'll invite Ed to join you."

"Sounds good, Baby."

Chapter 15

Jack rode comfortably behind Faraday and his men so as not to be noticed. Suddenly he pulled hard on the reins and came to a quick stop. He looked ahead; the men had stopped at the fork in the rode near Jed Orton's place.

Jack rubbed the horse's neck to keep him calm as he quietly rose up and dismounted. He grabbed the reins and headed for cover in a clump of Joshua trees near the road. Jack looked through the branches toward the fork in the road. He saw Faraday and his men talking and pointing at the woods where Orton was killed. Butch Canady jumped off his horse and ran into the woods. The other men stayed put, looking around nervously. A few minutes later, Canady ran out of the woods with something in his hand. He held it up to the other men. Some hundred yards away, Jack strained to see what it was.

Canady's head was moving as his explained his find to the other men. Jack pulled some twigs apart to get a better look. He couldn't be sure, but it looked like a spur. Canady had a habit, as some men did, of engraving his initials on just about everything he owned. Vagabonds like Canady were easy game for robbers, their initials were a way to claim their goods later. If it was a spur Canady was holding, it may have gotten caught in the thick brush and ripped off during the fatal beating of Jed Orton. It would be damning evidence if found by the law.

Suddenly, Jack's horse leaped into the air. A sidewinder slithered across the clearing, frightening his horse. She whinnied loudly, ears flicked; her hind legs stepped back toward the road. Jack tried desperately to calm the terrified charger, but to no avail. She backed toward the road.

Jack was now out in the road, in full view of the men as he struggled with the horse. He was grabbing for the reins, trying to mount the panicky steed. He saw Norton pull his Winchester out of its holster and level the powerful rifle at him, as he struggled mightily to get his foot in the stirrup.

Two shots rang out. Frightened by the loud noise, Norton's horse reared and danced nervously in the road; he couldn't set for another shot.

The first bullet whizzed by Jack's head. The second bullet hit the saddle horn, blowing it to bits. Lead flying, Jack struggled to mount up. His frightened horse finally stood still, Jack hopped aboard and rode quickly back to town.

Norton, atop his jumpy steed, tried to get off another shot; but it was too late. He gave momentary chase and then retreated.

Chapter 16

The fork clanked as Jon tossed it on the empty plate. He patted his belly. "Pretty darn good lamb chops," he said. He lifted his cigar up to his lips, took one more big drag and coughed up some pretty good smoke rings. He snuffed it out in the metal ashtray.

"Finally got a couple good ones." Ed laughed, squinting through the thick smoke.

"I get lucky every once in awhile." Jon smiled at his old friend. "Ready to go?"

Ed nodded.

The two men stood up and headed for the door. Jon smiled as he nodded at Libby as she watched play at a distant Keno table. "See you tomorrow, Darlin'," Jon shouted.

Libby smiled warmly, too ladylike to shout good-bye across the room.

The batwing doors popped open, and the two lawmen descended the steps to the dusty street.

"Let's straighten things up at the jail and call it a day," Jon ordered.

"Okay--"

Ed was interrupted by the sound of nearby rifle shots.

"It's Jack!" Jon shouted. The two friends looked at each other.

"Let's go!" Ed shouted.

The worried lawmen sprinted down Pecos Street to their horses. Fleet a foot, Jon arrived first, peeled the leather strap off the post and mounted up.

"Gitty up!" The big Palomino reared up; her powerful hind legs pushed forward. She was at full gallop within seconds. Ed was close behind.

Near the outskirts of town, Jon saw Jack riding frantically toward them. He pulled hard on the reins, and Babe jumped to a stop.

Jack pulled up; his horse pranced around nervously in the road, soon surrounded by Jon and Ed.

"You okay Jack?" Jon yelled, worried that his friend had been hurt again.

"Yea, I'm fine!" Jack shouted.

"What the hell happened out there?" Jon shouted.

Jack, out of breath, struggled to speak. "I was hidin' and watching them and my horse got spooked and whinnied. Web heard us and before I could get away, he took two shots at me with his rifle. Just missed my head, blew my saddle horn off."

Jon's face flushed red with anger at yet another attempt at his good friend's life. "Let's go get that bastard!" Jon said. The three men reined around and charged rapidly down the narrow road to Faraday's compound.

* * *

"You damn fool!" Faraday shouted at Norton as he galloped along the winding trail. "You don't shoot at lawmen in broad daylight, unless you are sure you can kill them!"

"I thought I could get him!" Norton shouted back.

"At one hundred yards away?" Faraday was incredulous. Norton didn't answer, his face red with embarrassment at the dressing down.

"Now we are going to have one fuming Sheriff Stoudenmire after us. The thought frightens me," Alex replied as they pulled up in front of his mansion.

"Leave the Sheriff to me; I'll take care of him!" Clive Cook replied, chest puffed out.

"Oh my, yes! It's been absolutely breathtaking watching the way you've manhandled that poor sheriff!" Alex said sarcastically as he slid off his Stallion and tied up.

"Gather round boys," Alex said.

Norton, Canady and Cook quickly dismounted and surrounded Faraday

"We have ourselves quite a problem here. My plan to take over all the gaming in this county is in jeopardy. The sheriff is on to us and he's one bloody tough hombre, as you cowboys would say!"

"Ah, bull! He ain't that tough!" Canady sneered.

Faraday's eyes narrowed at his hired gun for a second. He continued, "As we all know, Web here just took a couple shots at Jack Malone, a deputy sheriff. Deadly assault against a lawman is a serious offense and we need to find a way out of this, so here's our story boys, listen close!" Faraday quickly glanced at each man to be sure he was paying attention. He continued. "We were riding home from town. A man was hiding and following us, we felt threatened. We shouted at him several times, but he didn't reply. So Web here fired two warning shots to get the sneaky varmint off our tail. The shots scared him and he turned tail and ran. Satisfied that the bloke was no longer a threat, we rode on to the compound." Alex smiled smugly, seemingly impressed by his own ingenious plan.

"There's only one problem with your plan, Alex," Canady said as he spit on the ground.

"What's that?" Alex said, very annoyed at the surly gunman.

"Malone's got the only Red Dun within a hundred miles of here. We had to know it was him."

"Hmmm good point," Faraday replied. His eyes looked up as he thought for a minute. He smiled smugly and continued. "No problem Butch. If presented with that scenario, we'll simply say that our view of the perpetrator was diminished by the huge cloud of dust that our four horses had created when we rode down the trail. By the time the smoke had completely cleared, the shots had been fired and the man had evacuated the area. We had no idea what kind of horse he was riding, the visibility was horrible."

The men looked at each other and nodded their heads in approval.

"The sheriff is going to be here shortly," Faraday said. "So just act normal, like nothing happened. Go on about your usual activities. After all, we just shot at a potential robber, right?"

"That's right, Boss," Norton replied. The others nodded.

Web and Cook walked the warm steeds to the stable for a rub down. Alex pushed the big red oak door open as he and Clive retired to his study.

* * *

The three lawmen raced toward Faraday's compound. About five hundred yards away, Jon's hand moved into the air and he pulled to a stop. "Hold on!" he shouted. "Might be a trap!"

Ed and Jack reined hard on their steeds.

"Easy girl," Jon gently nudged Babe forward, eyes scanning the big rocks around the mansion for any sign of trouble. "Looks okay, let's move on in." Jon didn't really think Faraday would want gunplay over this incident. It might disrupt his plans to take over the county. The men rode down to the front of the mansion.

Bam! Bam! Jon slammed the big gold knocker on the front door. Too impatient to wait for an answer, he pushed the door open and charged into the corridor, knocking a startled Cook backward. Ed and Jack were close behind.

"Where's Faraday?" Jon asked.

"I will get--"

Jon interrupted the big Englishman. "I didn't ask you to get him, I asked where he was!" Jon's anger was palpable.

Cook looked away.

"Is he in the study?" Jon demanded.

A reluctant Cook nodded yes.

Jon and Ed charged toward the study. Jack stayed back to guard the front door. Jon's forearm slammed into the door, it flew open.

The startled Faraday shook the match out quickly. He stuck his pipe, still smoking, in its holder. "Why Sheriff, how good to see you again," Faraday said nervously.

"Cut the crap, Alex!" Jon shouted, as he moved over in front of Faraday's desk. He bent over, his fists hit the middle of the desk. Faraday looked frightened, as an angry Jon leaned toward him. Their faces were only inches apart. Ed was in the corner of the room watching Cook.

Cook was back by the door, clearly not anxious for another run in with Jon.

"Norton tried to kill Malone out on the trail. Where is he?" Jon growled.

"Now just one minute there, my friend," the frightened Brit protested meekly. "We didn't know it was Malone trailing us. Web fired two warning shots, that's all! We thought he was a robber or something! You've got no right..."

"I'll decide what's right or wrong around here," Jon said calmly, controlling his anger. He grabbed Faraday by the gold necklace around his neck. He pulled him up from his fancy chair, the slender nobleman was gasping for breath. "I said, where is he?"

Faraday was a pathetic sight, face red, eyes wide with fear. The humiliated Clive Cook felt he had to protect his boss. He moved quickly across the room toward an unsuspecting Jon.

"Not so fast, Cook!" Ed yelled as he drew his gun and pointed it directly at the huge Englishman. Cook stopped dead in his tracks.

'B..b...bunk house." Faraday struggled to speak.

Jon pushed the frightened Englishman down into the leather chair. Faraday rubbed his sore neck as Jon spun around.

"Let's go Ed," Jon said as he hurried toward the door and into the corridor. Ed dropped his bead on Cook and backed out the door. A red-faced Cook rushed over to aid his shaken boss.

Jack was holding the front door open. Jon and Ed hurried out. Jon yanked his guns out as the three men rushed toward the bunk house.

Jon saw Norton looking out of a small window, as he and the others approached. Norton's face disappeared from the window as the men got closer. The front door popped open slightly and then moved shut again. Jon could hear the sound of spurs on the other side of the bunk house. He tilted his head to the left, signaling Ed to go around back.

The front door swung open; Canady stepped out to face the sheriff, hands above his guns.

The sight of Canady inflamed Jon. He quickly dropped his Colts in their holsters and charged toward Canady. Caught off guard, Canady didn't draw. The back of Jon's left hand crashed into Canady's face. The nasty gunman's body flew back against the wooden bunk house. He fell to one knee; his fingers touched his lips, red blood appeared.

"Get up," Jon said angrily as he leaned down and wrapped his fingers around the red handkerchief on

Canady's neck. He yanked the heartless killer to his feet. There was a look of pure hate on Canady's face as Jon pulled him close.

"Our day is comin' Canady, and I can't wait. But right now I've got an arrest to make, so today you live!" Jon's free hand slid down and unbuckled Butch's gunbelt. Jon ripped it off and tossed it to Malone.

No match for Jon physically, the notorious gunslinger was smart enough not to provoke him. He wanted to kill him in the worst way, but now was not the time. He spoke quietly, "You'll see me again Sheriff, I promise you that." Jon's eyes narrowed, he looked hard at the evil gunman.

"Look here what I found!" Ed announced as he walked briskly around the side of the bunk house, Web Norton in tow.

"Good work, Ed." Jon grinned at his friend. "Go find a pack horse, Jack, and we'll take this varmint into town."

Jack emptied the chambers on Canady's guns and threw them over the wire fence next to the bunk house; he hurried over to the stable to find a pack horse. He hurried back and helped Norton up on the pack.

Jon stared at Canady as he mounted up. "Your pack will be at Camp's stable," he said calmly as he reined around and started toward town. Ed and Jack were close behind.

Canady's black eyes never left Jon. His square face looked dark and intimidating. "You're a dead man," the humiliated gunslinger said quietly.

As the lawmen rode by the mansion, Faraday and Cook stepped out on the front porch. "Don't worry

Web, the territorial judge is coming to town, we'll have you out by Friday!" Faraday shouted, still rubbing his sore neck.

Ed looked over at Jon. "Is that so?"

"Might be, it's Jack's word against his. Depends on the judge." Jon frowned.

Chapter 17

Jon plopped his foot up on the window sill as he leaned back in the chair. "How long do you have to--"

"Alright! Alright! I'm comin'! Just calm down!" Auggie shouted as he lifted the steaming metal pot off the stove and hurried over.

"Howdy Boys! How are you today?" Auggie poured the hot coffee into their waiting cups.

"Just fine Auggie, how 'bout yourself?" Ed replied, his fingers wrapped around the warm cup.

"Couldn't be better."

"Is that you Sheriff?" A shrill voice came out from the kitchen area.

"Sure is, and how's Lucy today?" Jon grinned and winked at the Irishman's chunky wife as she stuck her head out of the kitchen door.

"Just wonderful, Sheriff, just wonderful!" Lucy giggled. She batted her eyes at him and ducked back in the kitchen.

"Alright, alright, that's enough of that." Auggie laughed nervously. "What'll it be boys?"

"Eggs over, ham, and biscuits, Aug," Jon said.

"Couple of slapjacks and sausage for me Auggie," Ed said.

The friendly restaurant owner scribbled down their orders. "Comin' right up!" Auggie smiled as he ripped the order page off and hurried for the kitchen.

Ed looked over at Jon. "When's Judge Oliver comin' in?"

"Supposed to be hear tomorrow, but it isn't Judge Oliver. He took ill awhile back."

"You know who's comin'?" Ed asked.

"Yea, got a wire yesterday. Judge Walker's his name. Don't know him."

"When's the hearing?"

"Thursday." Jon's eyes narrowed a little; he looked over at Ed. "After breakfast, let's take a ride out through Dead Man's Canyon."

"Dead Man's Canyon?"

"Yea, I got a hunch about something," Jon replied.

"Well ain't that just dandy!" Ed bellowed. "You got a little hunch about somethin' so I gotta risk my hide ridin' through the scariest canyon this side of the Colorado River! Is that what you're tellin me?"

"Aw, don't worry Ed. You don't have to go!"

"Why not?" the incredulous deputy replied.

"I'll just grab one of the girls over at the Barbee, they're not afraid of a little canyon." Jon smiled at his old friend.

"Why you no account sodbuster!" Ed shouted as he reached down for his six gun. He put the steel barrel next to his temple. "A coward like me don't deserve to live!" Ed joked. "Boom!" he shouted. His head fell on the table.

Jon laughed hysterically at his old friend's antics.

The men were interrupted as Auggie hurried over with their breakfasts; the steam rose off the eggs and flapjacks. "Breakfast is served fellas," the businesslike Auggie announced. "And hurry up and eat before it gets cold," he ordered.

"If you say so, Aug," Ed laughed.

"All this fun reminds me of the old days, back in the camps," Jon said sincerely. He lifted his hand and pointed his cup toward Ed. "You're like a brother to me."

Tears welled up in Ed's eyes and he raised his cup, "I don't...ah...know...!"

"Pull yourself together, Ed!" Jon' grunted. He cupped his hand and slapped Ed gently on the side of the head. "We got us a canyon to ride through."

Ed smiled warmly at his old friend.

Jon took a sip of coffee, as the two lawmen hurriedly finished breakfast and headed for the cash register.

Auggie punched awkwardly at the keys. He pulled down on the iron handle, the bell rang and the door popped open. "Two bucks," he said.

Ed dropped a couple of silver dollars into Auggie's waiting hand.

"Thank you, Ed,"

"My treat tomorrow," Jon offered as the two men hurried out and mounted up for their trip to the canyon.

"Let's ride!" Jon shouted. The dust flew as the riders galloped down Pecos Street toward their precarious destination.

* * *

The curtain moved back on the office window at Faraday's saloon. Butch Canady watched the two lawmen hightail it out of town. Alex Faraday was doing some paper work nearby in his small, cramped office.

Canady looked over at Faraday. "Stoudenmire and his deputy just rode by," he said. "They're goin' some place in one big hurry."

"Hmmm." Faraday dropped his pen and leaned back in his chair. "It's hard telling what those two are up to. Tail them, Butch, and find out what they're going," Faraday ordered. "And for God's sake man, don't let them see you under any circumstances."

"Don't worry, Alex, I know what I'm doin'," Butch said defensively. He quickly moved around the Brit and stepped out the side door to the alley. His six guns bounced as he ran to his waiting horse. With one motion, he planted both his hands on the horse's rump and jumped aboard. He landed squarely in the saddle and rode out of town. The race to catch up with the sheriff was on.

Canady leaned to the side of the galloping Stallion; his eyes went to the ground. *The canyon,* he thought as he looked at the tracks, *They're taking the trail to the canyon.*

* * *

Up ahead, the cool morning breeze felt good on Jon's face as he and Ed rode on. The beautiful desert lilies that lined each side of the narrow trail were in full bloom. After about an hour the canyon was in sight.

"Pretty big hole!" Ed exclaimed as he looked into the deep canyon.

"Yea, it sure is," Jon replied as he pulled up next to Ed.

The ancient canyon, formed over thousands of years by a tributary of the Gila River, was a sight to behold. The walls on each side were exceptionally steep. Over time, the frost, wind, and rain had molded the sedimentary rock in the center of the canyon into several large formations. These formations had taken on rather odd shapes; some of them looked a lot like large daggers or pitch forks. They cast long shadows on the canyon walls, making for an eerie sight to the occasional traveler who was brave enough to try and negotiate its narrow pathways. The dreamlike nature of these formations helped explain why some of the local Indians thought the canyon was haunted and filled with evil spirits.

Jon and Ed rode carefully down the steep trail that led into the canyon. Babe's front hoofs edged along the narrow trail as they moved slowly along the edge of the canyon. Ed's nervous Buckskin whinnied and hesitated, frightened by the steep drop. Suddenly Babe whinnied, her big hoofs pushed violently backwards.

"Easy girl, easy," Jon said, trying to reassure his frightened steed. The edge of the trail had given way; several rocks went plummeting toward the bottom. Ed and Jon's necks craned, their eyes wide as they watched the falling rocks bounce along the steep rock wall. It seemed like forever before the rocks hit bedrock at the bottom of the canyon.

"Sure wish I'd a notified next of kin," Ed cracked.

"You mean, you didn't?" Jon laughed. He rubbed Babe's neck, calming the powerful charger. After a breathtaking few minutes of navigating along the treacherous ledge, the trail finally widened. They rode on for a few hundred yards, and then Jon pulled up and dismounted. Ed did the same.

"Let's walk them awhile," Jon said. As he looked ahead, his eyes focused on a cut out in the rocks ahead. A small desert ironwood stuck out from between some rocks next to him. He wrapped the leather straps around the protruding limb. "Leave your horse here," Jon said as he looked down at the dusty trail.

Ed tied up and followed.

The loose sedimentation crunched under Jon's feet as he walked along the canyon trail, eyes down.

"Look here," he said.

Ed moved in close.

"There's no hoof prints on the trail; rains washed 'em away."

"Maybe there weren't any tracks," Ed said. "Could be we're the only ones that have been up here lately."

Jon took a couple of steps toward a cut out area and kneeled down. "Look over here, Ed."

Ed stepped over.

"This area's covered, rain doesn't hit back here. Look here at all the hoof prints."

Ed bent over, his eyes examined the prints. "Yea,, and they're plenty fresh, just a few days old. We got boot prints, too. You're the tracker Jon. How many horses and men?"

Jon studied the area for a minute. "Looks like three horses and three men. Three men came in, but only two went out."

"What?" Ed sounded puzzled.

"Over here," Jon said as he moved to his left.

Ed stepped over and leaned down next to his partner.

"There's three horses comin' in. One's a pack, see the smaller prints?"

"Yea I see 'em," Ed replied.

"The small prints are deeper coming in then going out, see that?"

"I guess they are," Ed replied. "Go on!"

"That means the pack was heavier coming in than going out. Something went off of him," Jon replied.

"Hmmm." Ed rubbed his chin.

"There's two different sets of boot prints, but look here." Jon scooted over near the edge of canyon wall. "There's a line grooved out in the dust, see that?"

Ed moved over and looked down. "Yea."

"Looks like the two sets of boots drug someone over here to the edge of the canyon wall," Jon continued.

Ed nodded.

"The groove's smooth and wide, not narrow and deep. The person they drug was wearing moccasins, not boots."

"Little Bear?" asked Ed.

"Think so. The groove goes right off the edge. Faraday's henchmen killed Little Bear and then they dumped his body in the canyon thinking nobody would ever find him."

"Let's go get those no accounts!" Ed barked.

"Hold on Partner, we still can't prove it was them.

We need more evidence," Jon said. He stood up and walked over to his horse. He reached inside his saddlebag and pulled out a pair of field glasses. He stepped back over to the canyon's edge and scanned the steep wall below for any sign of Little Bear.

"Ummm.... I think I got something, take a look," Jon said as he tossed the glasses to Ed. "See that formation that looks like a pitch fork? Just to the right of that."

Ed's eyes scanned the area, suddenly he looked away. "My God!" he said. "Is that him?"

Half way down the canyon wall, a body was impaled on a sharp, dagger-like formation. Unfortunately for Faraday and his gang, the body never made it to the bottom.

"It's Little Bear alright, brown leather head band and three white Eagle feathers," Jon said.

"It's gruesome," Ed said somberly. "Little Bear was a good man."

"The best," Big Jon shook his head. "We'll never get him out of there."

"Maybe we can," Ed said. "The Piutes get in and out of this canyon all the time; it's sacred to them. I'll ask Chief Yellow Dog to try and get the body. He liked Little Bear; I think he'll do it."

"Sounds good, Ed, but we still got a problem," Jon said quietly.

"What's that?"

"I still can't prove Faraday's boys did it." He frowned.

"We need to squeeze a confession outa one of them," Ed said, as he handed the field glasses to Jon, untied and mounted up.

"We'll let Faraday's boys know what we got. One of them may think its enough, get nervous and start singing," Jon said as he put his foot in the stirrup iron and mounted up. "Okay girl, it'll be over fore we know it!" He gently patted Babe's neck. He and Ed inched along the treacherous trail on the canyon's edge.

* * *

Butch Canady sat sunning himself on a big rock about two hundred yards from the canyon entrance. He reached inside his black vest and pulled out a strip of jerky. He clamped onto the jerky, ripped a piece off and began to chew. Hearing voices, he sat up, looking down to the mouth of the canyon. Jon and Ed were just coming out. Canady slid off the warm rock and fell quietly behind some bushes.

"Dry run," he whispered, confident that Little Bear's body had not been found. He cackled quietly as he sat and watched the two lawmen ride out of sight.

* * *

The sheriff and deputy galloped into town, hooves pounding. Jon looked at Ed. "Stables," he shouted.

Ed nodded. They thundered past the jail to the livery stable, and reined to a stop.

"Howdy Camp," Jon said as he got off Babe.

Sweat dripped off Camp's face as he walked out the big door, hammer in hand. "Howdy Jon, looks like you worked 'em a little," he said as he rubbed the foam off Babe's neck.

"Yea, we've been out to the canyon." Jon scowled as he looked around the stable. "Anybody here?" he asked.

"Nope, I'm alone," Camp replied as he moved closer to Jon and Ed. "What's up?"

"Found Little Bear."

"In the canyon?" Camp asked.

"Yep, impaled about half way down the canyon wall," Jon replied.

"Faraday's boys?" Camp asked.

"Think so; can't prove it yet. Keep this under your hat."

"No problem, Jon," the young stable hand replied. "By the way, I was down at Faraday's last evening."

"Uh....huh," Jon said. He yanked the billet straps loose and pulled the saddle off.

"Canady was there, drunker'n skunk. He was tellin' everyone that'd listen that your days are numbered," Camp's eyes widened as he looked over at Jon.

"That so," Jon replied.

"Yep."

"I'll take care of Butch Canady soon enough. Right now I got me a murder to solve," Jon replied calmly. "Cards at noon?"

"I'll be there," an excited Camp exclaimed.

"Can't play long," Jon said. "We'll take a few deals."

Ed grunted as he lifted the saddle off Ed's horse. His fingers gripped tightly to the saddle as he carried it over and dropped it next to Jon's. "Hurry it up Camp," Ed prodded the youngster. "I can't wait to get in the sheriff's pockets."

"Soon as I groom these two crowbaits, I'll be there." Camp grinned as he gathered up the reins and led the warm steeds inside.

"Crowbaits, you say?"

Camp ducked as a tin can flew by his head. Jon and Ed roared. Jon pulled out a fresh cigar; he drug a match along the leg of his levis, it exploded into flame. He cupped the flame and moved it up to the waiting cigar. Jon took several hard drags, tipped his head back and blew smoke into the air. "Let's go buddy," he said to Ed. The two men walked slowly toward the Barbee.

The swinging doors flew open as they entered the raucous saloon. The faro and keno tables were humming; most every poker table was full. It was noon in the desert - gambling time.

Several heads turned, voices could be heard coming from around the bar.

"Howdy Sheriff!" "Howdy Ed!" the men shouted at he and his deputy. They moseyed on over to the end of the bar. Sam put a couple of shots in front of them.

"Good to see you fellas," Sam said. "Got ribs and taters taday."

"Sounds good." Jon looked at Ed.

"Make it two," the deputy replied.

Smoke rose as Jon poked his cigar out in the metal ash tray and downed his shot. "What's new round here Sam?"

"Nothin' much. Bill Webster said he saw you ridin' by his store this morning."

"Yea, Ed and I took a little ride out to the canyon." Jon scanned the room looking for potential assassins. With his reputation, he couldn't be too careful.

"Bill said Canady rode out a short time later."

"Hmmm... is that right?" Jon was puzzled. "Probably

just coincidence."

"Could be, but Bill said he came back 'bout the same time." Sam looked intently at Jon.

"That probably isn't a coincidence." Jon scowled. "Nice to know, but I can't book a man for leavin' town and coming back."

"Guess not," the amicable bartender replied. "Just seems funny to me.

The cook stepped out of the kitchen, the smell was delicious as the hot food hit the bar in front of the men. "Couple of beers," Jon shouted as they picked up the hot plates and headed over to their corner table.

* * *

Down at Faraday's, Alex fidgeted nervously with his black silk tie. He, Cook and Canady were seated at his large black oak table on the mezzanine overlooking the gambling tables, a favorite perch for Faraday. It was just above the casino and gave a full view of the goings on in his popular saloon.

"Judge will be here tomorrow," Faraday said. "Web should be out by evening."

"You sound awfully confident, Faraday," Canady snapped.

"Yes, Butch, I am. The judge and I have a little history." The smoke rose, his cheeks pruned, as he took a drag off his pipe.

"Oh yea, what's that all about?" Canady pressed.

"If he wanted you to know, he'd tell you!" Clive Cook said as he glared at Canady.

Canady's eyes shot back at Cook, his hand went to

his gun.

"Calm down, boys! It's okay, it's okay." The angry stares slowly subsided. Both men looked back at Faraday; he continued.

"Tom Baldwin tells me the judge's name is Tom Walker. I knew Walker back in Colorado, long before he became a judge. I staked him in a land deal up in Cripple Creek; the deal went bust. So far, he's only paid me nickels on the dollar. He owes me big time!"

"Don't mean he'll lie for ya." Canady sneered as he twisted his handlebar mustache.

"My dear man, I am not asking for a lie. I'm just asking that he see things from our point of view," Faraday said smugly. "And I'm sure when I remind him of the ten thousand dollars he owes me, he'll do just that."

"Hope so, Commissioner," Canady said sarcastically.

"I'm sure he will," Faraday replied. "Meanwhile we've got a much bigger problem."

"Sheriff Stoudenmire?" Cook asked

"Yes Clive, who else? Alex sneered at the embarrassed Cook. "With the special election less than a week away, our fearless sheriff is doing everything he can to pin those murders on us. He has to be stopped!"

"What do you have in mind?" Cook asked as he nervously fiddled with a stack of poker chips.

"I don't know yet," Alex said quietly. Ashes flew as he emptied his pipe bowl in the metal ashtray. "I don't know, but that man has to be stopped - the sooner the better!" He pounded the warm empty bowl in the palm of his hand and repeated, "He must be stopped!"

Chapter 18

Jon squinted in the hot desert sun; he wiped the sweat off his face and neck and stuffed the handkerchief in his pocket. He looked over and smiled at the old chief. "Thank you, Yellow Dog."

Yellow Dog nodded, and Jon handed the Chief two bags of coffee and sugar. Yellow Dog grunted something to his men; two warriors carefully laid the stiff body of Little Bear in the coroner's wagon. The latch clicked as County Coroner Jake Nussbaum pushed the tailgate shut.

"Good bye, Brave Bear," Chief Yellow Dog said, raising his spear to the legendary lawman. Brave Bear was the name given to Jon by the Piutes for his courage and size.

"Until we meet again," Jon replied, tipping his hat.

The friendly chief and his small band of Piute warriors rode quickly away.

Jon tuned toward the meticulous coroner, "Bullet in the head?"

"Yes, it appears as though there is gun trauma to the

back of Little Bear's head," Jake replied.

"I'd like to keep this quiet 'til we know more," Jon suggested.

"No problem Jon. I'll take the back way into town. It should be okay. Besides, I'm always bringing bodies in; no one will think much about it," Jake said as he carefully unfolded a wool blanket and laid it over the rancid body.

"Preciate it, Jake, see you later," Jon replied.

Jake jumped up on the wooden seat, cracked the whip and the two horses leaped forward. The wagon turned and headed for the little used back road to town.

Jon turned in the saddle, searching the surrounding rocks. "I think somebody's watching us," he whispered to Babe. A bright, blinding light flashed. Jon's hand went up to his eyes as he struggled to locate the light. "Gun barrel," Jon said under his breath.

He grabbed the butt of his rifle and slid it out of the holster. He jumped off Babe; he hit the ground and rolled toward some nearby rocks.

The dust flew as two bullets crashed into the ground near Babe's hooves. The brave horse whinnied but didn't move. "Go Babe, go!" Jon shouted. Hearing his command, she reluctantly moved behind some rocks.

Jon fired a shot to establish his location and then he rolled up on all fours and crawled rapidly around the rocks.

Sparks flew as hot lead ricocheted off the rocks above Jon's head. *That's a Remington, first two were a Winchester, got two shooters,* Jon thought. Sweating profusely, Jon moved swiftly to his left. Ready to climb, he found a notch in the rock above. His finger tips slipped into the notch, and he pulled himself up to the ledge. His belly pushed up the rock as he moved up to eye level for a look. Hat in hand, he peeked over the top of the large boulder. Once again, a bright reflection temporarily blinded him. He squinted into the light and saw a shadowy figure near the domed rock. Jon ducked down; his Carbine went up to shooting position. Time only allowed for a couple of shots, he had to make them good. Breathing rapidly, Jon rose up, took aim and fired two shots at the shadowy figure.

"Uhggg!" The shootist grabbed his chest, his rifle dropped out of his hands. As if in slow motion, his body rolled off the side of the rock. With an awful thud, it landed on the hard, jagged rocks below.

Jon sat still for a minute and then he heard a voice.

"Gitty up!" A voice came out of the rocks, the pounding hooves of a galloping horse could be heard leaving the scene. The second man had lost nerve and ran away.

Jon grabbed his hat and slipped off the ledge. He ran back to the opening. "Babe!" he shouted. The big steed charged from between several large rocks and stopped at her master's side. Jon's boot hit the stirrup iron; he quickly mounted Babe and rode up the hill toward the shooters. They came to a sudden stop, Jon jumped off and sprinted toward the domed rock, looking for any sign of the downed gunman.

"Gawd!" he exclaimed loudly, his eyes looked away. The bloody, battered body of the attempted assassin lay in a grotesque position in the middle of the jagged rocks.

Face contorted, Jon stepped over near the body. He

pushed on the dead man's shoulder with the barrel of his gun. The body rolled over on its back, his arms fell to the ground, his face pointed skyward.

Don't know him, must be a hired gun, Jon thought as he looked at the lifeless face.

Jon hurried back down the hill. His boot hit the top of a large boulder as he hopped onto Babe. "Let's do a little tracking," he said.

* * *

Back at the Barbee, Ed and Camp were enjoying a noon day game of stud with a couple of miners.

"Need a good one," Camp said, waiting on his next hit. The dealer flipped the next card, an ace of hearts landed face up in front of the young stable hand. His right thumb bent up the corner of the hole card ever so slightly revealing the ace of clubs.

"Two dollars," he said, the two shiny silver coins landed on the growing pot.

"I'm out," Camp said disgustedly. He flipped his hole card over. "Got nothin' again."

Four dollars hit the pot as both remaining players called Ed.

"Aces up," Ed said quietly.

"Beats me," one of the miners said.

"Kings up," the other man said as he dejectedly tossed in his cards.

A grin broke out on Ed's square face as he drug the pot in. He glanced over at Camp, "Gotta go, got a court hearing in ten minutes," he said.

"Oh yea!" Camp replied. "That's why you ain't

drinkin', huh?"

"Yea, Judge Walker's havin' a preliminary hearing on Web Norton's case," Ed said as he carefully tossed his winnings in a wooden cigar box.

"Hmm... Faraday promised to get 'em off."

"Yea, he sure did," Ed replied. "I guess the judge was down at Faraday's for over two hours last night. Someone said he and Alex are old friends."

"Uh oh! That doesn't sound good." Smoke rose to the ceiling as Camp poked out his cigarette. "We better get down to the jail, Jon should be back soon."

The two men folded and headed down to the jail to wait on the sheriff.

Jon arrived a short time later. His eyes immediately went to Web Norton's empty center cell. "Well, I'll be. The son of a buck did it. What happened, Ed?"

Ed frowned. "The judge said there wasn't enough evidence, it was our word against his. He said he would be derelict in his duties if he held a man for trial on no more evidence then we had. So he dropped the charges. Web Norton got off scott free. Clive Cook came in a few minutes ago and picked him up. I sure hated to open that cell."

"I'll bet you did," Jon replied. Jack handed him a cup of hot coffee. Jon walked over and plopped down in his swivel chair. He disgustedly tossed his hat on the desk. "They've gotta be stopped," he said quietly.

"How'd it go out there with Little Bear?" Jack asked, anxious to change the subject.

"Okay at first. I tell you, it was something watching those Injuns climb down in that canyon." Jon frowned. "Had a little problem later on."

"Oh yea, what happened?' Malone asked.

"The Piutes put Little Bear's body in Jake's wagon and he headed for town. Then the Injuns hightailed it out of there. When I mounted up to leave, I had a funny feeling someone was watching me." Jon took a sip of coffee. "First thing I knew I was ducking rifle shots."

"What'd you do?" Jack asked.

"I got off Babe and moved around behind some rocks. There were two shooters; I heard a Remington and a Winchester. I took one of 'em out. The other one got scared and rode off. I tracked them for awhile, but it looks like he flew the coop. His tracks headed west toward Tombstone. I guess he didn't want to face Faraday, so he skedaddled on outa here."

"Just as good, now he can't tell Faraday we found Little Bear's body," Ed said.

"Yea, I know."

"Did you know the dead man?" Ed asked.

"Nope, I never saw him before," Jon replied. "'They were probably a couple of hired guns from Tombstone. Keep an eye on things, Jack. Ed and I are goin' over to the Coroner's office."

"Okay Boss," Jack replied.

* * *

Jon and Ed hurried over to the Jake Nussbaum's office. Jon pounded on the door.

"Come in," a voice from within shouted.

Jon carefully pushed the door open; he and Ed stepped in. Jake stuck his head out of the back room. "Oh hi Sheriff." The coroner peeled the rubber glove off his right hand as he approached the two lawmen. His hand extended for a shake.

"Got another one for you, Jake," Jon said. He and Ed shook hands with the friendly coroner.

"Oh really?" Jake replied.

"Out by the canyon, near the large domed rock." Jon frowned.

"You know, I heard some rifle shots when I was riding into town. Just thought you were doing a little hunting or something," the surprised coroner replied.

"I wish. After you and Little Bear left, a couple of shooters tried to take me out. I got one of them. He's layin' out there in those rocks."

"Oh my, sorry to hear that. Are you okay?"

"Yea, I'm fine," Jon said. As usual the smell of embalming fluids permeated the little office. Jon's eyes began to water.

"I'll run out and get him soon as I can," Jake promised.

"Just charge it to the county," Jon said.

Jake nodded and tipped his head to the left. "Come on back here for a minute."

The three men stepped into the back room. Little Bear's body lay stiff on a long table in the center of the room. Jake walked over to a small metal table next to the body. The coroner slipped his hand back into the glove and pulled it tight with the other. He carefully picked something off the table, lifted it and showed it to the men.

"Took this bullet out of the back of Little Bear's head," Jake said.

Jon and Ed examined the bullet.

".38 caliber," Ed said.

"That's right," Jake replied.

"Cimarron's use .38 caliber bullets, Butch Canady carries Cimarrons," Jon said as he rubbed his chin.

"Only one problem," Jake said as he looked over at Jon.

"What's that?" Jon replied, curious.

"There's a whole lot of guns that use .38 caliber shells. Canady's a real bad actor, but this doesn't make him the shooter." Jake frowned.

"Doesn't eliminate him either," Ed said as he carefully dabbed his watery eyes with his handkerchief.

"Sure doesn't," Jon replied. "Thanks for the info Jake. We gotta be goin'."

Jon and Ed nodded as they hurried across the front room to the door; anxious to get away from the pungent odors of the coroner's office. Jon quickly pushed the door shut behind him.

"Whew!" the two men said in unison, their chests welled up as they breathed in the fresh out door air.

"How'd you like to work in that all day?" Jon exclaimed.

"Bout as bad as havin' to look at that ugly sheriff's picture all day," Ed shouted.

Both men joined in a big belly laugh. Jon playfully pushed Ed toward the jail.

Chapter 19

"Now once again, Butch. Just who were these men you hired to take care of our fine sheriff?" Alex Faraday asked as he pulled the curtain back on the front window.

"Two friends of mine from down Tombstone way," Canady replied. Alex was slumped down in the leather chair in front of the stone fireplace. He pulled out an ivory handled pocket knife from his jean pocket.

"And you say they are dependable and very good shots?" Faraday said as he looked nervously out the front window.

"That's what I said, Alex. Give 'em a good look and they'll take you out," Butch said, as he fidgeted with his knife.

"Well that's good, that's good," Alex Brit replied. "We don't need any failures at this point."

"Don't worry, if they don't get him, I will," Canady said confidently.

"Let's hope you don't have to do that. I would rather have him killed by strangers." Alex dropped the curtain and walked over in front of the fireplace. As he gazed at the dancing flame, he contemplated the situation. He needed to eliminate Jon without any connection to him. He wanted to build his power base in the area as a respectable businessman. Any connection to the popular sheriff's murder could make it difficult to gain the support of the folks. He also knew that an angry Jon Stoudenmire was a daunting foe indeed and if all else failed he may have to turn Canady loose on him.

"I hear somethin'," Canady said.

"Oh yes, someone's coming," Alex hurried over and glanced out the window. "It's Web," he announced. "Maybe he has some news. Let's go greet him, Butch."

Butch looked over at Alex as he pushed the blade shut with the palm of his hand and put the knife back in his pocket. He slowly stood up and followed the Englishman as Alex hurried through the corridor and out the front door.

Web quickly dismounted, tied up and hurried toward Alex.

"Tell me my dear man, what do we know?" the fast approaching Alex asked.

The newly freed Web was almost out of breath. "Well they didn't get him." Web leaned against the door slowly getting his breath.

"They didn't what?" Alex screamed.

"Some of the miners at the...uh...saloon said they're ridin' toward town today and heard several shots out by the canyon. A little while later Sheriff Stoudenmire rode into town from that direction."

"He what?"

"I guess Jake Nussbaum rode out with his wagon a little later and returned with a dead body. Nobody knew the man." Dreading the response, Web's eyes went to the floor.

"What kind of idiots do I have working for me?" Alex screamed. He wheeled around to confront the slowly approaching Canady. His bony finger shot toward the gunman. "I'm paying you one hell of a lot of money to kill people and this is what I get!" Faraday screamed, finger shaking.

The fearless Canady's eyes narrowed. "I know I got a job to do Alex, but this Stoudenmire's a horse of a different color. It's like he's got nine lives or somethin'."

"That special election is on Saturday. Web here will win the election and I will then appoint Clive as sheriff. I want Stoudenmire dead in 48 hours; I don't care how you do it. It has to be done!" The haughty Brit stormed by Canady.

Faraday stopped by the door to his study, he turned back toward Canady. "48 hours! Do you hear me?" he shouted.

"I hear you Faraday," Butch replied as he spit on the parlor floor.

Chapter 20

"You got an extra pack horse in their Sonny?" Butch Canady asked.

Busy shoeing, Camp looked up at Canady. He let the hoof slide gently to the ground and stood up. "Just a minute," Camp said curtly. He hurried to the back of the stable to retrieve Faraday's pack.

Canady was leaning against the side of the stable door as Camp approached with the horse in tow.

"Thought maybe you forgot about him," Camp said, making conversation.

"Naw, we just ain't had a chance to come in and get 'em," the stoic gunman replied.

"That'll be ten dollars please."

Canady slipped his hand into his jean pocket and pulled out a ten dollar gold coin. He flipped it to Camp.

Camp handed the reins to Butch.

"Hear the sheriff had a close call yesterday," Canady inquired as he grabbed the reins.

"I guess word travels fast around here," Camp said.

"Yea, one of the boys was in town and heard about

it," Canady replied.

"Sheriff's fine, the lowlife missed, the other coward ran away." The muscular young stable hand stared hard at Canady.

"Lucky man," Canady replied, as he spit on the ground. The gunman's shoulders slumped as he mounted up and slid down in the saddle. "I kind of get the feelin' you're in cahoots with this sheriff."

"Maybe I am, so what?" a testy Camp replied.

"So... that can be harmful to your health Sonny," Canady replied.

Unarmed, wearing his leather work apron, Camp stepped over near Canady's horse. His face was red with anger. "Do me a favor Mister."

Canady's eyes narrowed, his cheek bone twitched nervously as he replied, "What's that?"

"Don't ever call me Sonny again!" Camp folded his hands into fists.

Canady's square dark face cracked into a nasty grin, "Now, now Son..."

Camp lurched forward and moved his right arm up for a punch. Canady went for his gun like a flash; he drew it out and slammed the barrel hard against Camp's face.

Camp's body fell against the side of the horse. Dazed and disoriented, he went down on one knee.

Canady raised his arm again and bashed the metal cylinder against the back of Camp's head. He fell hard to the ground and lay moaning, disoriented by the hard blow.

"Bad move Sonny, now go tell that sheriff of yours to put his badge away and fight me man to man. I'll be in at sundown," Canady said, a brownish spit ball splashed next to the Camp. His horse pranced nervously as Butch looked down at the battered youngster. He reined her around and galloped rapidly toward Canady's mansion, pack in tow.

Camp struggled over to the hitching post. He pulled himself up to a sitting position, leaning against the post. His eye was swollen and throbbing, his head ached horribly. He staggered to his feet and headed for the center of town. His knees wobbly, he stopped and leaned against a tree. He glanced up and saw Babe in front of the Barbee. He pushed away from the tree and staggered on. His legs were shaky but he struggled up the stairs in front of the saloon. Suddenly, he fell forward, his hands grabbed hold of the batwing doors. He hung face down between the doors as he swung forward into the saloon.

* * *

Jon's eyes darted to the door. "My God!" he shouted as he rushed over. Libby screamed. Jon caught the young stable hand before he fell and sat him gently on the floor of the saloon.

"What happened, Camp?" Jon said.

"Ca... Canady came in to g...get their pack horse, we h...had words. T....Then the coward pistol whipped me. He wa...wants to meet you at s....sundown in the st....street."

"Sam, take Camp down to Doc's," Libby ordered.

Sam quickly took off his apron. He hurried over and dropped down on one knee next to Camp. "You think you can get down to Doc's okay if I help you?" the concerned bartender asked.

"Yea, I th...think so," Camp replied weakly.

Jon slid his arm out from under Camp as Sam's went under. Sam pulled him to his feet; they headed for Doc's office.

Jon was furious.

Libby squeezed his forearm. "Let's go sit down for a minute."

"Sorry Libby, I got a rat to kill," Jon said as he started for the door.

Libby pulled hard on his arm. "Please Jon listen to me!" she pleaded. "It's a trap. Canady came to town and pistol whipped Camp on purpose. He knew you wouldn't wait until sundown. They're waiting on you, Jon. As soon as you get out there, they'll open fire."

Jon stood still for a second, his eyes glazed over with anger. As strong as this rage could be, Jon always felt he could control it. Libby was right, it was a trap.

"Call their bluff, Jon," Libby spoke aggressively. "When Sam gets back, I'll send him down to Faraday's. He can tell them that you'll be ready at sundown. They'll ride out and tell Faraday and Canady and you'll get your fight. Fair and square, right here in town."

Jon looked over at Libby, "You're right," he said quietly. "As bad as I want to kill that nasty snake, I've got to wait. We'll have our fight at sundown."

Libby smiled warmly at her powerful lover.

"Thanks," Jon said as he pulled out his pocket watch. "It's three o'clock; I'm going down to the jail and meet with Ed and Jack." Jon tipped his hat to Libby and hurried out of the saloon.

* * *

Butch Canady's dark eyes squinted into the sun. "Should be here any time now," he shouted to nearby Web Norton. Both men were waiting to ambush Jon in the large rocks near the mansion. Two hands took aim across the road.

"You sure he's comin'?" Web sighed. "It's been quite awhile."

"From what I've seen of this sheriff, when he gets mad, he kind of goes off. And nothin' makes him madder than seeing' one of his friends get hurt. He should be comin' shortly."

From where they were sitting, the men had a bird's eye view of the trail. Plenty of time to set their sights.

Suddenly, hooves could be heard pounding off in the distance. "He's comin!" Canady shouted. "Get ready boys!" he commanded. "He's on his way."

Canady lifted his rifle up to eye level and took a dead bead on the trail, some hundred yards out. The others did the same.

The sound of the hooves got closer; soon a horse and rider were in sight.

"Wait 'til about a hundred yards," Butch commanded.

The rider shouted out, "Don't shoot, it's me Slim Wilson." He held his hands high above his head.

"What the..." Canady yelped. "Hold your fire!" He slid off the rock as he recognized the approaching rider. He dropped to the ground and ran out to greet Wilson.

The rider approached rapidly, hands held high.

"It's okay Slim, we know it's you," Canady shouted.

"Put your damn hands down."

"Okay, okay. Just didn't wanta get my head blown off," Slim said nervously.

"We had a greetin' party here for the sheriff, what're you doin' out here?" Canady demanded.

"That's what I'm here about; I gotta message from the sheriff."

"Oh yea! What is it?"

"Sam came down to the saloon and said Sheriff Stoudenmire would meet you out in the street at sundown. Just like you said." Slim waited anxiously for the gunman's reply.

"Hmmm... that sheriff's just full of surprises." Canady scowled.

"What you gonna do now?" Web asked, approaching from behind.

"I'm gonna meet 'em at sundown, what else?" Canady snapped. "I never really liked this ambush idea anyhow, it's a coward's way."

"Now you got your chance Butch." Web grinned at the nasty gun.

"Yea, I know. I been itchin' to kill him ever since that..." Canady's voice trailed off, too embarrassed to mention the beating.

"It's four thirty Butch. We got an hour's ride."

"Yea, let's get back to the mansion. I want to heat my six guns up a little. Then we'll ride."

Norton nodded.

* * *

The door to the jail slammed shut. Ed and Jack

hurried in.

"Got the word out Jon, told everybody to stay in and get the kids off the street," Ed said.

"Thanks fellas," Jon said, feet on the desk. He slid fresh bullets into the cylinders of his Army Colts as he sat slumped in his chair. Jon was in the darkness now, anxiously awaiting the pain and violence of the coming exchange with Butch Canady. Constant beatings by a cruel father had prepared him well for such events. He was in his element now, there would be no quarter asked, no quarter given.

"It's five thirty, Jon. Faraday and Cook just rode into the saloon. Canady and Norton weren't with them," Ed said.

"They came in to see me get killed." Jon scowled. "Web will probably come with Canady. They'll all meet up at Faraday's.

"Tell me, Ed, what are the folks out there thinkin' of Faraday and his boys these days?" Jon asked, his eyebrows raised a little as he waited for the answer.

"From what I hear, they still like Faraday and Cook okay. Folks love havin' that saloon in town. He's got more girls than Libby and he brings in more entertainment," Ed replied. "Also, some of them think you're putting the heat on Alex to help Libby out at the Barbee."

"Hmmm...that's interesting. What about Canady?"

"Nobody likes Canady much. But they accept him cause he works for Faraday. They think Alex brought him to town to help protect his money."

"What about the murders of Jed and Little Bear?" Jon asked, somewhat annoyed.

"Most of the folks think Little Bear killed Jed and then ran off. They don't know about the body, remember?" Ed grinned at his big boss.

"Yea, I guess we have kind of kept things quiet. And to tell you the truth, I kind of like it that way for the time being. We need more evidence any how." Jon took his legs off the desk and stood up. "Why don't we head on down to the Barbee, Ed. We'll set up there."

"I'll watch the shop," Jack said.

The door closed behind them, the two lawmen ambled toward the Barbee. As they walked slowly down the dusty street, Jon's mind went to his vineyard in Southern California. It was soothing to think of his distant paradise at times like this. His mind pictured the beautiful vineyard nestled in a valley at the base of the Sierra Madre Mountains. Row after row of lush green vines being pulled downward by shiny bunches of deep purple grapes. All glistening in the morning sun and warmed by the soft ocean breezes. *Just like heaven!* he thought. *I'll settle there when my fight'n days are over.*

A familiar voice broke the trance.

"Howdy Jon," Sam shouted as he and Ed approached the bar and moved quickly to the end.

Sam slid a shot of Early Times in front of them.

"Thank you Sam," Jon said. The patrons got quiet as the music died, all eyes were on Jon.

"No need to be so quiet," Jon said as he looked around the room. "Just got me a snake to kill, that's all. No need for worry!" Jon raised his shot to the crowd and smiled. "Bottoms up!" he said as he downed the shot. Many in the crowd tipped their glasses to Jon, conversation began again; the piano started to play.

Libby strolled over from the gambling tables. She looked gorgeous in her dark blue gown and pearl necklace.

"How are you doing, Jon?" she said as she sat down next to him.

"I'm ready to go," Jon replied confidently. His senses were on high alert; he couldn't wait for the fight.

"Do you think he'll show?" she asked.

"Yea, he'll show," Jon said as his eyes looked into his empty shot glass. "He thinks he's the best. Plus a man like him feels no fear, because he doesn't feel anything. The thrill of killing somebody is what drives him. Taking me out will make him feel good for a little while, that's all he wants."

"Maybe you shouldn't be fighting him, being sheriff and all," Libby said quietly, tears forming in her lovely green eyes.

Jon smiled; he raised his hand and tenderly stroked her cheek. "You know me better than that, Libby, I've got to fight him. It's for the town and for the people and try not to worry; everything will be fine."

"I know it will," Libby replied. She smiled bravely.

"Canady's comin'!" a voice shouted from out in the street. People began to scurry about. Jon glanced through the doors. The steady beat of Butch and Norton's horses could be heard out front. All dressed in black, Canady looked straight ahead as he and Norton rode slowly past the Barbee.

"They're headin' for Faraday's," Camp said. "It's almost sundown. It won't be long now!"

* * *

Alex Faraday fiddled nervously with his gold cuff links as he awaited Canady's arrival. He and Cook were sitting at their usual spot on the mezzanine.

"For God's sake Clive, say something." He was annoyed at the lack of conversation by his old friend.

"Not much to say, Boss," Cook replied.

"Not much to say? My dear man, we are about to kill the most famous sheriff in the southwest and you can't think of anything to say?" Alex was incredulous.

Cook frowned and looked down at the table.

"Well, tell me this Clive, do you think we're doing the right thing?" Faraday pressed.

Cook looked up at his boss. "We don't have much choice."

"Yes, we do have to kill him, but then we still have to get Web elected. Will the townspeople turn on us?" Faraday nervously bit on his pipe.

"I don't think so; it's going to be a fair fight. No one can accuse us of bushwhacking our fine sheriff."

"Well yes... yes, that's a good point," he replied nervously.

Suddenly, shouts could be heard coming from out in the street.

"What on earth is that, Clive?"

"Sounds like Butch and Web are here." Cook pivoted in his chair; his eyes went to the front door. A black glove appeared on the top of the door, Canady walked slowly in, Web was right behind.

"Butch!" Clive shouted.

Canady's eyes went up to the mezzanine; he nodded and walked toward the stairs.

Alex watched Canady approach the table. "He has a

scary look about him," he whispered to Cook, "and those eyes are pure evil."

Butch and Web arrived at the table and took a seat. Canady slumped down in his chair, his face hidden under his hat.

"We need to talk, Butch," Faraday said.

"Okay, then talk," Butch replied, his shadowy face looking dark and menacing.

"I realize you have a difficult task in front of you my dear man, but..."

"Cut the crap Alex, just spit it out," Canady snapped.

Alex glowered at Canady. "Okay Butch, I'll cut the crap! I've invested a fortune in this area, with my estate, this saloon and other holdings. If Stoudenmire is able to implicate us in the deaths of Jed Orton and Little Bear; we could all go to jail, or worse yet, be hung. Our plan to dominate the gambling and prostitution in the southwest will go up in smoke. The sheriff must be stopped and it's your job to stop him!" Alex was angry, seething from Canady's insult.

Canady's black eyes shot back at him. "I know what I gotta do Alex, I'm the best. Just have the money ready, five hundred dollars."

"What?" Alex exclaimed. "I never bargained for this! Are you crazy?"

"You heard me; pay it or I'm ridin' outa here," Butch said calmly.

Alex's face was flush with anger, but he had no choice. He needed Stoudenmire dead and Butch was one of the few men who could do it. "Alright! Alright! Five hundred it is." His pipe rattled as he tossed it on the oak table and slumped back in his chair. "That sheriff must be killed," he said quietly.

"I need a drink," Canady said. He stood and walked down to the bar. The patrons watched quietly as the notorious gunman maneuvered his way to the end of the bar. The bartender slid a glass of Scotch, his favorite, in front of him. He downed the shot, slammed the thick glass on the bar and demanded another.

* * *

Meanwhile, preparations were being made at the Barbee. Jon and Ed were at the bar talking.

"Watch my backside out there, okay?" Jon said directly.

"No problem, Boss, I was plannin' on it," Ed replied.

"Faraday wants me out of the way real bad, I think he'll have a second shooter somewhere. I got the street covered. Check the roof tops for me."

Ed nodded. Jon smiled at his trusted friend.

The sun was almost down. Jon's mood was darkening with the desert sky. He thought of Jed Orton, a fine and good man, killed for no reason. He thought of his friend Little Bear, gunned down by a heartless killer. He could feel himself getting angrier and angrier at Alex Faraday, Butch Canady, and the rest of that rat's nest. He thought of the attempts on Jack Malone's life and the awful beating of his young friend and cohort Camp Wilson. Soon, Butch Canady would be dead; Jon had no doubts about that. As much as he loathed the killing and violence, he lived for these moments.

Chapter 21

Inside Faraday's Saloon, Butch Canady stood alone with his thoughts. His thin fingers surrounded the thick glass; he downed the last shot of Scotch. He stepped back from the bar and tied down. He raised his six guns slightly and dropped them loose in the holster. His eyes went up to the Mezzanine. Alex Faraday nodded at him as he stood up. Canady walked slowly toward the swinging doors; everyone in the saloon sat quiet.

Faraday and the boys walked quickly to the second story balcony to watch the showdown from above. Canady stopped at the doors, his eyes scanned the dusty street. It was sundown, plenty of light for a fight, but no glare. He pulled his black gloves tight and pushed the door open.

There were shouts out in the street as the gunman emerged. Butch was ready; it was his chance to kill yet another man. He had no doubts he would prevail, he had fought the best. The wooden steps creaked as he stepped out on the street.

* * *

Jon heard the commotion out on the street. "Sounds like he's comin'," Sam said.

Jon's head tipped back as he downed his final shot. He pulled the metal Sheriff's badge loose and dropped it on the bar. "I'm off duty," he said. He pulled out his pearl handled Colts and spun the cylinders out of habit, knowing they were fully loaded. Libby smiled from the end of the bar; he nodded and smiled back at his lovely lady. No time for sentimentality, she stayed her distance. Jon walked toward the street.

"Kill the bastard!" one man shouted, followed by several yea, yeas! Shouts of good luck reverberated throughout the saloon. Jon stared straight ahead as he pushed through the swinging doors. Ed wasn't far behind. The patrons rushed over for a better look.

Jon stepped deliberately down on Pecos Street; Ed hurried down the walkway toward the alley.

The wood frame buildings cast long shadows across the street as Canady walked slowly forward, stopped and turned toward Jon. They were now about three hundred feet apart. Jon glanced up at Faraday and Cook on the balcony; he looked over and saw Ed in the open alley way looking high. A small puff of dust flew up as Canady spat tobacco on the street.

The two warriors walked slowly toward each other down Pecos Street. At fifty feet, both men stopped, their legs spread apart. The crowd was stone quiet.

Jon stared through the shadows at Canady. Both men stood perfectly still, any unnecessary movements could start the lead flying before they had their say.

"I'm gonna take all of you today, Jon, it's a shame." A sly grin broke out on Butch's square dark face. His hands hung loose over his guns. "All you had to do was mind your own business, and you just couldn't do it!"

"You talk too much, Butch! Make your move!" Jon's anger grew as he looked over at the nasty varmint. *This man needs killin'!* he thought.

Canady's eyes narrowed. A nearby horse reared up and whinnied, temporarily distracting the men. Butch went for his guns.

Jon's six guns flew out of their holsters. Yellow flames shot from the barrels, as two bullets from Jon's six guns blasted into Canady's gut. His skinny body blew backward and slammed against a railing. The crowed screamed as blood squirted from the holes in Canady's stomach. Jon rushed forward through the smoke for a better look.

Canady, struggling mightily to stay on his feet, lifted one of his six guns waist high for a shot.

He was too slow, another shot from Jon's Colt blasted into the gnarly gunman's chest. His body spun violently backward over the wood rail and he slammed face down on the other side. His gun fired harmlessly into the dusty street. Brownish red blood streamed out from under him. The evil man's body jerked a couple of times and fell still. The killer was dead.

A shot rang out from near the General Store. Jon ducked as a bullet whizzed by his head. He saw a man standing on the second floor porch of the store.

Ed took dead aim and blasted away at the culprit. The man jumped over the wood banister, as his rifle fell to the street. Ed had shot the rifle out of the would-be assassin's hand.

Still enraged, Jon ran after the escaping man. It was a foot race. The man headed for the Mesa behind the store with Jon in close pursuit. Suddenly the man slipped on some loose gravel and stumbled. Jon dove on the fallen man, grabbed hold of the handkerchief around his neck and yanked him to his feet. He doubled his fist and blasted the varmint hard to the jaw. Screaming in pain, the man fell to one knee.

"I've had enough!" The man's arms covered his head as he begged Jon not to hit him again.

"Jon!" an approaching Ed shouted.

Once again the sound of his good friend's voice kept him from administering more punishment.

Jon pulled back and took a close look at the man. He was shocked to see Slim Wilson. "What are you doing here, Slim? You're no killer."

"Sorry Jon, I had to do it. Faraday told me if I didn't kill you, he'd kill me!" a somber Slim Wilson replied.

"You fool!" Jon said angrily as he let loose of the kerchief. "Take him to jail Ed and book him for attempted murder."

Ed pulled Slim's arms behind him and cuffed him. By now a large crowd had formed in the street. Jon looked up at the balcony at Faraday's saloon; it was empty. Faraday and his boys had flown the coop. Distant hoof beats could be heard out in the mesa.

"They can run, but they can't hide," Jon said under his breath.

Ed grimaced and pushed Slim toward the jail.

Libby pushed through the gathering crowd and hurried over to her man.

"Are you okay?" she asked.

"Yea, I'm doing okay," Jon replied.

"Was that Slim Wilson Ed was taking to jail?" she asked.

"Sure was. He tried to kill me," Jon replied.

"That's not like Slim. I guess you never know." Teary eyed, Libby looked up at him. "I'm glad you're okay; I better go, I got work to do." She smiled warmly, turned and started to leave.

Big Jon gently grabbed her arm, she stopped and looked back. "Love you Baby," Jon said tenderly. She kissed two fingers and touched his cheek and then faded into the crowd.

"Forget something, Sheriff?" an apron clad Sam shouted as he pushed his way through the crowd and pinned the metal sheriff's badge on Jon's denim shirt. The crowd applauded. "Sam, would you run down to Baldwin's Barber Shop and tell Tom I need to see him right away at the jail?"

"Sure thing, Sheriff." Sam hurried off.

* * *

Ed pushed the small gate open and walked Wilson into a cell. "Sit down!" Ed ordered as he took the cuffs off the frightened man. Close behind, Jon walked in the cell and sat on the cot across from nervous ranch hand.

He looked over at Jon. "I ain't no murderer, I want you to know that, I come from a good family!" Slim pleaded.

"I know you do, Slim," Jon said. "Just calm down a little; I need to talk to you."

"O...Okay Sheriff, I'll try," Slim replied.

"Jack made a pot of coffee a few minutes ago. You want a cup?" Jon asked.

"Yes please Jon, thank ya," Slim replied.

Steam rose as the Jon poured a cup and handed it to Slim. Slim took a sip and looked over at the Sheriff.

"You're in a whole heap a trouble here Slim, but I'll go lenient on you if you tell me the truth," Jon said sternly.

"Yea, you'll go easy, but Faraday'll kill me!" Slim lamented.

Jon leaned forward, elbows on his knees. "If you don't talk, Faraday won't have to kill you."

"I'm darned if I do, darned if I don't," Slim sighed as he leaned back against the wall. He was quiet for awhile and then looked up at Jon. "Go ahead," he said quietly.

"Do you know who killed Jed Orton?" Jon asked.

Slim's brow furrowed, he hesitated. It seemed like forever before he spoke.

"Canady," he said quietly.

"Who ordered Canady to kill Jed?"

Slim shook his head nervously as he stared at the floor. "Faraday," he mumbled. The frightened man rung his hands. Beads of sweat formed on his face.

Jon looked over at Ed and smiled.

"What about Little Bear?" Jon pressed.

"I dunno. I think he just got'n the way, I guess," Slim replied.

"What about them two varmints who tried to take me out over by the canyon?" Jon said.

"Faraday hired 'em, they were friends of Butch's

from down Tombstone way." Slim's face was white with fear. "That's all I'm sayin' Sheriff, that's enough!"

"Thank you, Slim, you've been a big help." Jon patted the terrified man on his knee. "And don't you worry, we'll keep you under guard 'til Faraday's either dead or in jail." Jon promised.

"Thanks Sheriff. Tell my folks I'm sorry, will ya?" He looked at Jon with anticipation.

"One of us will, I promise, Slim." Jon smiled.

The heavy door clanged shut as Jon hurried over to his desk. The front door swung open and Commissioner Tom Baldwin hurried in.

"Howdy Tom," Jon said.

"Howdy Jon, how are you?" Tom asked. "I heard the gun shots, but I couldn't see much from my end of town."

"I'm fine, Tom, sit down," Jon ordered. "Cup of coffee?"

"Thought you'd never ask." Tom slid a chair out and sat down.

Jon plopped down in his swivel chair. "We need to talk, Mr. Commissioner," Jon said seriously.

"Fire away, Sheriff!"

"Slim Wilson tried to take me out today after I shot Canady," Jon said matter-of-factly. "Ed here, shot the rifle out of his hands. He tried to run; we caught him and put him in jail."

Tom looked back in the cell area, "That's a shame, it's not like Slim."

"I know and he's scared stiff, and he just spilled the beans on Faraday," Jon said, leaning forward.

"That's good; what'd he tell you?"

Ed handed Jon a hot cup of coffee; Jon squinted through the steam. "Glad you're sitting down," Jon said. "Seems as though Alex ordered Slim to try and kill me today. That sidewinder also ordered Jed Orton's murder, which implicates him in the murder of Little Bear. Slim also told us that Alex set that trap for me out by the canyon. Looks like our fine new commissioner is implicated in two murders and two attempted murders - one on Jack and on me!" Jon scowled.

"Doesn't surprise me. I always thought those two Brits were a little bit too good to be true!" Tom frowned.

"What about the special election scheduled for tomorrow?' Jon asked.

"Under these circumstances, a special election would be out of the question. I'm going to postpone it indefinitely until we get this mess sorted out." The natty barber went on. "More importantly, we can't have violent men like these living among us. Faraday, Cook and his bunch must come to justice. I will give you all the support you ask for."

"Thanks Tom." Jon reached forward for a quick handshake.

"Good luck my friend and please be careful! The town needs you!" He smiled and left the jail.

"Great!" Jon exclaimed as the door closed behind the Commissioner. "Now we have time to round up those nasty varmints."

"Yea, but something tells me it ain't gonna be easy," Ed replied. "Faraday's mansion is going to be an armed camp. Alex, Clive, and Web Norton are all crack shots, and he'll get a few hands to join in. They'll take up positions in the rocks on both sides of the road in. If we try and charge them, we'll be sitting ducks."

"You're right," Jon replied.

"What are we gonna do?"

"Dunno yet," Jon said, "I'll have to think about it. Has anybody heard anything about Camp? We're gonna need all the help we can get."

"He's doin' better, heard him out shootin' this morning," Jack said.

"Run down and ask him if he's ready to ride with us, Jack," Jon ordered.

"Sure thing Boss." Jack grabbed his hat off the peg and headed for the stables.

"Judge is due in next week," Jon said. "I'll wire him to be sure he shows. It's almost dark. First thing in the morning let's take a ride out near Faraday's and look things over. And no gunplay tomorrow, too many would be killed."

"Okay, Jon, but what if he's gone?" Ed asked.

"He's got too much invested to run away now. He'll try and get out of this mess first. If he can't, then he might run," Jon said decisively.

* * *

The ranch hands ran out to meet Faraday and the boys as they came charging in the compound. They pulled up and quickly dismounted.

"Run these horses over to the stable," Alex ordered. "Then I want Cliff and Bill to load their rifles and take up positions in the rocks in front of the mansion. If anybody tries to ride in here, shoot them!" Faraday shouted. The men nodded. Alex tilted his head toward the house, Cook and Norton followed him in to the den.

Clive and Web took seats by the desk as Alex paced in front of the fireplace. He ran his fingers through his hair. "We better hole up here in the compound until we get this mess straightened out. Clive, I want you to send Cliff into town tomorrow and bring our attorney out here. We'll use him as our liaison with the sheriff."

"Okay Boss," Clive replied.

"We've got big problems men. Stoudenmire's probably got Slim singing like a bird. He--"

Web interrupted. "You shoulda never put Slim on the balcony, that was a huge mistake! Up 'til then it was a fair fight, now we could be charged with attempted murder!" Web said forcefully.

"What's done is done, Web! It seemed like a good idea at the time. I wanted to be sure that Stoudenmire was dead," Alex said defensively.

"Well he ain't dead and we're all gonna hang!" Web shouted. "I didn't bargain for all of this when I signed on with you Mr.--!"

"Shut up, Norton! You knew damn well what you were getting into. Quit acting like a bloody coward and pull yourself together. We haven't been hung yet!" Faraday screamed.

"Okay Alex, then what are we going to do?" Clive interrupted.

Alex and Web stared at each other for several seconds, and then Alex spoke up. "The District Judge is due in next week..."

"Judge Walker or Judge Oliver?" Clive asked.

"I'm not sure. Tom Baldwin told me the other day that Oliver was feeling better and might be coming in. But that won't work; we have to get Walker here." Faraday bit hard on his pipe stem.

"How are you gonna arrange that?" Web asked.

"I want you to ride to Mesa first thing in the morning. Tell Judge Walker we're in a big mess over here and we need his help. Tell him, if he can get us out of this predicament, I will forgive his entire debt -the whole ten thousand. I know him pretty well. I think he'll go for it." Alex grinned.

"I'll ride out in the mornin'," the loyal Web replied.

Alex went on. "Meantime we have to keep Sheriff Stoudenmire at bay. I'll use Attorney Brown for that." He turned toward Norton, "You're free to go now, Web."

Norton hurried out to prepare for his trip through the desert to Mesa.

Faraday motioned for Cook to come closer.

Cook stepped over. "Yea Boss?"

"Slim's a big problem. He knows too much. We can't have him on the stand no matter who the judge is. Take care of it!" He looked menacingly at his big cohort.

"You want me to kill him?" a surprised Cook asked.

Alex struck a match, lit his pipe and shook the match out. The smoke drifted to the ceiling. "I'm afraid we have no other choice my friend!"

Chapter 22

The cock crowed as a shivering Ed Morgan rode down Pecos Street to meet Jon. It was a cold winter morning in the desert. A light flickered through the window at Auggie's. As usual Jon was already there waiting. Ed tied up, his black duster drug over the post as he walked up the steps to the cafe.

The yellow flames danced in the pot belly stove; it felt warm inside.

"Mornin' Ed," Jon said enthusiastically. "Sit down; I'll get you a cup a coffee. Lucy's not in yet, Auggie told me to get the coffee."

Ed sat down and took a sip. "You're disgustingly happy for this early in the morning, you know that, don't ya?" Ed frowned.

"I'm just so glad to see you, Ed." Jon laughed. "Plus, I got good news!"

"Oh yea! I'm ready for some good news. Let me have it, Partner!"

"Well I got to thinking about today's trip and--"

"Uh oh," Ed exclaimed.

"Can I finish, please?"

Ed frowned.

"Like I said, I got to thinking about today's trip and with all those guards and stuff out there at Faraday's, there's no way we can go down that main road. Why, we'd be sitting--"

"Oh no! Oh no! Not this early in the mornin', with all the dew and everything. Ain't no way I'm going through that canyon this early in the morning!" Ed shouted. "Noooo way!"

"Why that's one of the most beautiful canyons in the world," Jon said with a sly grin. "I thought you'd be excited about it!"

"Breakfast served," Auggie shouted as he hurried out of the kitchen. "Two eggs over with bacon!"

"I took the liberty of ordering your breakfast, Ed; hope you don't mind."

"You mean my last supper don't ya?" Ed replied.

Laughter filled the little cafe as the two men finished their breakfasts and prepared for their trip through the canyon.

* * *

Out at the mansion, Alex Faraday was busy putting his new plan into action.

His loyal foreman, Cliff, had just returned from town with Faraday's Attorney Pat Brown.

"Welcome Pat, have a seat." Faraday gestured toward the oak chairs.

"Thank you Alex," The stocky, well dressed attorney settled in the chair. "It's awfully early; you must have something pretty important on your mind."

"Well, yes I do, Pat. It seems our fine sheriff, Mr. Stoudenmire, is becoming quite a problem," Alex replied.

"Oh, is that right?"

"Yes, let me explain. It seems like ever since Clive and I arrived in town and opened my new saloon, Mr. Stoudenmire has been doing everything he can to run me out of business. And as you probably know, his love interest is none other than the lovely Elizabeth Thompson, owner of the Barbee Saloon. It's no secret that we've taken a lot of business away from her. I do believe the man is on a mission to protect his lady friend's interests at my expense!"

"Has he accused you of any wrong doing?"

"Not yet, but I believe he is preparing to charge us with the murder of Jed Orton. He may also try to implicate us in the disappearance of Little Bear."

"Hmmm... is that right?" Brown said thoughtfully. "I hear Slim Wilson's in jail, what did he do?"

"He was covering Canady's backside during the shootout with Stoudenmire. He got nervous and his gun went off accidentally. Ed Morgan took a shot at him; he jumped off the porch of the General Store and ran. The sheriff ran after him and caught him. First thing I know, Slim's in jail. It's hard telling what they've forced him to say. I hear the Sheriff can play plenty rough if he wants to. Alex's eyes narrowed as he awaited Brown's response.

Brown grimaced. "Hmmm... that's interesting! I've never known Sheriff Stoudenmire to threaten prisoners, but I guess he could. Also, if Slim's gun went off near a lawman, we've got problems. They could charge him with attempted murder."

"Who's bloody side are you on?" Faraday asked.

"Why, yours of course, it's just that--"

Faraday interrupted. "Now listen to me, Pat, you've had a lot of big pay days with me, and some of things you done for me have not been completely honest. If I go down, my friend, you'll go with me!"

"Well now, no need to get upset, Alex. I guess I was just thinking out loud." Brown laughed nervously.

"That's better," Alex replied. "Here's the plan. Web is on his way to Mesa today to speak with Judge Walker. I want to be sure he is the Judge of record next Tuesday at the hearing. In the meantime, I want you to act as our intermediary with the sheriff."

"I see." The nervous attorney squirmed in his seat.

"I don't want Sheriff Stoudenmire to try and arrest any of us before the hearing. I need you to reassure him that we will come into to town for trial on Tuesday when the judge arrives. Meanwhile, for our own protection, we will stay here."

"Hmmm... don't know if he'll buy that," Brown replied.

"That's your responsibility; he has to buy it!" Faraday was irritated. "Ride back out after you talk to him and let me know what happened."

"Okay Alex," the attorney said quietly.

"I'll send for your buggy." He nodded at Cook; his big partner hurried out to get Brown's buggy.

* * *

Nearby, Jon and Ed were just finishing their trip through the canyon.

"That wasn't too bad, was it?" Jon asked as he climbed up the final, treacherous incline.

Ed, close behind and white with fear, scowled. "Yea that was great, can't wait to go back through!"

Jon grinned as Ed pulled up along side him. "We're on the back side of the compound, let's climb these tall rocks. We can see the road from there," Jon said quietly.

They dismounted and tied down. Jon slid his hand into a crevice and he pulled himself up. Ed was close behind. They reached the top of the rock and Jon's arm went up; Ed ducked down next to him.

"This is the last big rock," Jon whispered. "Take your hat off."

Ed's hat slid off.

They scooted on their bellies a little farther and stopped.

"Great view," Ed whispered. "You can see the whole compound from here."

"Isn't that Pat Brown's buggy sitting by the front door?" Jon asked.

"Sure is; he's got the only fancy buggy in town."

"Shhhh!" Jon's finger went to his lips. "Someone's coming out!"

The two watched as Alex and Lawyer Brown stepped out the front door and shook hands. Brown jumped in his buggy; he cracked the whip as he rode off. Alex watched for a second and stepped back in the house.

"Well, I'll be damned!" Jon said. "Alex is lawyering up. Hard telling' what he's up to."

"Look Jon," Ed whispered. "There's two riflemen in

those rocks there near the entrance."

"Good, now we know where they are." Jon smiled. "Looks like Faraday's going to be here for awhile. Let's get back to town; I think we're going to have a visitor."

"Yea, and we're gonna have to hurry." Ed frowned.

"You're right, Partner." Jon laughed.

Chapter 23

It was a hard day's ride to Mesa. Web Norton cantered and galloped, saving his borrowed horse's strength. The hot sun was rising in the desert sky; beads of sweat were forming on Web's forehead. Suddenly the path narrowed; he pulled up to take a look ahead. The path tapered dramatically between two huge rocks. Web had reached the infamous "Rattler's Junction" - so named because of the large number of rattlers that sunned themselves on the warm rocks on either side of the path. It was scary and the only way through the rocks. Web's horse whinnied, sensing the pending danger.

"It's okay, girl, its okay." Web patted the foamy neck of the jittery horse. His spurs gently touched her backside, urging the reluctant steed slowly down the slim pathway. Web touched the rocks; they felt warm. It was a hot winter day. *Oh no, there's going to be a lot of them today,* he thought. The horse and rider inched along the path. Web saw a couple of rattlers but they were higher up on the rocks. After several tense minutes, he saw a light at the end of the narrow trail. Suddenly, his horse jerked to a stop, her ears pricked and stood erect. She heard something, Web strained to hear.

"Hiss!" The quiet sound came from a rock just above Web's head. Ready to bolt, the steed's ears began to flicker. Web sat still, his eyes looking over at the eerie snake. The rattler was only a few feet away, curled and ready to strike. Sweat poured off Web's face, his denim shirt was soaked. Hand shaking, he carefully lifted his gun up for a shot at the scary critter. He turned slowly and blasted away. Sparks flew off of the rocks near the snake. A dead hit, the snake blew backward off the rock. The terrified steed, already in a fit of panic, reared up on her hind legs and bolted down the narrow stone trail.

"Whoa!" Web screamed as his body flew backward off the frightened horse. The back of his head crashed on the stone pathway, his body rolled left and fell still. The gun, still spewing smoke, fell next to him.

* * *

"Let's go Ed, we've got to keep moving'," Jon prodded his good friend.

"I know, I know!" Ed replied.

"Gotta beat Brown back to town."

"Ut oh!" Ed shouted. His steed's hoof slipped on the narrow trail. Several small rocks tumbled over the side of the canyon. It seemed like forever before they hit the bed rock at the bottom.

"We're out!" Jon shouted. Babe's powerful hind legs pushed up the final grade. Jon cracked his whip; the horse and rider galloped toward town. Ed bounded from the harrowing canyon and ran close behind.

"Whoa, girl!" Jon shouted as he and Ed pulled up at the jail a half hour later. Camp's horse was out front. They quickly tied down and hurried in. Camp was sitting on the corner of Jon's desk talking with Malone.

"Howdy, Jon," Camp said as Jon and Ed hurried in.

"Howdy, Deputy." Jon smiled, his hand shot forward for a shake.

How are you feeling?"

"Head's a little sore, but I'm okay," the gritty youngster replied after a quick shake.

"Glad you could help out, Camp."

Camp nodded.

"Pat Brown's going to be in town any minute. I don't want him to see our warm horses." Jon glanced at Camp.

"No problem, Clem's down at the stables. I'll run 'em right down." Camp rushed out for the stables.

"Hurry back!" Jon shouted as the door banged shut.

"How's Wilson doing?" Jon asked Ed.

"Seems down, says he's gonna die one way or another. If we don't hang 'em, Faraday's gonna kill 'em. Says he disgraced his family and won't be able to face them again. I'm sleeping on the bunk in the back room and watching him day and night," Jack replied.

"That's good Ed, and Slim's right about one thing."

"What's that?"

"Faraday would love to have Slim out of the way." Jon frowned.

"I thought Brown would be here by now," Ed said impatiently.

"That Dapple Grey's his pride and joy, he never pushes him," Jon said as he pulled out his pocket watch and checked the time. "He should be here any time."

All of a sudden, the front door swung open. Attorney Brown removed his hat as he stepped in.

Ed raised his eye brows at the smiling Jon.

"Good mornin', Pat. Didn't expect to see you today," Jon said as the two men shook hands

"Well Jon, something has come up, we need to have a little talk."

"Okay Pat, have a seat." Jon's hand waved toward the chair. "Coffee?"

"No thanks," the dapper attorney replied. He pulled the oak chair out in front of Jon's desk and sat down. He looked around at Ed and Jack. "My or my, we've got quite a crowd in here." Brown laughed nervously. "I thought we might speak alone, Sheriff."

"These men are all my deputies, you can say anything you want if front of them," Jon said firmly.

"Hmmm... all deputies, huh? I see! Well, if you insist." Brown dropped his hat on Jon's desk.

"Fire away Pat, I'm a busy man," Jon pressed.

"Oh sorry, Jon, I'll get to the point. I have been put on retainer by Mr. Alex Faraday," Brown said, as he nervously tapped his fingers on Jon's desk. "As we all know, there has been a lot of violence around here lately. His man Slim Wilson is sitting here in your jail due to a shooting incident. Alex is very concerned for the safety of Mr. Wilson and for his own safety. He is so concerned that he is currently seeking sanctuary at his home just outside of town. He feels the incident with Mr. Wilson can be explained in a court of law, and Mr.

Faraday will be happy to come into town for a court appearance on Tuesday with the District Judge arrives, but not before," the wealthy lawyer said smugly.

"You're right about the violence, Pat. There have been two possible murders and two attempted murders in the past few weeks. And your client should be concerned; we just filed an attempted murder charge against his hired gun, Slim Wilson. We also have reason to believe that your client is involved in the murders of Jed Orton and the disappearance of Little Bear!" Jon scowled.

"My client thinks otherwise. He advised me that any charges you bring against Mr. Wilson or himself have been trumped up. He feels that you have unfairly singled him out due to the success of his saloon," Brown said, nose in the air.

Ed, Camp, and Jack all winced at the accusation by Lawyer Brown. They quickly glanced over at Jon for his reaction.

Jon felt his anger rise. He was trying desperately to control himself as he came up out of his chair. His fists dropped on the desk as he leaned toward Brown.

The attorney, faced with the daunting specter of an angry Jon Stoudenmire, shook in his seat.

"Is your client saying I'm after him because he's taking business from the Barbee?" Jon said as he leaved over the desk top. "Is that what you're saying?"

"Well... uh... yes, I believe--"

Jon grabbed the attorney by the tie and yanked him up to eye level. Brown was shaking all over. "Now you listen to me, Mr. Brown. Tell Alex that he better be here Tuesday morning at ten. If he's not here, I'll come out to his mansion with both barrels blazing. If he tries to leave before then, I'll hunt him down and bring him in. Do you understand?"

"Yes... uh... I will tell him."

"Ahhh!" A loud cry came from the cell area.

"What the..." Jon shouted, he pushed Brown back in his seat and hurried to the cell area.

Ed arrived first. "Oh no!" the deputy exclaimed loudly. "Slim hung himself!" Ed unlocked the door and rushed in. The body hung motionless in the center of the cell.

Jon came in the cell; he and Ed untied the leather belt Slim used to hang himself and laid the man gently on the bunk.

"He's gone," Jon said solemnly.

Jon pushed the huge cell door aside and rushed through the small gate.

Attorney Brown stood shaking by his chair as Jon charged over. "Get the hell outa here, Brown," Jon barked. He shoved the terrified man toward the front door.

Brown, rubbing his sore neck, staggered through the door to his buggy.

"Damn, we just lost the best witness a man could have!" Jon said dejectedly.

* * *

Just over an hour later, the traumatized lawyer Brown rode up to Faraday's mansion. He hurried over to the front door and banged the knocker several times; Clive Cook answered directly.

"My God, what happened to you?" Clive exclaimed. "You're white as a sheet!" Cook gestured toward the back porch. The two men hurried through the living room to the porch where Alex was relaxing with a book.

A surprised Faraday looked up from his book. "Back already, Pat? You look like you've seen a ghost. What on earth happened?"

Attorney Brown sat carefully on the arm of a wooden chair. Cook arrived with a snifter of brandy. The anxious attorney took a sip to try and calm his nerves.

"Out with it, man. What did our fine sheriff have to say?" Faraday prodded.

"He said he had information that you were involved in the killing of Jed Orton and the disappearance of Little Bear. I told him you didn't see it that way and you felt there was a vendetta against you because of the success of your saloon."

"Yes, that's bloody right! What did he say?"

"The sheriff became very angry. I thought he was going to knock my head off. He can be a frightening man."

"Why, that's a perfectly legitimate defense," Alex replied, apparently oblivious to Brown's personal trauma. "He's trying to intimidate us into not using it against him. But it won't work. It's our strategy and we're staying with it."

"That may be, Mr. Faraday. But rest assured, he won't like it one bit."

"Consider me forewarned," Alex replied. "Did you buy us time until Tuesday?"

"Yes, you have until ten Tuesday morning. He said if

you don't show up, he will come after you."

"Good, good. That buys Web the time he needs to talk to Judge Walker in Mesa. Everything seems on track," Alex replied. He stuffed tobacco tight in the pipe bowl, a match exploded. The coals burned red-orange as he lit up.

"Oh yes Alex, there's was one more bit of news."

"Oh yes... well, what is it?"

"While I was there, Slim Wilson hung himself." Pat managed a slight smile. "And he did a good job; he's very dead right now."

"You're kidding; how convenient!" an elated Alex proclaimed. "Things are looking good, very good indeed!"

"Indeed, Alex! A man did die, you know!" Cook scolded his over excited boss.

"Why yes, I meant no disrespect. Very sorry to hear about poor Slim," Alex said clumsily.

Brown continued. "I'm sure they have written testimony, so we'll still need Judge Walker on the bench. But having Slim out of the way will help immensely. But may I caution you against underestimating the sheriff? He's a very determined man!"

"Yes... he's a powerful adversary indeed, but the poor sap's too honest for his own good. We'll win this case and then he'll do whatever Judge Walker tells him to. Then we'll be free to go!"

Brown sighed. "I hope so!"

* * *

The silent flight of the turkey vultures filled the

bright, blue sky above. The lifeless body of Web Norton lay motionless on the stone pathway below. Gradually more birds joined the ancient dance of death; their routes sank lower, closer to the man. A few of the ugly red-headed birds landed on the rock above, their long necks craning toward the fallen messenger.

Suddenly Web's crusty left eye lid moved open, then his right. Dazed, but still alive, he felt something warm and dry slide over his face. His body froze in sheer panic as a rattler slithered over the terrified man and moved quickly between the rocks. Web blinked several times; his hands moved along his warm body checking for more snakes. Feeling none, he rolled to one side and pushed up to a sitting position. The hiss of a nearby vulture caught his attention. Angered, he struggled to his feet and waved his black hat at the huge birds. "Get outa here! Get outa here!" he screamed. The disappointed scavengers hastily took flight and soared away.

Sunday afternoon! he thought. His swollen hand pushed against the rock wall as he righted himself. He whistled, but his horse didn't come. He looked around; the silence was deafening. Shoulders slumped, he gazed at the trail ahead. *Over a day's walk, one water hole,* he thought as he contemplated the dangerous journey back to Faraday's. He took a couple of steps and picked up his dirty hat. He placed the hat gently on his sore head. "I better get goin'," he whispered to himself.

The setting sun gave way to the cool evening breezes. They felt good as they blew across Web's hot, dry face. The sandy gravel crunched under his stiff leather boots as he struggled along. His legs ached;

blisters were beginning to form on the soles of his feet. His lips were dry and parched.

"Where the hell's that water?" he moaned. Finally, the large round boulders that surrounded the water hole appeared. Still a couple of miles away, they seemed closer. Exhausted, his pace quickened. The desert sun was almost gone as he finally reached the elusive hole. He fell to his knees on the sandy bank; his hat flew to the side. He ripped open the snaps on his blue denim shirt, cupped his hands and threw water over his head and chest. The cool water felt wonderful as it splashed against his hot, sweaty body. He drank until saturated and then laid on his side. The sun was down and the temperature was dropping rapidly. Weary, he lay still for a couple of minutes and then rolled up on all fours. His swollen eyes scanned the surrounding terrain. He was becoming very cold; he needed cover for the night. He saw some fallen branches from a nearby tree. He crawled around picking up the scraggily, leaf covered branches and drug them to a dugout in the corner of the rocks, away from the chilling breeze. He piled the thin, makeshift protection over himself, giving him some cover from the cold desert night. A strip of jerky slid out of his pocket, and he chewed it away. His eyes dropped shut as sleep overcame him.

* * *

The reddish-yellow sun rose above the dark sandy landscape. Web's tired arms carefully pushed away his leafy cocoon. Morning was upon him; the back of his head still ached from the awful fall on the stone passageway. His body hurt all over as he crawled to the water hole, his dry, parched lips sucked the water in. The Indians taught him that a good saturation in the morning can last up to a full day in the desert sun. One jerky left and a full day's walk ahead, his feet were already blistered. It was a daunting task indeed, but deep inside he dreaded Faraday's anger even more. His failure to secure Judge Walker for the hearing on Tuesday would infuriate Alex and by the time he got back it would be too late to do anything about it. He ripped two strips of denim off the bottom of his shirt, dampened them and carefully wrapped them around the blisters on his sore, swollen feet. He slipped on his boots and stood up, his eyes squinting into the hot morning sun. He limped forward, starting the last agonizing leg of his tortuous journey.

Twelve hours later, Web heard voices off in the distance. Totally exhausted, he struggled mightily to keep from falling. His feet were bloody stubs, his face horribly swollen and cracked. His eyes were oozing slits. His boot slid forward and caught on a protruding rock. The dust flew as his aching body fell hard on the rocky trail.

A rider approached rapidly, slid off his racing steed, grabbed the canteen and dropped to one knee next to the fallen man. He slid his hand gently under Web's neck and lifted his head. Web's parched, puffy lips opened slightly; the canteen tipped, the water flowed in.

"My God Web, what the hell happened?" the man asked as he moved his body to protect Web from the evening sun. Water gurgled from Web's mouth as he tried to speak." "Rattler," he said almost inaudibly.

Another man arrived with a pack. They gently lifted Web up and sat him on the horse. He slumped over, his head bounced from side to side as they walked him to the compound.

The front door of the mansion pushed open. Clive Cook, hearing the commotion, had come out to see what was going on. He approached the sentries.

"Oh my! He looks awful!" Cook exclaimed as he stopped next to Web. "Are you okay?" he asked.

Semi-conscious, Web didn't reply.

"Did he say anything?" Cook asked.

The sentry shrugged. "All he said was rattler."

"A rattler must have spooked the horse and thrown him off," Cook surmised. "Take him to the bunk house, clean him up and let him rest. I'll hold Alex off. He's in no condition to talk right now."

Cook hurried back to the house to tell Alex. He rushed into the living room and approached Faraday. "Web's back!"

"Web's what?" Alex shouted.

"He's lying in the bunk house unconscious," Cook replied. "His horse must have thrown him off. Looks like he's been walking in the desert for a couple of days. He's very weak, can't speak."

"That means he never got to Mesa and Judge Walker and it's Monday evening," Alex mumbled to himself. He paced nervously in front of his living room sofa. "Send Cliff Nestleroad into town to await the judge. Soon as he knows which judge is here, have him ride back out." Faraday scowled as he cracked his horse whip on the oak coffee table. "Damn!" he shouted.

Chapter 24

Libby sighed, "Hey Big Boy, you don't look too happy," she said as she joined Jon at their corner table.

Jon looked up at the lovely Miss Thompson. "Oh, I'm okay, I guess." He patted her tiny wrist.

Libby slid a shot of whiskey in front of him as she took a sip of her wine.

"Thanks," Jon said. "Attorney Brown came to the office today."

"What did he want?" Libby asked.

"Faraday's lawyerin' up. He's saying I'm just picking on him cause his saloon's doing so well."

"Why that's ridiculous Jon, you would never do that." Libby frowned.

Jon downed the shot and sat the empty glass on the table. "I know, but he's got somethin' up his sleeve." Jon grimaced.

"Is the judge in town yet?" Libby asked.

"Not yet," Jon replied.

"Who's coming?" the pretty saloon owner asked.

"Dunno," Jon replied. A thought came to him, and

he smiled. "That's it," he said excitedly. "That's it!" He jumped up and began pacing near the table.

"Are you going to let me in on the secret, Jon, or am I going to have to sit here in the dark?" Libby chided him.

"That's it! The judge," Jon replied. He pounded his fist in the palm of his hand. "If Faraday and Brown can get Judge Walker here, they can use that bogus defense and possibly get off. I hear Walker owes Faraday big time."

"What if Oliver shows up?"

"Judge Oliver's an honest man. Alex would be in deep trouble." Jon shook his head. "That snake."

"I'll bet he tried to contact Walker to be sure he showed up," Libby said.

"I'll bet he did," Jon replied. "But something tells me Judge Oliver's on his way. He'll smell a rat and he'll be here."

"I hope you're right," Libby smiled. Sam rushed over and poured them both another drink.

* * *

Out at the mansion, Faraday nervously tossed his fork on the large oak dinner table. "What's taking Cliff so long?" he said, becoming exasperated by the wait.

His servant approached tentatively. "Dessert?" he asked.

"No, Jonathon, no!" Alex shouted. "Just leave Clive and me alone." The servant nodded and hurried out.

"I think I hear something," Cook said. "Sounds like a horse is approaching."

They tossed down their cloth napkins and hurried out to the front. Nestleroad rode up to the door. The smallish foreman dismounted and hurried over to them.

"Well man, for God's sake what's going on?" Alex shouted, his face pushed forward, anxiously awaiting the reply.

"He ain't here, yet!" Cliff replied.

"Why on earth not?" an enraged Faraday asked.

"The sheriff just got a telegraph a little while ago. The stage broke an axle near Cactus Bend. It won't be in 'til mornin'."

"It won't be in until morning? That's disastrous!" Alex exclaimed.

"Did he say which judge was coming?" Cook asked expectantly.

"Nope, I asked 'em which judge was comin' and he said he didn't know," Cliff said sheepishly.

"Oh my, everything is falling apart! We are all going to hang!" Alex screamed.

"Now calm down, Alex," Cook said. "I've got a plan!"

"What is it?" Alex barked. "It better be a good one!"

Cook's eyes rolled toward the door.

"Oh... uh, that will be all. Cliff, tell the boys to get ready. We will be riding into town tomorrow."

"Okay, Mr. Cook." the loyal foreman hurried away.

"Now, go ahead Clive," Alex said, annoyed by the delay.

"Where was I?"

"You said you had a plan," Alex grumbled.

"Oh yes... yes, When that stage gets in tomorrow, it's going to take the judge, whoever it might be, and hour or so to get around after he arrives." Cook paced confidently on the front porch.

"Yes, yes man! Go ahead!" Alex waved the back of his fingers at Cook.

"Well, we'll ride in early and wait over at the saloon..."

"Yes... and!"

"And if Walker shows up, well, then we're okay."

"Why of course my dear man, we all know that!" Alex exclaimed. "What if it's Oliver?"

"If it's Oliver, then we still have an hour to get out of town. It will take him that long to clean up and get ready for court." He smiled smugly. "I'll have one of the boys station four fast horses out back of the saloon for a quick, quiet get away. No one will suspect a thing. We can come back out here, load up and move on down the road. If worse comes to worse, we'll go to Mexico and hop a freighter back to merry ole England. Anything's better than hanging."

"Oh yes, hanging's not good," Alex mumbled. "And you're right, the sheriff might be expecting us to leave town if Oliver arrives. He will probably be watching the street. So you and I, Web and Cliff can slip out the back unnoticed. Hmmm... then we'll go to Mexico, England, or whatever... huh!" Alex replied, thinking out loud. "But how do we get word of our predicament to Judge Walker if he does in fact show up?"

Cook smiled. "I've thought of that, too. The owner and day clerk at the Westwood, Les Pemberton, is a friend of mine. I'll write a letter to Walker explaining the situation. Les has a little spread between here and town. I'll ride out to Les's place tonight and deliver it in person. If Judge Walker arrives tomorrow, I'll ask Les to take the letter to his room. The judge will have plenty of time to read it before court goes into session. To be certain Pemberton goes along with us, I will promise him exclusive rights to any new hotels in town after we take over. That will be irresistible to him." Cook's eyebrows rose as he smiled confidently at his boss.

Alex digested it all for a minute and then spoke up. "Hmmm... good plan my dear man, good plan!" Alex smiled broadly. "Shall we retire to the veranda for a brandy?"

Cook nodded as the two Englishmen strolled confidently toward the back of the mansion.

Chapter 25

The first light of day beamed through the small milky pane on the jailhouse window. A narrow white line fell across the corner of Jon Stoudenmire's oak desk. It was eerily quiet at the jail. Slim Wilson's suicide hung over the room like a bad dream. Jack and Ed were down at Auggie's. Camp was at the stables. Jon was alone with his thoughts and he knew what was coming. The telegram the night before had mentioned Judge Oliver as a passenger on the stage. Of course, he didn't tell Neslteroad, but he now knew that Oliver was coming. He looked out at the tranquil street, not sure how many would die this day, but knew that blood would flow. When Faraday found out it was Judge Oliver, he and his men would try to leave town; Jon would have to stop them; several could die. He prayed silently for the well being of his brave friends, Ed, Camp, and Jack. All of whom would be with him 'til the very end, he knew that. He tried hard, but couldn't think of Libby; the emotions were too strong.

He thought of how Alex Faraday and Clive Cook

had fooled the fine people of Logan's Crossing. He thought of the murders of Jed Orton and Little Bear and the attempts on Jack Malone's life, and he grew angry. His goal today would be to stop Alex Faraday and Clive Cook from hurting anyone else, while protecting his friends from harm. The darkness was coming over him. Soon, the power of his tortured soul would be unleashed again with great fury - a fury driven by the memory of a brutal father. Often in the heat of battle, his father's face would appear to him - the same cruel, heartless face that terrorized him throughout his childhood. *How long?* Jon thought. *How long will this rage live inside of me?*

He spun the cylinders on his Army Colts, still warm from early morning practice. He was fully loaded. He stood up and straightened his tie, donned his brown felt hat, and stepped out of the jail. He turned and quietly locked up. The dew glistened on the roof tops as Jon marched toward Auggie's. It was dawn in the desert, cool and wet.

Jon pushed open the door to Auggie's, stepped in and walked over to their favorite table by the large front window. "Howdy Boys," Jon said as he sat down, back to the wall.

"Mornin' Jon," the deputies replied, already seated and waiting.

"We've got some plannin' to do, fellas," Jon said as Auggie handed him a hot cup of coffee. "We gotta make sure Faraday and Cook don't leave town." Jon's elbows hit the table; he made eye contact with each man. "Here's the plan."

Chapter 26

"Wake up Web," Clive shouted.

Web's aching body rolled left on his bunk, his crusty eyes broke open. He looked up at the massive Cook.

"We're riding into town; we need your gun," Clive said firmly.

"Go to hell!" Web retorted, as he slid the covers up over his head.

"Listen Web, Alex is madder than a hornet at you for not making it to Mesa. He said if you don't get up, I am to whip you."

Web grumbled. He rolled up to a sitting position. His muscles ached and he had a terrible headache. The night's sleep had helped; he felt a little better as he stood and stretched. The back of his head still hurt from the hard fall, but everything else seemed to be working.

"We're having breakfast at the house; the boss wants to go over a few things." Clive motioned toward the mansion.

"Lead the way." Web scowled as he followed Cook to the house.

Chapter 27

Ka....ching! the cash register door slid shut. "Be careful," Auggie said. "I'm kind of gettin' attached to you boys."

"Thank you, Aug," Jon replied. The others nodded as they left the cozy eatery.

Jon saw the silhouettes of six riders move silently across the horizon as the men walked to the Barbee. Jon stopped and stuck his arm up; the men pulled up behind him, all eyes went to the distant riders.

"They're comin' in force," Ed said.

"Sure looks like it," Jon said as he motioned the men toward the Barbee. "Spread out," he ordered. The men all stepped up on the walkway and spread out facing the street.

Dust clouds appeared on the edge of town as the riders approached; they looked dark and menacing against the morning sun. The brave lawmen stood motionless.

It was eight o'clock. The town was coming alive; people scurried to get out of the way of the approaching riders.

Faraday sat tall in the saddle; his beautiful thorough-bred pranced nervously as he led the group through town. Clive Cook's broad shoulders looked huge as he rode next to and slightly behind, Alex. Web Norton and the others spread out behind the two Brits.

Quite a show!! Jon thought. *I hope I don't have to kill'em!!* He stared hard at the riders, his heart growing dark.

Alex looked over at Jon. "Top of the morning to you Sheriff," he said with a sly smile.

"Mornin' Alex," Jon replied calmly, never taking his eyes off the wily Englishman.

The riders pulled up at Faraday's Saloon, dismounted and tied down. Jon watched as Faraday slid his rifle out of its holster, hid it under his long duster and walked in his saloon.

"Faraday took his rifle inside; looks like he means business," Jon said.

The other men nodded as they turned and walked in the Barbee.

"Howdy boys," Sam shouted as the men strolled in.

"Morning Sam," Jon replied as he moved to the end of the bar.

Sam poured four cups of hot coffee as the boys lined up along the bar. He dumped a shot of whiskey in each cup. "Good for the nerves," Sam said with a grin.

The saloon's doors flew open, Fred from the telegraph office rushed in. "Telegram for the Sheriff," he announced.

"I'm over here," Jon said. Fred hurried over.

"Thank you Fred." Jon tossed him a silver dollar. Fred laid the gram on the bar and hurried out.

Jon ripped it open, his eyes scanning the message.

"What's up?" Ed asked.

"Stage should be arriving any time now," Jon said calmly. "It's right on time!"

Jon looked over at Camp. "Coroner Jake told us he saw four horses behind Faraday's on his walk this morning. Better go pick them up. I think they're getaway horses for Alex and his gang."

"Sure thing, Jon." Camp took a quick sip from his cup and hurried out the door.

"Good morning, boys," Libby said as she walked out from the kitchen and leaned on the bar.

"Mornin Libby," Jon replied. "Are your new girls comin' on the stage today?"

"They should be," she replied softly.

"Stage is on schedule, it should be here any time," Jon said.

"Oh good, I can sure use the help: I've been a little shorthanded around here lately." Libby's brave smile couldn't cover up the tears in her eyes.

Jon moved in close and gently wiped the tears away, "Don't worry baby, it'll take more than these lowlifes to take this cowboy out." The two lovers sat and talked quietly for several minutes.

A short time later, Camp rushed in. "The horses are gone," he announced. "I took 'em down to the stables and stationed one of the boys up in the rocks behind Faraday's, just in case."

"Good work, Camp! I'd like to see Faraday's face when he finds out his getaway horses are gone." Jon laughed.

"I do believe he will be bloody mad." Camp said

sarcastically, followed by a hardy laugh from the men.

* * *

Down at Faraday's, Alex and his boys were sitting around the big oak table on the mezzanine, planning their next move.

"Cliff!"

"Yea, boss!"

"The stage should be coming soon. Go down near the hotel and wait in the alley. As soon as you know which judge it is, get back here as quickly as you can!"

"Sure thing, Boss." Cliff hopped down the stairs and hurried out the front door.

"Hiya! Hiya!" The stage driver's voice could be heard just outside of town. The wooden wheels rumbled as the Well Fargo stage charged into town, window shades drawn.

"The stage is here!" Alex shouted. "Clive, go out back and check on our four horses."

Clive jumped up and ran down the back stairs.

The two hands sitting at the table grimaced and looked at each other. "Four Horses?" one whispered.

"There's six of us! That SOB don't give a damn about us, let's get outa here while the gettin's good," the other hand said quietly. "I'll say somethin' to Faraday."

"Hey Boss," he said.

"Yes, yes, what is it?"

"We're goin' down to the bar and grab a quick drink."

"Hurry up, there may be trouble," Alex replied.

"Okay, Boss," he replied as he smiled mischievously

at his fellow hand. The two men hurried down the stairs and exited through the swinging doors.

Alex glanced up from stuffing his pipe just in time to see the two hands scurry out the door. "Damn cowards!" he shouted.

* * *

Jon and his men hurried out of the Barbee to meet the stage just as the two hands were leaving Faraday's.

Camp saw them out of the corner of his eye and went for his gun.

Jon quickly grabbed Camp's shoulder. "It's okay," he said. "It's just a couple of boys from the ranch. Let 'em go. They probably decided they didn't want to die."

Camp slowly dropped his six gun back in the holster. He watched as the two hands mounted up and galloped out of town.

"Jack, you and Camp stay here. Ed and I'll go down to the stage and greet the judge. Keep an eye on the comings and goings over at Faraday's," Jon said as he walked hurriedly toward the Westwood. Ed was close behind.

* * *

"You won't believe it!" Clive shouted as he raced up the steps to the mezzanine. "The horses are gone, every damn one of them."

"They're what?" Alex screamed. He tossed his pipe and it bounced across the table. "What the hell kind of idiots do I have working for me?"

"You should've had a guard out back, Alex! Now we're in big trouble, they're on to us and we got no where to go!" Web shouted.

Faraday stared at the insolent Norton, his face hot with anger. "Shut your mouth, Web, this was Clive's idea. Besides, it's too late to worry about it now. We have to hope that Judge Oliver's not on that stage; if he is, Stoudenmire will be coming after us, you can bet your bloody life on that. We need to be ready for anything; grab your weapons, men, and follow me.

Alex picked up his Winchester; Clive and Web spun the cylinders on their six guns as the three men raced down the steps.

"Get out of the way!" Faraday shouted as he pushed aside several chairs and tables on the way to the bar. "Get out of there!" he shouted at the bartender. The bartender ducked out from behind the bar as Alex rushed in. "I'll take the middle, you boys go to either end," Alex shouted. "If they come after us, shoot to kill."

Dust filled the street as the stage rushed past the Barbee. "Whoa! Whoa!" the driver shouted as six horses and the wooden carriage pulled up in front of the Westwood. The driver tied the straps on the brake handle and quickly jumped down. He grabbed the metal handle and yanked the cabin door open. A small hand reached forward from inside. Two young girls in long dresses stepped out to greet the sheriff.

"Welcome to Logan's Crossing." Jon tipped his hat to the pretty ladies. They giggled as they nervously waved their fans in front of their faces. "Your rooms are waiting. Miss Thompson will be down later to meet with you," Jon said quickly. "The driver will escort you to your rooms." The shotgun driver tossed their luggage to the driver, he and the girls hurried inside.

Jon's eyes went immediately back to the stage door. Just as expected, out of the corner of the dark cubicle, the thin figure of Judge Oliver emerged. He smiled and shook hands with Jon.

"Mornin' Jon, sorry for the delay, we had a little--"

The judge was suddenly interrupted by Ed Morgan.

"Hold up there, Cliff!" Ed shouted as Faraday's lookout jumped out of the alley and began running along the walkway toward the saloon.

"Excuse me, Judge." Ed tipped his hat and charged after Cliff Nestleroad. Camp and Jack picked up on the action and joined in the pursuit.

"I cut him off!" Camp yelled from the middle of the street, He took the angle to the walkway to cut him off before he reached Faraday's. "Get their horses out of here," Camp shouted at Jack. Malone nodded and ran toward the hitching post.

Nestleroad shouted, "Oliver!" as he dove under the doorway to the saloon; trying to warn Faraday and the boys inside. Ed and Camp were in close pursuit.

Out in the street, Jack yanked off his hat and smacked the behinds of the horses. "Get!" he shouted. The frightened horses snipped at each other as they began to move away from the post. "Get, now get on out of here!" Jack continued to shout and wave his hat as the horses ran in every direction. Suddenly, Jack was alone and isolated in the middle of the street in front of Faraday's. Realizing that he was a sitting duck for the shootists inside, he turned to run.

Two loud rifle shots reverberated from inside the saloon. Splinters flew as the bullets blasted through the batwing doors and hit Jack square in the back.

"Uhggg!" Jack screamed. The force of the shots blew his body to the center of the street, he rolled over on the rutted street and then fell face down. Dark red blood oozed from the smoking holes in his back.

Ed and Camp were now in front of Faradays.

More rifle shots could be heard as the big front window blew to pieces; Ed was blasted off the walkway as he and Camp ran past the window. He crashed onto the dusty street. Holding his limp left arm, he quickly rolled back toward the wooden walkway for cover.

Unharmed, Camp dove under the hitching post and stood up facing the saloon. The angry youngster pulled out his six guns and began blasting away,.

In a fit of rage, he fired randomly into the saloon.

Jon raced down the middle of the street toward Jack; his heart was breaking at the sight of his wounded friend. Bullets whizzed by Jon's head as he slid to the ground next to Jack; his big arm went under Jack's stomach as he gently rolled his bloody friend over and lifted him up.

"I guess they finally got me," Jack said softly. He smiled at the sheriff; his chest stopped heaving, his eyes fell shut.

"Jack! Jack!" Jon shook his friend, trying to bring him back, to no avail. Jon laid Jack's limp body on the dusty street. His eyes glazed over with rage, he turned and looked toward the saloon. Suddenly a rifle shot blasted into Jon's shoulder. He barely felt it as he stood up and faced the fire; a dark blood stain appeared on his blue denim shirt. He glanced inside the saloon; he could see Alex in the middle of the bar. He drew his Colts and walked toward the bar, guns blazing. He looked down at Ed below the walkway. "You okay?" he asked, as the bullets whizzed by.

"Yea, I got a pretty good one, but I'm gonna make it." Ed grinned at his old friend.

Jon looked over at Camp." Stay here with Ed."

"Ed's okay, I'll go with you," Camp replied.

"Damn you, do what I say!" Jon barked.

Camp frowned as he slammed his smoking six guns back in their holsters and kneeled down next to Ed.

Jon quickly reloaded, the pain of Jack's death once again shot through his heart like a dagger. He was almost overcome with rage as he moved in front of the swinging doors, and walked forward gun blazing.

Bellows of smoke from Jon's gun blasts filled the air. He continued to fire toward the bar as he leaned forward and dove through the swinging door and rolled up under a fallen table.

Two loud blasts came from the bar area. Splinters flew above Jon's head. He waited a minute and then peeked over the top of the table. The barrel of Cook's six gun was pointed directly at him,

Cook fired again. Jon ducked quickly behind the table; he felt the wind as the bullets flew past his head. Jon saw his chance; he rose up and took aim at a reloading Cook.

The hot lead blasted into the center of Cook's forehead. His huge body flew against the wall, glasses breaking as the wall shelves collapsed; he bounced off the wall and fell hard to the floor. Blood and brains spewed out of the hole in Cook's forehead. The horrific scene terrified the nearby Faraday; he began shaking and looking for a way out.

"At the other end of the bar, Norton fired wildly toward Jon.

Hearing the continuing gunfire and worried about Jon, Camp couldn't wait any longer. He busted through the front doors, firing in the general direction of Norton.

The addition of Camp's gunfire filled the saloon with smoke. All hell was breaking loose as the youngster scanned the room looking for targets.

Suddenly, two shots rang out from the balcony, the bullets crashed into the door frame next to Camp's feet; he ducked quickly to the left!

Jon returned fire, as he blasted away at the hidden gunner.

"Oh hell!" the shooter screamed,. "I'm hit!" Cliff Nestleroad staggered out from a dark corner of the balcony. He stumbled over to the wood railing and fell head first over the railing toward the floor below. The sound of his neck cracking as he hit the hard wood floor could be heard throughout the saloon.

Jon stood slowly, his left arm hung limp from the shoulder wound. He motioned with his right gun hand for Camp to go outside. An unhappy Camp stormed back through the swinging doors. Jon's six gun was still smoking from the shots at Nestleroad. He surveyed the situation, like a cat ready for the kill. All the firing had suddenly ceased; the room was eerily quiet as the thick smoke drifted to the ceiling.

* * *

Norton was reloading. Faraday inched along the floor behind the bar, shaking violently, terrified at the prospect of facing an angry Jon Stoudenmire. He reached the end of the bar and looked out at the alley, shocked to see his faithful steed standing just outside the back entry. The loyal horse was waiting on her master. Alex's pulse quickened; he now saw a chance to escape.

"Throw your guns over the bar, put your hands up and come out, Web!" Jon shouted.

"Promise me I won't hang and I'll come out," Web countered.

"Can't promise you that, but I'll see that you get a fair trial," Jon replied.

Faraday's eyes darted left and right. Under the cover of the bar, he started to crawl quietly toward the back door.

Web's voice bellowed out from behind the bar. "It's a trick, you just wanna get me out in the clear so you can kill me. I'm gonna hang and you know it!" The agitated man jumped up and fired again at Jon.

Jon ducked to the right as the bullet whizzed past. "You fool!" he shouted as he fired two shots at Web. Sparks flew off the cylinder of Web's six gun as it flew out of his hand.

"Ahh!" He screamed as he leaped up, shaking his shooting hand.

Jon moved quickly through the thick smoke to the end of the bar near Web. He looked outside and saw Camp standing next to Ed.

"Take Web to jail," Jon shouted out the door to Camp. Camp rushed inside and cuffed Web.

Meanwhile, Faraday crawled quickly through the back door and mounted up.

* * *

"Damn!" Jon yelled as he saw Faraday start to ride away. He darted toward the front of the bar; busted through the swinging doors and whistled for Babe. The giant Palomino ripped the leather loose from the hitching post in front of the Barbee and charged toward her master.

Doc Fletcher was kneeling on the street bandaging Ed as Jon ran by. He jumped up and grabbed Jon by the arm."You're not going anywhere, young man, I need to bandage that wound!"

"Sorry Doc, I don't have time right now!" Jon shouted as he leaped on Babe. "Let's go girl!" he shouted as he charged after the fleeing Englishman. *He's got about a five minute head start,* Jon thought, as he raced out of town. He looked down at Faraday's tracks; they ran toward the ranch.

* * *

After an all-out ride through the desert, Alex dropped quickly down the final incline to the mansion; he jumped down and rushed inside, rifle in hand. His heart was racing as he pushed open the heavy door to the den, hurried over to the safe and dropped to one knee. He frantically worked the combination on the safe; moving the dial back and forth.

"Okay, bloody safe, open!" The dial spun toward the final number; he grabbed the metal handle and gave it a yank, but nothing happened. Suddenly, he looked toward the front, his eyes wide, as he listened to the sound of an approaching rider. "He's almost here," he mumbled. He looked back at the safe; sweat covered his hands as he tried once again. Hands shaking, he mumbled, "right to 32, two lefts to 9, right to 24."

He frantically grabbed for the handle once again and pulled, but shockingly, it failed to open once again. Sweat was pouring from his face as he stopped to listen for any sound of the approaching rider. The hoof beats had stopped. *HE'S HERE!* A bolt of fear shot up his spine.

* * *

Jon, weak from loss of blood, dismounted and surveyed the scene around the mansion. He knew Faraday was inside, his horse was grazing nearby. It would be suicide to charge the mansion; Faraday would hear him coming and kill him from ambush. He moved around to the side of the house and walked quickly to the nearest window and looked inside. He saw Faraday bending over the safe on the other side of the room, his back to Jon. Jon stepped silently through the large open window, his foot gently touching the floor inside.

The devious Brit, working feverishly on the combination, didn't hear Jon step in. He frantically turned the dial, grabbed the handle and pulled down. The heavy door creaked open. He reached inside and pulled out a large canvass bag, took a firm grip on it, jumped up and started for the back door.

"Going somewhere, Alex?" Jon said calmly.

Faraday stopped dead in his tracks and looked straight ahead. Jon stood in the corner of the room near the window, the front of his shirt soaked red with blood.

"Why uh... how are you, Jon?" the wily Brit said nervously. "I didn't hear you come in."

"You seemed busy, I didn't want to bother you," Jon replied, his heart dark, his anger growing. "Drop the money and put your hands up, then turn around so I can see you!" Jon ordered.

The bag fell to the floor, and the nervous Brit turned to face Jon, hands up.

"Were you going somewhere, Alex?"

"Why no I... uh... wasn't... Now listen Sheriff, I don't see why we can't work this out, no need for anymore bloodshed." the Englishman was sweating profusely.

Jon started to walk slowly toward the safe, gun pointed at Faraday. Blood from his shoulder wound dripped on the wood floor as he moved across the room. Jon reached down near the safe and picked up Faraday's rifle with his left hand. "Here," he said coldly, "I want you to be armed when I kill you!" He tossed the rifle to Faraday.

Alex, a bright man, let the rifle bounce off his shoulder and fall to the floor; to catch it would have been suicide.

"That was smart Alex; you know I won't kill an unarmed man. But I'm thinking about killing you anyway and putting the gun in your hand. It would look like self defense." A nasty grin broke out on Jon's face.

The frantic Englishman spoke quickly. "There's forty thousand dollars in that bag on the floor, Sheriff. Let me go and it's yours."

"You just don't get it, do you Alex?" Jon replied. "You just killed one of my best friends and you think you can buy me off with gold? You make me very angry Alex!"

"So sorry about Malone, I thought somebody was stealing our horses and..."

"Cut the crap Faraday, you don't give a damn about Jack Malone. The only person you care about is yourself. Jack's death was cold blooded murder!"

Suddenly a buggy rattled to as stop out in front of the large house.

"Jon! Are you in there?" Doc shouted through the open front door as he and Ed jumped down and ran toward the mansion. Faraday's prayers were answered as Jon turned toward the sound of Doc's voice.

The Derringer Faraday kept hidden up his sleeve slid down his arm and into his sweaty palm. He lifted his thin arm for a shot, but shockingly Jon's Colt was pointed directly at him.

"I'm not that stupid Alex." Jon grinned at the doomed man.

The terrified Brit's arm was shaking like a leaf as he pulled the trigger. Jon ducked to the left, the kerosene lamp just behind his head burst into a thousand pieces.

Jon opened fire. Flames shot out of the warm barrels as Faraday's thin body flew across the room and slammed against the back door. Jon staggered forward through the smoke, holding his aching shoulder. Getting weaker by the minute, he stooped over the fallen Brit. The acidic smell of burnt gun powder filled the air; blood was oozing from several bullet holes as he looked down at the dying man.

Shockingly, Faraday sat up.

"You bastard!" he screamed. Derringer still in his grasp, he raised it for a final shot.

A wobbly Jon reacted quickly. He fired away at close range, emptying his gun.

"Uhggg..." Faraday moaned. The Derringer bounced on the floor as his body fell limp.

Jon, weak and angry, stood over Faraday's riddled body. He raised his gun and pulled the trigger twice again. Click! Click! Suddenly, Jon stepped back, his eyes wide with fear, *My God, I just tried to shoot a dead man!"*

Ed raced across the room; Doc was close behind.

"It's me Jon!" Ed shouted. "Doc and I are here."

Jon blinked a couple of times as if coming out of a trance; his gun dropped to his side. Weak from blood loss, he fought to stay on his feet. Ed hurried over and put his arm around his friend.

"Ya okay?" Ed asked. He fought hard to hold the huge man on his feet.

"I'm better than he is," Jon replied quietly.

Doc knelt down and quickly checked Alex for a pulse. He shook his head. "Don't know why I'm checking him," Doc mumbled. "He looks like a pin cushion."

Doc stood. "You've lost a lot of blood, Jon. We better get you back to town."

"Okay Doc," Jon said quietly

Jon and Ed reached the door and stepped outside. Ed helped Jon into the buggy, he slumped down in the back seat. Doc tied Babe to the back of the buggy and the three men started for town.

Chapter 28

Auggie planted his leg firmly on the window sill and looked out at the empty street. Some tumble weed bounced past, pushed by a cool morning breeze. A sense of malaise had settled over this desert town after the violent confrontation of a day earlier. It was nine o'clock in the morning, usually a busy time. Today the only sound in Logan's Crossing was glass breaking down at Faraday's Saloon as the workers busied themselves cleaning up the mess. A sign saying, "Closed until further notice," was posted by the front door of the saloon. Auggie looked to his left and noticed some comings and goings down at the coroner's office, a busy place for sure. The sunlight reflected off Jon's second floor window at the Westwood Hotel. Auggie wondered how the sheriff was feeling after his gunshot wound in the shoulder and all the bloodshed of the day before.

"Need some help back here!" Lucy shouted from the kitchen.

"Okay, okay, I'm coming!" Auggie replied. "Heaven forbid I have a little time to myself," he mumbled as he hurried back to the kitchen.

* * *

Over at the hotel Jon's arms reached toward the ceiling as he yawned mightily. His eyes blinked open as rolled up and sat on the side the feather bed. His heavily bandaged shoulder ached as he stood slowly, walked over and dipped his hands in a pan of water, splashed his face wet and patted dry.

There was a gentle knock on the door. Jon dropped the towel next to the pan and hurried to the door. "Can I help you?" he asked.

"It's me, Jon," Libby announced.

Jon quickly opened the door. "Come in Libby, please come in." Libby stepped in, the two lovers embraced as the door swung shut behind them.

"How are you?" she asked softly.

"Doc says I'm gonna be okay. The bullet went clear through my shoulder, it'll be fine in due time," Jon replied.

"Well that's good. And how are you feeling otherwise?"

"Ehhh.....okay I guess!" Jon said quietly.

"You don't sound too sure," Libby replied.

Jon walked over and looked out the open window at some children playing in the quiet street.

"Bang! Bang! I'm Sheriff Stoudenmire and I shot you dead, Faraday!" a little boy shouted as he pointed a wooden gun at his friend.

The other boy rolled on the ground holding his stomach. "You got me Sheriff!" he shouted.

Jon was very troubled by the scene. Libby walked over and gently laid her hand on his back as Jon leaned out the window and shouted at the boys. "That's enough of that, boys. Now get on out of here!" Jon barked.

The boys giggled as they looked up at the big man in the window. "It's him!" one of them shouted. "It's big Jon,"

"Wow!" the other boy shouted. He pointed his wooden gun at Jon. "Bang! I got him," he screamed. "I killed Jon Stoudenmire." The boys ran away squealing.

Jon slammed the window shut. "Damn!" he said.

"You're their hero, Jon," Libby said calmly.

"I know I am, but I shouldn't be," Jon muttered as he sat on the feather bed and hung his head.

Libby nestled in next to him, her arm slid around his shoulder. "I'm not so sure about that," she said tenderly.

Jon's eyes narrowed, he grimaced as he spoke. "I rolled around in bed all night last night, Libby, I couldn't sleep. There's something inside of me, something dark. I pulled the trigger twice yesterday on a dead man. It's not right. I've done a lot of thinking, and I've made up my mind about something."

Libby's eyebrows rose.

"I'm resigning today as Sheriff of Mesquite County. I'll be heading west to my vineyard in California in the morning, at the crack of dawn."

Libby looked intently at Jon, shocked and dismayed by the stunning announcement. "I've been dreading this day for a long time, Jon. I was afraid you'd be leaving me at some point."

"It's not like that, Libby! I want to be with you more than anything, but I've got a lot of healing to do, my heart's not right. Even the love of a good woman like you can't fill this hole deep inside of me. The faces of all the men I shot, the smell of death, it's too fresh in my mind right now! I need some time away from all this, some time alone. When I get to California, I'm going to build a large cabin near the mountains and when it's done and when I've become the kind of man you deserve, I'm going to send for you. And I'm hoping and praying you'll come be with me."

"It was always my dream to come out west and own my very own saloon, Jon, that's all I ever wanted. I was so happy, and then you came along, with those rugged good lucks and proper manners. And what do you know? I went and fell in love. I tried to fight it, but every time you gave me that boyish grin and I looked into those big blue eyes, I just melted. I knew it wasn't right, but I couldn't help myself. Go build your cabin Jon; Sam will buy the Barbee when the time comes and I'll come to California. I got no choice, I just plain love you too much to say no. In the meantime, during our time apart, I'll hold tight to our memories!"

Jon stood and pulled Libby gently into his arms. "Your new kitchen will have a view of the mountains," he said tenderly. A long passionate kissed ensued followed by a long embrace.

Suddenly there was a loud knock on the door. "You better answer it," Libby said, "It might be someone important."

Jon hurried to the door. "Yes?" he shouted.

"Tom Baldwin, Jon, I need to talk to you. Got a minute?" Jon looked at Libby, she nodded yes. "Just a minute Tom."

Libby walked over and squeezed his hand. "I best be going," she said. "A respectable girl shouldn't be alone in a hotel room with her man - people might talk!" She looked directly at Jon for a moment. "Sorry for staring," she said. "I just want remember that handsome face until we meet again." She tenderly kissed his cheek. "Better not keep the Commissioner waiting," she said quietly.

Weak kneed, Jon turned the handle and opened the door. *What a lady!* he thought.

The waiting commissioner's eyes brightened when he saw Libby. "Good Morning, Libby. Surprised to see you here. How are you?"

"I'm fine, Tom. I just stopped in to see how Jon was doing, I best be going now." She smiled at the friendly barber, lifted her lovely gown and stepped out of the room.

Jon slid the metal badge off his denim shirt. "Come on in Tom, you're just the .."

The door clicked shut behind Libby as she hurried back to the Barbee.

* * *

The cool breeze sent a chill down Pecos Street as Jon walked to the jail to clean out his desk. Evening was falling. As he passed Baldwin's Barber Shop, he thought of his friend, Tom Baldwin, a friendly and principled man. The hitching post was empty in front of Auggie's as he walked past his favorite eatery. He remembered all the good times there, the practical jokes and laughter. His heart sank as he walked past the Barbee. The thought of leaving Libby, even for a short time, was gut wrenching. His heart raced as he walked past Faraday's Saloon, the horror of the gunfight the day before sickened him. He looked over at the jail; Ed's horse was out front. He hurried over and stepped inside just as Ed was walking out from the back room.

"Evening, Ed."

"Howdy, Jon, good to see ya. I didn't think you'd be up and around so soon. How are ya feelin'?"

"Shoulder's a little sore, otherwise I'm feelin' okay, thank you. I'm leaving for California in the morning," Jon said matter-of-factly.

"Tell me it ain't true," Ed replied, eyes wide with surprise. "My good buddy's leavin' me again? I can't believe it, you're finally gonna do it, turn tail and run off to California. And just when I was gettin' used to having you around?" Ed smiled warmly.

"I'm sorry Ed, but I got a lot of thinking to do, I have to get my heart right," Jon said sincerely.

"I know Partner, you've sure had a tough go of it here," Ed said somberly. "I had no idea that things would get this rough when I asked you to stay on and be--"

Jon interrupted. "It's not your fault Ed, I'm a big boy. I knew what I was getting into when I took the sheriff's job. And its not just here, my whole life's been one fight after another. I gotta get things straight, that's all."

"I understand, partner. How's Libby handling it?"

"Like the wonderful lady she is. I'm building us a cabin near my vineyard in the mountains; she'll join me there someday."

"Hope so, she's a fine woman," Ed said.

"The best," Jon replied as he emptied his desk drawers into one of his saddle bags.

"I got an early ride in the morning, so I best be going Sheriff." Jon smiled at Ed.

"Sheriff?" Ed exclaimed loudly.

"You heard me right, friend. This town needs somebody like you right now! Tom Baldwin and I talked about it this morning; he'll be in to see ya tomorrow."

"Well, thank ya, Jon. I'm flattered. I'll do the best I can, but nobody can replace you. As far as I'm concerned you'll always be the Sheriff of Mesquite County!"

Jon nodded at his dear friend, "Thank you Ed," Jon replied. "I got just one bit of advice, if you don't mind."

"Fire away!"

"When trouble starts, move in fast; don't let some no account get the jump on you. You'll live longer that way," Jon said.

"I'll take that to heart my friend, I promise ya!"

Jon smiled as his face softened. "There's one more thing Ed."

Ed nodded.

"When the time comes, could ya take a little time off and bring Libby over the mountains to me. She's precious cargo and you're the only man I would trust."

"I was already plannin' on it," Ed said with a grin.

"Thanks Ed," Jon replied. "I'd like to stand here and talk all day, partner, but I got things to do." Jon punched the new sheriff on the arm. "Take care buddy," The two old friends shared a quick embrace; Jon turned and hurried out the door.

Chapter 29

The cold wind stung Jon's face as he walked to the stable early the next morning. It was still dark. Jon pulled the collar up on his duster for additional protection from the cold. Two full saddle bags and two bags of water were draped over his right arm. He could hear laughter nearby, the all night gamblers were still at it at the Barbee. Libby had probably just gone to bed a few hours earlier; his heart ached to see her, but a proper lady needed time to prepare herself, he wouldn't disturb her.

Jon's heart was heavy as he walked along the darkened street. Logan's Crossing had been an epiphany for Jon. During his time spent here, he had come to grips with the very forces that tortured his soul and darkened his heart, while at the same time experiencing the greatest love he had ever known. It was with great conflict that he departed from this town, knowing that the year spent here had been the most significant in his life.

Camp tossed a saddle on a rail as Jon approached.

"Morning Camp!"

A surprised Camp looked up. "Mornin', Jon."

"You got a big Palomino in there?" Jon asked.

"Sure enough do Sheriff." Camp smiled broadly as he stepped over and shook Jon's hand.

"You may not have heard," Jon said.

"Well probably not, I was out shoein' all day yesterday," Camp replied. "What's up?"

"I resigned as sheriff yesterday. I'm leaving town this morning if Babe's ready."

"Babe's fine, I... ah groomed her real good last night," he mumbled, clearly shocked by the news of his mentor's departure.

"Thank you, Camp," Jon replied.

"I guess you'll be goin' to California, to that vineyard," Camp said almost inaudibly, visibly shaken. Camp popped the latch open on Babe's stall; he stepped in and threw a blanket on the excited steed. He lifted Jon' saddle and sat it gently on the blanket, yanked the straps tight and led her out. He looked down at the ground, apparently so upset by Jon's departure that he couldn't look his hero in the eyes.

Jon walked over and tossed the water and saddle bags over Babe's hindquarters. Then he laid both his big hands on Camp's slumping shoulders. "My fighting days are over, Camp. I put my Colts away."

Camp glanced down at Jon's empty waist. "You what!" he barked. "You took your guns off!" Camp's eyes were wide with amazement. "What's the matter with you, Jon? Have you gone chicken or something?" Camp tried to pull away; Jon grabbed tightly on his shoulders.

"Now just hold on there," Jon said firmly, scolding the young gunman. "My guns have caused me nothing but pain and sorrow and those guns of yours will do the same to you. I'm forty years old Camp, and it's a miracle I'm alive. Most every gunman I've ever known is already dead. I should have hung my guns up long ago, but my pride wouldn't let me."

"You're an old man and you're giving up," an angry Camp shouted. "That's the way I see it!"

Jon was shocked by the hurtful remarks from the youngster. His hands slid off Camp's shoulders; he frowned. "It's no use. Camp, there's nothing I can say. You're just like I was when I was your age. You think you're too tough to be killed, you won't listen!" Jon's eyes softened as he looked back at his loyal friend. "You're a brave man, Camp Wilson, and I'm proud to call you friend. I hope someday you'll understand."

Camp's head dropped. He kicked the dirt with his foot.

"I'm sorry, Jon! I'm truly sorry!"

Jon smiled warmly at the young gunman.

"It's just that....I...uh.. I just can't believe you're leaving and that you're not packin' and all!" Camp said quietly, still looking down.

"I guess I kinda shocked you!" Jon said sincerely.

"Just about everybody around here knows how I feel about you Jon. They know how I look up to ya and all. I feel like somebody just punched me in the gut!" Camp said softly.

Jon grinned at his somber friend. "I understand, but just remember, you're welcome at my vineyard any time."

Camp looked up at Jon. "Well I guess that's what I'll have to do; I guess I'll just have to cross those mountains."

"I hope so," Jon said as he gently punched his young mentor on the chin.

"You can count on it Jon," Camp said as he gave Jon a quick, hard embrace and then stepped quickly back.

"Bout noon time today my heart's gonna start achin' for our daily game of stud. I'm really gonna miss ya buddy," Jon said as he mounted up. A single tear rolled down the tough young stable owner's cheek as Jon reined Babe around and rode slowly away.

The sun was just breaking into the morning sky as Jon rode toward the outskirts of town. There were smiles and nods from the few townspeople who were out and about as Jon headed for the desert and his long journey to California. Jon tipped his hat and spurred Babe forward to a canter. He was leaving Logan's Crossing as he had arrived: alone!

Several miles down the trail at a high point, Jon reined up and turned around for a last look at the distant town. The wood frame buildings looked dark and isolated against the desert sky; a strong feeling of melancholy fell over him. The emotions of the past year raced through his mind once again: the pain, the violence, his love for Libby. *What a hell of a year!* he thought, as he reined Babe around and rode on toward his vineyard paradise, gradually disappearing into the lush desert landscape.

Unbeknownst to him, the devil that he so loathed and despised; still lie hiding deep in his heart.

About the Author

Armed with a vivid imagination and a love for the gun fighting days of the old west, R B Conroy developed and conceived his main character Jon Stoudenmire. The resulting story is a unique and compelling tale about a charming and violent gunman in the turbulent days of America's early west. As *Devil Rising* goes to press, R B is hard at work on the sequel. He lives in Leesburg, Indiana with his wife Cheryl.

www.ingramcontent.com/pod-product-compliance
Lightning Source LLC
Chambersburg PA
CBHW020614260626
47157CB00003B/1014